S0-BOK-125

He loved her face.

When he touched her, trailing his forefinger down the sweet line of her cheek, he was surprised at the strength of his emotional response. He wanted to be Rhett Butler or Mr. Darcy or at least one of Louis L'Amour's Sacketts and take her in his arms. Maybe carry her up a flight of stairs since the Dower House had such a nice wide set. This wasn't a book and he was definitely no hero, but he wanted to protect her from all harm, to lend peace to her soul tomorrow and tomorrow and tomorrow.

Regret worked its way inexorably into his thoughts. Regret because they didn't have tomorrows.

But they did have now. He lowered his mouth to hers, keeping the kiss light, almost friendly. But more.

Dear Reader,

I've never written with a partner, although I kind of envy those who do. How cool would it be to have someone cover for you on those days when every word you write needs to be unwritten as quickly as possible! However, when I started *Every Time We Say Goodbye* and I couldn't seem to name *any*thing, the then-mayor of a town near me, friends on Facebook and Cole Porter took care of that for me. I'd never been in flag corps, cheerleading or marching band, so more friends lent me some of their considerable knowledge. When it came time to choose a title, a genius in Marketing came up with *Every Time We Say Goodbye*. (I was completely torn between being in love with the title and being jealous because I didn't think of it—love won. It always does.) My name is the only one on the cover, but a lot of other people helped "put music to my words."

I hope you love Arlie and Jack's story—and Miniagua and its residents—as much as I do.

Liz Flaherty

HEARTWARMING

*Every Time
We Say Goodbye*

———

Liz Flaherty

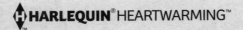

If you purchased this book without a cover you should be aware that this book is stolen property. It was reported as "unsold and destroyed" to the publisher, and neither the author nor the publisher has received any payment for this "stripped book."

Recycling programs
for this product may
not exist in your area.

ISBN-13: 978-0-373-36786-3

Every Time We Say Goodbye

Copyright © 2016 by Liz Flaherty

All rights reserved. Except for use in any review, the reproduction or utilization of this work in whole or in part in any form by any electronic, mechanical or other means, now known or hereinafter invented, including xerography, photocopying and recording, or in any information storage or retrieval system, is forbidden without the written permission of the publisher, Harlequin Enterprises Limited, 225 Duncan Mill Road, Don Mills, Ontario M3B 3K9, Canada.

This is a work of fiction. Names, characters, places and incidents are either the product of the author's imagination or are used fictitiously, and any resemblance to actual persons, living or dead, business establishments, events or locales is entirely coincidental.

This edition published by arrangement with Harlequin Books S.A.

For questions and comments about the quality of this book, please contact us at CustomerService@Harlequin.com.

® and TM are trademarks of Harlequin Enterprises Limited or its corporate affiliates. Trademarks indicated with ® are registered in the United States Patent and Trademark Office, the Canadian Intellectual Property Office and in other countries.

Printed in U.S.A.

www.Harlequin.com

Liz Flaherty retired from the post office and promised to spend at least fifteen minutes a day on housework. Not wanting to overdo things, she's since pared that down to ten. She spends nonwriting time sewing, quilting and doing whatever else she wants to. She and Duane, her husband of...oh, quite a while...are the parents of three and grandparents of the Magnificent Seven. They live in the old farmhouse in Indiana they moved to in 1977. They've talked about moving, but really...thirty-seven years' worth of stuff? It's not happening!

She'd love to hear from you at lizkflaherty@gmail.com.

Books by Liz Flaherty

Harlequin Heartwarming

Back to McGuffey's

Harlequin Special Edition

The Debutante's Second Chance

Many thanks go to Jim Walker, who named Lake Miniagua, to the Facebook friends who named Wally and Caruso, and to songwriter Cole Porter, whose song titles made Miniagua such a fun place to write about. A special thanks to Joey Kubesch, who helped put the right names with the right businesses.

A few miles from our house, sitting smack in the middle of the cornfields, is a school campus containing grades K–12 plus preschool. It's where my kids, some of my grandkids, and I all graduated from. It's where my daughter and son-in-law teach. It is one of the safest, best, most loving places I know. It's because of what I learned there that I grew up to write books—the best job in the world.

So it is to the past and present staff of North Miami Community Schools that this book, with my heartfelt gratitude, is dedicated. Go Warriors!

CHAPTER ONE

IT HAD BEEN sixteen years since he'd seen Arlie Gallagher. And three months and four days. Not that he was counting.

But he knew, as he stepped out of the rental SUV he'd parked in front of the Come On In hardware store, that the woman standing in front of the tearoom across the street was indeed Arlie. She was dressed in turquoise scrubs and wearing sunglasses that covered half her small, heart-shaped face, but he recognized her compact build, riot of red curls and hey-world-it's-me movements as though he'd seen her only yesterday. He thought the woman with her, whose dark hair was a perfect foil for the rich copper of Arlie's, was her stepsister, Holly. He couldn't look away long enough to be sure.

The coward in him urged him to hustle into the hardware before Arlie looked across Miniagua's gravelly Main Street and

saw him. But that would have meant looking away.

Which he couldn't have done under pen-
alty of, well, death, he guessed, because that
was something he knew. He'd looked away
from her once, actually walked away from
her, and dying would have been a whole lot
easier.

He closed the car door firmly. Sounds carried on the breeze from the lake, and Arlie
looked up, meeting his eyes. She raised her
arm, then dropped it with the wave unfin-
ished. Her smile, that wide, generous expression that grew like one of those sped-up
videos of a rose blooming, started but faded
before the rose made it out of bud stage.

He still couldn't look away. He couldn't
breathe, either, so he just drank in the sight
of her. This must be what a person would
feel like if he came in from the desert after
not having anything to drink for, say, sixteen
years. That first glass of water would be wonderful. It would be life-affirming and fresh
and would end way too soon.

The brunette, whose brisk, loose walk
didn't give away the fact that her left foot
was prosthetic, nodded in his direction. She
didn't smile, though, and he didn't either,

just lifted his chin and let it drop. When the women went into the Seven Pillars Tearoom, he was finally able to turn and walk toward the hardware store's front door. Mostly without seeing where he was going.

He and his half brother, Tucker, had been raised on the estate that filled a chunk of the frontage property on the south end of Lake Miniagua's six hundred acres, but Jack Llewellyn seldom came back. When he did, he paid his stiff respects to his grandmother and stood silent and stoic sentinel for an hour in the cemetery beside the Miniagua Community Church. He'd learned to move quickly on these visits, making it on the afternoon flight home so that by midnight, he'd be relaxing in front of the TV with a beer. He wouldn't have seen anyone but Margaret Llewellyn and her household staff.

This time, he didn't get off that easily. Not only would he not get back to Vermont today, he wouldn't make it tomorrow, either. From the looks of his grandmother's will and her estate, he'd be in Indiana for a good long time settling the estate.

That meant he'd have to see all those people whose lives had been irrevocably changed the night his father drove drunk and failed to stay to the outside on one of the tight curves on Country Club Road. Jack might have to try to explain things for which he had no justification. Things like why he'd left.

He'd known he would see Arlie, whose heart he had broken, but he had wanted—no, needed—time to prepare himself. Sometimes if he was ready, if he tightened his jaw and focused on other matters—any other matters— he could think about her with barely a twinge of the hurt he'd caused them both. Sometimes.

But that was before he saw her across the street. More than a twinge, the pain that ripped sharp and unexpected down the center of him nearly brought him to his knees.

The bell over the hardware store's door rang when he stepped inside. Sam Phillipy's voice, the deepest, truest bass the high school choir had ever heard, came from the back of the hardware store. "Can I help you?"

Jack had to catch his breath yet again. Why hadn't he thought about it longer before coming into the store? Before coming down to Miniagua's two-block business district at all? He should have known Sam would be here, should have been ready to face the only man who'd ever been as close to him as his brother. There had never been a better friend than Sam Phillipy. Or a worse one than Jack Llewellyn.

"I'll need a remodeling crew. I figured this would be a good place to start looking." Jack sauntered back, striving for casual. Hard to do on legs that still felt shaky.

The old wooden floors echoed with the same hollow sound as they had in high school days. He could almost hear the dribbling of basketballs on the boards. It was an indicator of just how small Miniagua was, he reflected, that teenage boys had hung out in the hardware store.

Sam met him in the middle of the store beside the endcap of paint colors. They sized each other up much as they had more than twenty years ago. Sam looked good even with a patch over his left eye. Lasting damage from the prom-night wreck. Jack had to stop himself from flinching. "Sam."

"Jack." Sam nodded, not offering his hand. "My condolences on your family's loss." If there was a sneer in his voice, Jack couldn't hear it, but there was no warmth in his old friend's expression, either. Nor even a hint of welcome.

"Thank you." Jack shuffled his feet on the worn floor, feeling as he had that first day he'd come to school at Lake Miniagua, the only eighth grader in high-dollar khakis and Italian loafers. Sam had greeted him then, walking through a gaggle of lakers with an outstretched hand and an offer to share his locker. The move had been both curiously adult and a harbinger of what was to come—they'd shared a locker until the day they graduated.

"When is your grandmother's funeral?" Sam poured coffee for them both, handed Jack a cup and lifted the pot in invitation to the pair of Amish farmers who were examining the harness that hung across the back wall. They came forward for refills, then went back to the wall.

Jack wasn't sure why Sam had given him the drink but was grateful nonetheless. Maybe the motivation had been pity because Jack was once again wearing designer clothing in a Levi's-and-T-shirt kind of place. It had been bad enough being the overdressed new kid at thirteen—it was worse at thirty-four. But he'd gone from a business meeting straight to the airport. His assistant had met him there with a suitcase. "Tomorrow at two."

"Will you be staying on? How about Tuck?"

"Looks like we both will." Jack drank

deeply. Sam definitely knew his way around a coffeepot. "At least until we can sell the plant and figure out what to do with the Hall." He smiled without humor. "Know anyone who wants a ten-thousand-square-foot albatross?"

Sam shook his head. "So, you're selling the plant?" His face was tight, his knuckles white on the curve of his cup.

Jack nodded, then remembered that Sam's father, Paul, was the production supervisor and had been since the boys had been kids. "Your father's job will be safe, unless he's ready to retire. There's no need to worry about that."

"I'm not worried. He won't be, either, I imagine, but those other fifty-some people who work there—they might have some concern." Sam's voice was mild, but the look in his good eye was anything but.

Irritation crawled along Jack's hairline, and he tightened his jaw. He'd bought and sold a handful of businesses since he'd graduated from Notre Dame. He'd made himself a success by flipping companies the way those guys on television flipped houses, and he hadn't done it by causing irreparable harm to labor. Didn't Sam know that?

No, of course he didn't. Why would he?

"We'll do what we can to protect all the jobs."

"Well." Sam nodded abruptly. "That's good. Did you say you were looking for a remodeling crew?"

"A couple of them, probably. If we are going to sell the alba...the house, it needs to become more like a home and less like a museum."

"Are you and Tucker living in it?"

"Tuck is. I'm in the Dower House." He looked at his watch. Not that he cared what time it was, but it was hard maintaining eye contact with Sam, as hard as it had been seeing the redhead across the street. "I'll check back with you, all right?" He set down his cup and headed toward the front door of the store, needing air, needing something to ease the grief of being back in this place he'd loved so much and being completely alone.

Sam's voice followed him. "I'll check around." He cleared his throat. "I'll see you at the funeral."

Jack stopped, turning around to meet Sam's gaze. "That's very kind of you." He knew the words were stilted, but he meant them.

"Your grandmother was a customer. Not

that she ever came in the store, but she'd call
and tell me what she wanted and I'd take it
out there. And she was your grandmother.
We were best friends in high school—all the
way through. You walked away and the truth
is I don't like you very much right now, but
on some level we're still best friends."

Jack smiled, but the expression felt cold on
his face. He doubted if it looked any warmer
than it felt. "Really."

"Yup." Sam sketched him a wave. "When
you drive down Country Club Road, those
little crosses that are all rough and the paint's
worn off? They're the only sign that the accident ever happened. The road's been repaved,
even widened a little. They couldn't do anything to straighten out the curves, but it's a
lot safer than it was then. Other than those of
us who were in the wreck and our families,
people have forgotten. The scars have healed.
I don't know why you saw fit to leave the way
you did. I may never know why. But you're
back now, at least for a while, and it's time
for the exile to end. It's been long enough."

"Long enough?" Jack kept his voice mild,
maintained the smile, but everything inside
him tightened. "For the Gallaghers and the

Benteens? The Worths and Linda Saylors's parents? For you, Sam?"

Sam hesitated, lifting his free hand to straighten the patch that suited his face so well it was as though it had always been there. "Maybe not. I don't know." He sighed. "The accident wasn't your fault. No one blames you for it."

"I know." Not that he believed it for a New York minute, but maybe if he said it often enough, he would. Maybe.

"SERIOUSLY. RENT-A-WIFE IS cleaning the Dower House and I drew the short straw? No one will be there while I'm working, right?" Arlie Gallagher filled her plate with a little more spaghetti than was probably good for her, but her stepmother was the best cook on the lake. "You told them that everyone should be out of the house so I can get the job done quickly?"

"Yes, I told them that." Holly, her six-months-younger stepsister, followed her, filling her own plate as full as Arlie's.

Gianna Gallagher topped off their wine-glasses and waited for the daughters she'd raised more alone than not to join her at the table. "I'm glad you girls are here." She swirled the liquid in her glass and took a drink. "I don't get lonely much—there's no time—but mealtime's when I miss your dad the most."

"We should come for dinner more often." Arlie covered her stepmother's hand with her own and smiled into her eyes. "It would be a struggle, but I could eat your cooking occasionally as opposed to standing over the kitchen sink scarfing a Hot Pocket. Goodness knows, Holly could use some more pasta, too."

"No, I couldn't." Holly shook her head. "If I gain more than ten pounds, my foot doesn't fit right and I have to get a new socket." She rapped the side of her prosthetic ankle, a result of the accident that had claimed her stepfather's life.

Gianna squeezed Arlie's fingers. "I wanted to talk to you both before you started hearing things. Lakers may blame the summer people for starting rumors, but the truth is that gossip travels even faster in the wintertime when people are bored."

"What is it, Mama?" Holly spun her pasta expertly onto her fork.

"The Llewellyns."

Arlie laid down her fork again, her appetite

gone. "We're cleaning the Dower House as requested, Gianna. We already know Jack's coming back for a while. He won't stay—he never stays." The words made her stomach twist, the way it had when she'd seen him on the street today.

She leaned back in Gianna's comfortable dining room chair and sipped wine, enjoying the immediate comfort of it. Sycamore Hill's red was extra good this year. Not that she could tell the difference, but Chris Granger's family owned the local winery and he said it was.

Gianna hesitated. "Apparently the estate is very complicated. I don't pretend to know what all's involved—the beauty-shop grapevine's intel wasn't that in-depth—and both boys will be coming back here to stay for a time." Gianna's eyes softened on Arlie. "Will you be okay with it?"

After the accident, there had been so much pain between them they couldn't seem to get through it. When he left for college, he never came back. It still hurt to think about it, though not as badly as it had then. *Nothing* hurt as much as it had then, but seeing him across the street today had opened the old wounds.

If Arlie gave the word, her stepmother was completely capable of telling Jack Llewellyn the streets of Miniagua weren't big enough for him and her daughter both and he needed to find his way back out of town.

She sipped her wine, enjoyed its warmth, then drained her glass. "It's not as though I've spent the last sixteen years in mourning. I've lived half my life since then. I have a career, my own house, and Chris is a sort-of boyfriend. I can deal with seeing Jack."

It sounded good, she thought, but her stepmother didn't look entirely convinced.

Gianna glanced at her watch, then poured the last of the red into their glasses. "We've buried our dead and gone on with our lives. Jack and Tucker are here to do the same thing. Miniagua is home to them just like it is to the rest of us. It's time for peace in all our souls." She firmed her voice and met Arlie's eyes, her dark gaze compassionate. "If you think you can welcome them back, then I know I can."

Holly nodded. "Me, too."

Arlie didn't think she was ready for that. Cleaning the Dower House was one thing. Seeing Jack from across the street without losing her lunch had been entirely doable.

Getting friendly with the Llewellyns was something else entirely.

"I'll try." Arlie stared back into the eyes that still held hers. "I promise I'll try."

Once dinner was over and they were standing in the driveway of Christensen's Cove, Gianna's house, saying good-night, Holly offered Arlie a ride. She shook her head. "I need some air. And maybe to think some."

"Don't *over*think it, sis." Holly hugged her hard.

Arlie nodded. "See you in the morning."

The evening was warm for mid-October. A full moon danced on the water, and Arlie could hear people chatting on their porches and docks, hanging on to all the comfortable outdoors time they could. Sometimes during the day, Lake Miniagua looked big, but in the evening it seemed to shrink, its streets becoming the bumpy and narrow throughways they actually were. People rode by on bicycles, calling out greetings as they passed. Golf carts whizzed along in near silence. Teenagers walked close together in couples and groups, both sibilance and new huskiness in their hushed laughter. The playground above the beach was deserted, although Arlie thought if she listened hard, she could hear echoes of the past ringing through it. But maybe that was just the rustle of dry leaves as they scuttled across the ground in the breeze.

Arlie's father had built the house she lived in, though he'd sold it when he and Gianna married. The red Cape Cod sat at the end of a narrow inlet that had been dubbed Gallagher's Foot. When Arlie bought the house three years ago, she painted Gallagher's Big Toe on the mailbox. The name had shrunk to "the Toe" and stuck.

When she'd opened the garage door the first time after she took possession of the house, she found a scrap of a kitten curled up in an old Easter basket. Jesse Worth, a veterinarian whose office was halfway between Miniagua and Sawyer, had said it wasn't old enough to leave its mother. He'd given Arlie enough eyedroppers and a recipe for formula to keep it alive.

The kitten, whose meow was so loud Gianna had christened her Caruso despite her gender, now weighed fifteen pounds and owned Arlie, body and soul. Caruso was not amused that her housemate was so late coming home, but a couple of treats accompanied by an intense chin-scratch and belly-rub helped matters considerably.

After showering, putting on a faded Ball State University sweatshirt and black flannel pajama pants, and wrapping her tumble of red hair in a towel, Arlie lifted a scrapbook from one of the bookshelves that flanked the gas fireplace. She clicked the fireplace's remote, then sat in the recliner, drawing a quilt over her legs—warmth had receded fast once darkness fell. Caruso settled in beside her, her purr a companionable roar in the cozy room.

"What do you think, Caruso?" The book of memories was her first effort, put together when she was trying to get her mind and hands to work together after the accident. Holly had replaced cheering and dancing with writing after losing her leg in the accident. Arlie had learned to scrapbook in lieu of singing and playing the piano and clarinet when neither her throat nor her hands returned to what they had been previously.

She'd been seventeen when she put together the first album, the one with covers in their school colors, so she shouldn't have been surprised that the first picture was of her and Jack. She shouldn't have been, but she was. Every single time.

She jumped when the doorbell rang. It

wasn't that late—just after nine—but visitors in Miniagua usually phoned or texted first and came by before dark unless it was summertime, when everyone was sitting outside anyway.

The cat accompanied her to the door, her ringed tail at stiff attention, and Arlie bent to pet her. "You're such a good girl. It's probably some of the senior class selling magazine subscriptions—that and car washes are the only way they get the prom paid for. Did you want to go with me if they ask me to chaperone? You saw that picture when Jack and I went. You and I would be at least that cute."

Caruso leaned against her legs when they reached the entryway. Arlie turned on the porch light, the wattage guaranteed to blind whomever was on the porch, and pulled open the door.

Somehow she wasn't surprised when she saw Jack standing on the other side of the threshold.

His hair, curly and unmanageable when he was a boy, was straight now, still blond but streaked with brown. She'd always accused him of wearing tinted contacts because his eyes were such a bright blue. They were still spectacular, still fringed by thick lashes, but the blue had darkened and he wore glasses with wire frames. His face had been a boy's when she saw him last, with all the softness of adolescence in it, but now his cheekbones were sharper, his jaw more square and covered with a well-trimmed beard. His build was lean, still broad shouldered and flat stomached, but more spare somehow than sixteen years before.

He wore jeans and a leather jacket that hung open over a faded blue cotton sweater. An earring glinted in his left ear, and she wondered for a suspended moment if it was the same one with his birthstone that she'd bought him for his September birthday. She'd given it to him early, before he left for college, and then she'd never seen him again.

"Jack."

"Arlie." He nodded, his gaze not leaving hers. "I just wanted to tell you, you don't have to clean the Dower House. I can't believe the lawyer's rep asked you. Well, I can, but I'm sorry she did." His smile was so slight it almost wasn't there. "I also can't believe that's the best excuse I could come up with for coming over here this late."

She didn't smile back. "She didn't ask me. She asked Rent-A-Wife, which is Gianna's business. I just help out once in a while. Unless you no longer need our services, we'll do the job." Angry for a reason she couldn't name, not to mention insulted, she started to push the door shut.

"Wait." He stopped the door with his hand around its edge. "May I come in?" He hesitated. "Please."

It's time for peace in all our souls. Gianna's voice echoed gently in Arlie's mind. She took a deep breath and stepped back, Caruso winding around her ankles. "Sure. Go ahead and have a seat. Would you like something to drink?" She made the offer grudgingly, but she wasn't Gianna Gallagher's daughter for nothing.

"Do you have coffee? I know it's late for that, but it's tasted good all day."

Friendly. That was how he was going to play it. *Let's just pretend the past sixteen years didn't happen.* Okay, she could do that. Sure she could. "There's an organic market on the lake. I think everyone buys coffee there now." She went to make a fresh pot, breathing deep when she opened the coffee canister. The scent was definitely therapeutic.

He leaned on the counter between the kitchen and the dining area. "I had supper at the Anything Goes Grill on the north end. I guess it's new? It was good."

"It is good. It's nicer than the Silver Moon, although the food's about equal on the quality scale, and it has booze." Chris's family had opened Anything Goes within the past year. He didn't work in the restaurant, but he spent a lot of time there. She wondered if he'd been there tonight.

Jack looked around. "Your house looks pretty. Was it nice to come back to where you lived as a little kid?"

"It was after a while. At first, until we painted everything and put down the hardwood floors, I just kept thinking of it as the house where we lived when my mother left." She lifted cups from the cupboard.

"Do you hear from her? Your mother?"

"No. Well, yes. At Christmastime. Usually. She's forgotten a few."

Arlie handed him his coffee, then filled a plate with cookies and led the way back to the living room, carrying the plate and her own mug. The cat glared at her from the seat of the recliner. "I didn't introduce Caruso, did I? She's my roommate."

"What a beauty she is." Jack had always loved cats. He set his cup on the table at the end of the couch and lifted Caruso into his arms. She leaned into him, purring politely and eyeing him adoringly with bright green eyes. "I thought Russian Blues didn't like strangers."

"She does. Especially males." Although the cat wasn't crazy about Chris. She always climbed onto her perch on the front windowsill and lay with her back to the room when he was there. Arlie wasn't so sure Caruso's instant adoration of Jack qualified her as a good judge of character.

When they were seated, Jack sipped from his coffee, closing his eyes for a moment in appreciation. "Rent-A-Wife?" He raised an eyebrow. "Weren't you wearing scrubs today?"

"I'm a nurse at the hospital in Sawyer. I just help at Rent-A-Wife when Gianna needs me." He was trying to make conversation, and she had to give him points for the effort, but she didn't know what to say to him.

He picked up the scrapbook that lay on the couch beside him. "I remember this. You made it that last summer, didn't you?"

She nodded, and quiet settled between them as he leafed through the heavy pages. Partway into the book, he began to ask questions.

She progressed from two-word answers—
"Sophomore year"—to short explanations—
"No, I was grounded"—to unwilling laughter
when he buried his head in his hands after
seeing a picture of himself in drag during the
high school production of *Hairspray*. After
that, they laughed more, argued over things
that didn't matter and played the "do you remember?" game. At some point, it was almost
as though he'd never left Miniagua. Never
left her.

They were on their second cups of coffee
and yet another plate of cookies when Jack
reached the end of the album. He fell silent,
looking at the five-by-seven studio shot of
the ten of them who'd driven together to the
dance. The last dance.

"Do you ever talk about it?"

She looked at where the book lay open
across his lap, then up at the clench of his
jaw, the set of his mouth and the tragic look
in the eyes behind his glasses. She set down
her cup and clasped her hands between her
knees. She kept her voice quiet and steady,
trying to downplay the huskiness of it. "We
mention it sometimes. We say 'the accident'
because you can't just pretend away something that changed your life to that extent. We

talk about Daddy—he was Superdad, after all." She smiled, feeling her cheeks wobble with the effort. "But we don't play the 'if only' game—at least not out loud, because it would drive us crazy."

Jack nodded and looked at the picture again.

"Do *you* talk about it?" she asked gently.

"No."

"Do you see Tucker?"

Grief darkened his eyes and stiffened his features once again. "Not often, though we're both here now."

She tried to imagine her life without Holly and couldn't. "Maybe *we* should talk about the accident. Gianna says it's time to let things go." She said the words, but she didn't mean them. She could be polite to Jack, even friendly. But she didn't think she could quite forgive him. At least, not yet.

"How is Gianna?"

"Wonderful. She had a heart attack three years ago—that's why I came back here to live—but she had surgery and has done great ever since."

"Maybe I'll get to see her."

Arlie didn't ask about his grandmother's last days or her death. She was afraid if she delved too deeply into the well-being of any of the Llewellyns, she'd never be able to come out of the morass of memory again.

But there was Jack, for the first time in nearly half her life, sitting so close she could feel the warmth of him. That same warmth she'd felt before—

Before everything changed.

"I remember screaming," she said without meaning to. "I didn't realize no one could hear me because my larynx was injured. I wanted to comfort Holly because her foot hurt so much. Daddy wouldn't answer us. I couldn't find you. That's all I remember." There was more. But she wouldn't go there. Couldn't.

The prom had been the event of the school year for high school juniors and seniors. They'd rented the ballroom at the country club, having car washes and selling magazine subscriptions and candy bars to cover the expense.

Even in a high school as small as Miniagua's, everyone knew there would be drinking at the prom, so the parents came up with the idea of hiring vans to provide transportation to the club.

Jack's grandparents, under the auspices of

Llewellyn's Lures, owned their own limo, but Margaret said it was needed for business. This was how Arlie, Jack, Holly and Tucker ended up riding to and from the country club in the back of a twelve-passenger church van. Jesse Worth and Linda Saylors sat in front of them with Sam's date, Cass Gentry. Sam, Nate, and Libby Worth sat behind Arlie's father and stepmother in the front seat.

No one was particularly comfortable, and hardly any of them fastened their seat belts around their formal clothing. Arlie's father—who always started every drive with the words "seat belts on?"—turned an unaccustomed deaf ear to the lack of clicking buckles from the backseats.

At first the girls had been embarrassed, but had joined in with the others when Dave Gallagher's rumbling baritone and Gianna's sweet soprano started singing "Dancing Queen."

The next thing Arlie remembered was screaming.

"One time," Arlie said, her throat aching, "Gianna came into Libby's tearoom while I was cleaning. I had 'Dancing Queen' playing loud and my mop and I were dancing away. When I saw her face, it just killed me what I was doing to her. I went to shut it off, apologizing like mad all the way, and she just said, 'Oh, no, honey, it's like singing with your dad again,' and turned it up some more. We danced through the whole song. I think I've played it a thousand times since then."

Jack's face was pale, his features set, and Arlie knew that whatever it had cost her to talk about that night, he'd paid a heavy price for listening, too.

"We've all healed," she reminded him, keeping her voice level and quiet. She got up quickly, needing to move, not wanting to remember anything else about the accident and its aftermath. "More coffee?"

"Yes." He followed her back to the counter. "The real reason I came here tonight was to apologize, but I don't have any idea where to begin with you or with anyone else. I don't know how to be back here. What to do when I run into Jesse or Libby or Holly. Do I say, 'Gosh, guys, sorry my family's limo came out on top when it did a head-on with the church van'? Or maybe, 'Hey, look at the bright side—at least you lived'?"

His pain was palpable. She felt it on her skin, in the dryness of her eyes and the heavy beat of her heart.

"You were the only person who ever blamed you for the accident, Jack. Your father was driving the limo, not you, and he died, too. It wasn't like your family didn't suffer loss."

She knew as soon as the words were out of her mouth that they were wrong. She set the coffee carafe back on its heating unit and came to lean her elbows on the bar between them. "One person blamed you, that is," she said quietly, holding his gaze, "but I didn't blame you for the accident. I blamed you for leaving me."

CHAPTER TWO

LAKE MINIAGUA WAS a small community. Most of its businesses and many of its residences were named with the titles of Cole Porter songs. The prolific songwriter had grown up in nearby Peru. The Anything Goes Grill and the Silver Moon Café were the primary restaurants. A salon and spa called It's De-Lovely was near Rent-A-Wife, Gianna Gallagher's business. Nate's golf course was Feathermoor. The greenhouse was Old-Fashioned Garden. The Sea Chantey Convenience Store and Bait Shop and Through Thick and Thin Barbershop filled Main Street storefronts. Even some of the wine bottles Jack had seen at Anything Goes had names like The Beguine and Midsummer Night.

On the other side of the lake, near the fishing huts and Hoosier Hills Cabins and Campground, there was a second convenience store, a Laundromat and a usually closed pizza parlor—Miniagua's abortive attempt at a strip mall.

At the end of the business district, before the bridge that led to the golf course, the old drugstore and sundry shop sat empty. Out for a morning run, Jack slowed as he passed the brick building, looking at it with eyes both contemplative and assessing.

He thought of the evening before. Of being in the same room with Arlie and wanting to stay and stay and stay. Of talking and laughing and drinking coffee that tasted like home.

They'd talked about the past and—to a lesser degree—about the present. Jack knew Arlie worked in a nearby hospital as a nurse but that her heart was with midwifery, even if she had little opportunity to practice those skills since returning to the lake. He knew and disliked—even though he had no right to even have an opinion—that she'd dated Chris Granger for two years. She'd said she loved quilting and cooking and working with Holly on choreography for the marching band.

He'd told her he loved woodworking more than anything else he'd ever done and that even though he'd lived and worked in several states, he liked the Northeast Kingdom and thought he'd stay there for at least the foreseeable future.

But he hadn't told her about the twelve-year-old who was the real reason Jack made Vermont his home and had done things like buy life insurance and stuff a college fund with conservative investments. The boy who'd made him understand, finally, why he'd survived the prom-night accident. Whose grandparents would drive him down from South Bend for tomorrow's funeral.

The geeky young genius who'd made him a father.

He hadn't mentioned Charlie. Not even once.

ARLIE HATED FUNERALS, especially when she was only there because it was the polite thing to do. She'd loved Jack Llewellyn with all her heart and soul when she was in high school. Tucker had been a great friend. But she hadn't loved their grandmother. Not even close.

"I still don't know why we're here." She pulled Gianna's car into a parking place at the large mortuary in Kokomo. "Margaret Llewellyn didn't like our family and we weren't all that cracked on hers, either." Her thoughts backtracked and it was as though she could feel Jack's blue gaze on her. "I mean, later on, we weren't. After the accident."

Gianna sighed. "She and I made our peace over the years, fragile though it was. Now Jack and Tucker are back here to stay, at least for a while. Judging from what I'm hearing on the grapevine, Jack is not being treated kindly." She patted Arlie's cheek. "I know you welcomed him when he stopped by last night, and I'm proud of you for that. I also know how much you were hurt. I think if we make our 'welcome back' public, it will be a good thing." Her dark eyes were damp, but her smile caught her stepdaughter in an aura of warmth. "I love you, Arlie."

"You already got me here. You can stop being sniffly over me." Arlie gave her a one-armed hug. "But I love you, too."

The service was dignified and brief. From where she sat between Gianna and Penny Phillipy, Arlie could see Jack and Tucker in the alcove reserved for family. Tucker's mother sat between them. A boy who appeared to be about twelve was in the chair beside Jack. Arlie wondered who he was. As far as she knew, other than his half brother,

Margaret Llewellyn had been Jack's last living relative.

Many people from the lake attended. When it was over, most of them spoke to Tucker, though there wasn't the exchange of memories that usually took place at memorial services. No one said, "If there's anything I can do..." or "She's in a better place now." No one hugged anyone. No one laughed or cried.

And hardly anyone talked to Jack. There were nods of recognition from townspeople. Sam, Nate and Jesse shook his hand. Even Jack and Tucker seemed to have little to say to each other. The boy stood between them, shaking hands when he was addressed.

The night before, when Jack had appeared at her door, Arlie hadn't wanted to talk to him, either. Seeing other people purposefully snub him broke her heart. She turned an anxious gaze to Gianna. "Can we fix this?"

Just as her stepmother had never led her astray, she'd also never failed her when it came to knowing the right thing to do.

With Arlie in tow, Gianna walked straight to Jack. "Oh, sweetheart, we've missed you so." She drew him into a hug he couldn't have avoided if he'd wanted to. "You remember that you and Tucker are expected for dinner at the Cove tonight, don't you?" She smiled at Tucker's mother. "Ellen, it's been too long. Can you come, too?"

"I can't." Ellen Curtis beamed at her, gratitude shining from her eyes. "I'm having dinner with other friends tonight because I'm flying back to England tomorrow, but I'm so pleased these two will be in your capable hands."

"Yes." Jack had to clear his throat. "Thank you, Gianna. Is it all right if I bring another guest?" He drew the slim-built boy forward, his hands resting either protectively or possessively on his shoulders. "Mrs. Gallagher, this is Charlie. My son."

The earth didn't move. Most of the people around them didn't even look surprised. Of course, they were probably too busy squirming from being shamed by Gianna's openhearted acceptance of Jack into their midst.

But Arlie couldn't breathe.

They'd spent two hours together the night before and he hadn't seen fit to mention a son. Or—*go ahead and twist the knife*—a wife. Not that being married was necessarily a prerequisite to parenthood; Jack and Tucker's father hadn't married either of their mothers. But the conversation the night before had been one that went well beyond the parameters of just being polite. They'd shared memories; they'd laughed. They'd talked about the accident and he'd apologized even though he hadn't specified exactly what he was apologizing for. He'd said he didn't know what to say to people now that he was back.

I have a son named Charlie would have been an extraordinarily good start.

"THEY DIDN'T KNOW I exist?" Charlie stood stock-still at the rear door of Tucker's car when they finally left the cemetery after the private graveside service Margaret Llewellyn had requested. "How could they not know I exist? I'm arguably the best thing that's ever happened to you."

"You're twelve years old." Tucker stared over at his nephew in disbelief. "No one uses the word *arguably* when they're still wiping their noses on their jacket sleeves."

They did when they were Charlie, who'd skipped third grade and was well on his way to passing over the eighth, as well. He was both brilliant and funny. Neither of those traits led to appropriate behavior, which he insisted against all parental objections was part of his charm.

"Get in the car, Charlie." Jack waited for him to obey, then closed the door behind him and got into the front passenger seat. "You know I never come back here unless I have to."

He was still trying to process the look on Arlie's face when he'd introduced Charlie. She had looked, for just a heartbeat in time, completely stricken. She'd paled so much that the spray of freckles on her nose had stood out in stark contrast to her skin. He'd reached to touch her, but she'd backed away a step, shaking her head slightly before turning a smile on Charlie.

Tucker looked at Jack from behind the wheel. "He's right, you know. Other than continuing to have me for a brother whether you wanted me or not, Charlie is probably the best thing to come into your life since you walked away from the lake."

"See?" Charlie spoke up. "Except for the brother part, Tuck's got it."

Jack turned enough to look at the adolescent behind him. "You know, I can probably get your grandparents to take you back to South Bend with them. They can run you over to O'Hare and put you on a direct flight tonight instead of me flying with you tomorrow afternoon. Your mother would be glad you weren't missing another day of school."

Charlie grinned at him, metal from his braces glinting in the afternoon sun sifting through the car window, and Jack grinned back. He could no more resist the boy, who really *was* the best thing in his life, than he could fly.

"We need to stop and get Gianna a bottle of wine or some flowers." He looked out the side window of the car. The autumn colors were beautiful. "Is there anywhere on the lake or do you need to stop in Sawyer?"

"We go right past Sycamore Hill, the winery the Grangers started up a few years ago. It's between the golf course and Jesse Worth's vet clinic on Lake Road."

"Chris Granger?" He'd been Jack's age and had lived next door, but they'd never been friends. The fact that he was Arlie's boyfriend made it fairly certain they never would be.

"Yeah." Tucker looked over at him, his expression undecipherable. "I guess he and Arlie have been seeing each other for a long time."

"They have." Jack continued looking out the window, noting the colors of the leaves as they went under the canopy of trees on the stretch of road they'd always called "the tunnel." Jesse's place would be next, where he'd opened his clinic on the family farm, and then the winery the Grangers owned.

Arlie and Chris Granger. Even thinking about them as a couple made his insides jump around. It had been so much better not knowing. In all the time he'd been gone, he'd managed not to call her, though he'd dialed the number at Christensen's Cove at least a thousand times. He'd thought maybe Gianna would answer and he could just ask about Arlie to make sure she was all right. But he always hung up before anyone picked up on the other end. He'd written letters all through his first two years at college, trying to explain, to make her understand. He'd never mailed any of them, but he hadn't thrown them away, either—they were in a wooden box he'd made, stuffed into the back of his closet in his house in Vermont.

Sometime during the summer after sophomore year, he stopped dialing her number, stopped writing letters he would never mail. He started dating again, albeit without his heart in it. He and Tracy, his study partner, shared a propensity for vintage TV shows and Chicago-style hot dogs. They spent most of their evenings together.

That winter, he married her, entering into a union they later referred to as the best marriage of convenience that ever took place on the campus of Notre Dame University.

Tracy was pregnant by a man she found out too late was married. When he was running one night, Jack found her standing on a bridge over the St. Joe River. "I can't get an abortion and I can't jump," she'd said, turning tear-filled eyes to him. "It's not the baby's fault its parents are losers."

As much as Jack liked Tracy and enjoyed her company, there was no real attraction there. Not to mention, he believed his time to love had passed him by. He didn't particularly want children of his own, but neither had his father—something he and Tucker had known every day of their lives.

What if this had happened to Arlie? What if she'd been alone and pregnant? She hadn't been—they had never been intimate after the accident—but what if she had and he'd never known? He'd have wanted someone to do what was right for his child.

Life had granted him no illusions about marriage, happily-ever-after or being a proud father at someone's graduation. But he'd hated that his father hadn't wanted him and Tuck.

"How can I help you?" He'd wrapped his jacket around Tracy and laughed, the sound nervous. "We could get married for a while. Get you through finals and decide what you want to do."

They'd spent the first months of their marriage studying, learning to cook without poisoning themselves, watching *Matlock* reruns and deciding what to do after the baby was born. Finally, eight months into Tracy's pregnancy, they'd made the decision to release the baby for adoption and have their marriage annulled. No harm, no foul, just gratitude for getting each other through a rough time.

But then there was Charlie. In the space of time between the obstetrician saying "you can push now" and a red-faced baby squalling his head off, Jack and Tracy learned that while love had definitely complicated their pasts, it just as certainly defined their future. They had ended their marriage, but that was the only part of the plan that came together.

Jack brought his mind to the present, looking back over his shoulder to smile at the boy who'd changed his life. Who'd made him decide maybe living was worthwhile after all. Whom he was afraid to spend too much time with.

"Did you bring homework with you?"

The boy rolled his eyes, their whiskey color reminding him of Arlie's. "I did. It's algebra and it's probably going to be the sole reason I'm never accepted to a reputable college."

"Good. Tucker can help you."

Tucker tossed Jack a look of outrage. "I flunked algebra. In my freshman year. Remember? He's in the eighth grade and can already run rings around me in anything mathematical."

"I know you flunked it, but you did okay when you took it the second time. I, on the other hand, only passed it because Arlie helped me."

"She's a girl and she helped you with algebra?" Charlie scoffed.

"She did." Jack unbuckled his seat belt when Tucker pulled in at the winery. "And I double dog dare you to take that tone with her. Unless she's changed a lot, you won't come out of it real well."

Charlie squinted. "Double dog dare?"

Tucker laughed. "Don't do it, Charlie. You'll be sorry."

Twenty minutes later, having bought two bottles of wine and a carryout pan of apple dumplings Charlie had salivated over, they pulled into the driveway of Christensen's Cove. Jack sat still in the passenger seat, a white-knuckle grip on the bottle of zinfandel in his lap. He met his brother's eyes across the seat. "I don't know if I can do this. Or if I should." He was aware, peripherally, that Charlie had got out of the car, but he was incapable of calling him back. He seemed to be just as unable to move. "I should go."

"No." Tucker gripped his shoulder hard. "You've done that. To her and to me both. It didn't work worth beans for any of us. It's time to stay, Jack."

Charlie was already taking off his jacket when they stepped through the front door of Gianna's house. "We brought enough apple dumplings for everyone, but if Dad doesn't eat his, I already called dibs on it. Did you really help him with his algebra?"

"I did." Arlie hung up his coat. "But in all fairness, he helped me with biology—I couldn't get the whole mitosis and meiosis thing—and Holly helped us all with English."

She grinned at her sister, the expression all delightful wickedness that made Jack's heart do the jumpy thing again. "However, she charged us."

Holly nodded. "Believe me, Charlie, I earned every nickel of it, too."

"Is there any chance you'd help me with my algebra?" Charlie asked Arlie. "Dad said Tucker could, but I don't trust him much."

"Well, sure. We'll let…uh…your dad and Tucker help Holly with the dishes and we'll do your homework." Arlie put an arm through his. "Let's go in and talk to Gianna. I hope you like spaghetti—she cooks enough for an army—and her bread sticks are the best thing since burgers and fries." She tossed a smile over her shoulder at Tucker, ignoring Jack entirely. When they walked into the kitchen, there was a definitive martial aspect to her posture.

Dinner was more comfortable than Jack expected, even though it was obvious Arlie had nothing whatever to say to him. It shouldn't have bothered him, since he knew very well it was his own fault, but it did. When they'd spent time together the evening before, it had felt as though one of the letters he'd written had been sent and delivered. She'd understood and he'd been forgiven.

But he hadn't been. Of course he hadn't. Forgiveness for sixteen years didn't come about in a single day, especially when a whopping lie of omission was added to the mix. He asked himself once again, in the long span of silence between Arlie and himself, why he hadn't just told her about his marriage and his son.

He knew the answer. Because it had been the ultimate betrayal. Raising a family had been the life Arlie wanted and he'd been ambivalent about, yet here they were in their midthirties and he had Charlie and she had a cat.

She was nice to Charlie, though, and that was what mattered. By the time dinner was finished, the kid had charmed her last bread stick off her plate and extracted a promise from Holly to show him how her prosthetic foot worked as soon as the dishes were done and he and Arlie had finished his algebra. When Jack objected to Charlie's over-the-top curiosity, the Gallagher women had all rolled their eyes at him, so he'd thrown up his parental hands and eaten another helping of spaghetti.

"You should either bottle this sauce for public sale or be arrested for leading innocent young men astray with it," he told Gianna.

She laughed. "I do bottle it, but not for public sale. I think the girls and I spend most of August canning tomatoes in the form of sauce, juice, salsa and catsup."

"Catsup?" Charlie's eyes widened. "You make catsup?"

Gianna nodded. "And Arlie and Holly help me. It's kind of like homework—they don't want to, but they do it."

"That is so cool. I had to google a tutorial to show my mom how to open the Heinz bottle."

"Charlie!" Jack objected, although he couldn't stop the snort of laughter that went with the remonstrance. Tracy was the worst cook in the Northeast Kingdom, and she made no pretense at being anything more.

"She's a lawyer," Charlie explained to his captivated audience. "She says she can't cook because she has to use her legal prowess to keep me from getting arrested for being a smart-a—"

"Charlie!" Jack and Tuck spoke together that time.

He gave them a withering look. "Smart

aleck. That's all I was going to say." He turned his orthodontic-wonder smile on Gianna. "May I have more?"

When the dishes were washed and Charlie's homework done, Holly demonstrated removing her foot, then put it back on and made Charlie dance the length of the house's center hall with her.

"We have to go," said Jack regretfully when Charlie fell against him on the deacon's bench near the front door. He hugged him, breathing in the scent of him. "You can come back for Thanksgiving. Your mom already said."

"Splendid." Gianna handed a bag of leftovers to Tuck and kissed his cheek. "Then you'll be able to spend the day with us."

"Thank you." Jack got to his feet and took her hands. "For everything."

Everyone hugged Charlie and the Llewellyns left on a chorus of goodbyes. The last one out the door, Jack finally caught Arlie's eyes and held firm, as if to say, *I'm sorry.* It was as though no one else was there.

She looked away, the stiffness of her demeanor making her taller, straighter. "Good night, Jack. Be safe."

Be safe. He wondered if she said those words whenever anyone left. He did; Tucker did. He wouldn't be surprised if the other survivors did, too. In some ways, prom night would never end.

CHAPTER THREE

JACK FLEW BACK to Vermont with Charlie the next day. Tracy met them at the airport and they all had dinner together before Tracy took Charlie back to the town house they shared.

Jack checked on his house, standing outside it for a long moment and reflecting that no matter how much he liked the two-hundred-year-old brick Cape Cod, it should have been a family house. And wasn't, because he only had a family on occasional weekends and vacations.

After a restless night, he drove his own car back to Miniagua, spending the night somewhere in the middle of Ohio. He pulled into the keyhole drive of the Dower House behind the Rent-A-Wife van late in the evening of the second day. There were lights on in both the first and second stories of the house—only the attic and basement windows were dark. He frowned at the clock on the dash of his SUV. He didn't know how long her workdays were normally, but he thought Arlie might be overdoing it. Twilight came early to the lake these days, but she didn't need to work after the sun had slipped below the horizon. Not on his house, anyway.

It felt strange to ring the doorbell of the house he was going to live in when the keys were in his pocket, but he didn't want to scare her by walking in unannounced. He could see her coming through the sparkling lights beside the heavy front door. She was wearing ragged jeans rolled above her ankles and a scrub shirt that had seen better days—maybe even better years. Her hair was tied into a messy ponytail and her face was completely devoid of makeup.

She looked wonderful.

And she didn't even check to see who was ringing the doorbell.

"You didn't look," he said, scowling as she swung open the door. "I could have been an ax murderer."

"Well, yes, I suppose so." She raised a questioning eyebrow. "Are you? I thought you were an entrepreneur and a weekend dad who was embarrassed to tell people he had a son."

He couldn't look away from her. After all these years and everything that had happened, he still couldn't look away from the lights in her eyes.

Something inside him shifted. They had laughed together through learning to ice-skate, sliding down snow-covered Sycamore Hill on the detached hood of a junkyard Chevy and being stuck at the top of the Ferris wheel at Indiana Beach. Was it realistic to think they could laugh together again without reopening old wounds? Was it even possible?

Not until he explained about Tracy. About Charlie.

"I'm not an entrepreneur. I just get bored easily. And I never get embarrassed about Charlie—only by my own parental inadequacies."

She stepped back, her expression not changing. "Come on in. It's your house, after all."

He went in, inhaling the fresh smells of vinegar and linen and something flowery. "It looks great."

"This floor does," she said. She looked cautiously pleased. "The basement is still an adventure, and I haven't even been in the attic."

"You have cobwebs in your hair."

"I think it's crummy of you to notice." She moved ahead of him through the clean rooms. "Have you been in here at all?"

He shook his head even though he knew she couldn't see him. "I haven't been in this house since the housekeeper and her husband lived in it. I don't know how long it's been empty."

"Four years. Your grandmother offered to let the housekeeper live in it even when she retired, but the woman wanted to live in Florida, so she turned her down."

Jack snorted. "Knowing Grandmother, she probably wanted to charge her an arm and a leg to stay in it, or better yet have her keep working without pay to cover rent."

They continued through the downstairs. "I can set up an office in here," he said, standing in the doorway of the dining room. "There's plenty of room in the kitchen for a table and chairs."

"That's what I did at my house. I had the counter built in to divide the kitchen from the dining area. It's not very big, but it's convenient." Arlie counted outlets. "Of course, my whole downstairs would fit into this dining room and kitchen. But you have plenty of outlets in here, and your wiring is up to date, so you won't darken the whole neighborhood the minute you start plugging things in."

"That's a plus." He smiled at her, hoping

the sheer comfortableness of being together would come back to them the way it had the night before his grandmother's funeral. Before Charlie had arrived. "What's upstairs? I don't really remember."

"Take a look."

The stairway was enclosed, but the stairs were wide and easy to climb. "It won't be too bad bringing furniture up." The handrail felt smooth under his hand, and he smiled. He didn't know where his appreciation for good woodwork had come from, but he was glad he had it.

There were four bedrooms and two baths upstairs. At the end of the center hall, lit by a wide window that overlooked the garden in the back, was a little cove of a library complete with shelves and a built-in desk under the window.

"I'd forgotten this." He stepped down three stairs into the area. "It's over the glassed-in porch off the kitchen, isn't it?"

She nodded. "You may have forgotten it, but I covet it. It's beautiful."

"Do you have a library in the Toe?" He knew she loved to read—it was one of the things they'd shared.

"Sort of. There was a closet under the

stairs I really didn't need. For my birthday the year I bought the house, Gianna hired a carpenter to take the door off it, line it with bookshelves and put lighting in it. There's even room for a chair, but when you sit in it your legs stick out in the hallway."

"Sounds great." He moved down the hall, peeking into the bedrooms. "I'll use this one—Charlie can be across the hall when he's here. How's the plumbing—do you know?"

"I checked it when I got here. It all worked, but I imagine you'll want to put showers in the bathrooms. All that's in there are eighties-era tubs. I do have the master bedroom and bath clean, though. I thought they'd be the ones you'd use. You can move in whenever you're ready."

"I don't want to get in your way." He frowned at the walls. They were clean and smooth. "Is the entire house painted this color? It's so bland, it makes off-white look exciting."

"Yes."

"Does Rent-A-Wife do painting?"

"No, but Sam's wife, Penny, does."

He'd heard that. "I'll see if I can get her in here first. Does Sam help her?"

Arlie laughed, and he felt the ice begin to

melt. "Not with painting. She won't let him. But he helps her set up scaffolding and hauls materials. She does great work and plays good music while she's doing it."

"That would be better than interrupting the crew that's going to work in the Hall. Tucker wouldn't want me to do that, either." He stepped into the walk-in closet and spoke over his shoulder. "I forgot. There was a reason I stopped by."

"I thought you were checking up on the work."

"No." He came back out, pleased with the storage space the house had to offer. "Why are you working this late?"

"Oh." She looked embarrassed. "The van won't start and my cell phone's dead. I went ahead and worked awhile, thinking Holly might stop by when they got back from the casino—she and Gianna took a group today—but I forgot they were staying for dinner. I was getting ready to turn off the lights and walk home when you got here."

"I'll take you home. Or, better yet, to dinner."

She shook her head. "There's chili in the Crock-Pot at home. If you'll give me a ride, I'll share it."

"That sounds great." He agreed before she could change her mind, as the look in her eyes told him she might have wanted to.

When they walked past the company van, Arlie patted its crumpled front fender. "We're going to have to give her a decent burial."

Jack gave the vehicle a doubtful look. "It looks as though she's had a long and hard life." He opened the passenger door of his car for Arlie.

"Don't hurt her feelings. She's been with the company from the first, when she already had a lifetime's worth of miles on her. She did look better then. Now I'm the only one who will still drive her." Arlie flipped down the sun visor and frowned at herself in the lit mirror, pulling at the cobwebs in her hair. "Of course, I looked better then, too."

"There's nothing wrong with how you look now." He meant it, and her eyes flashed something that might have been appreciation in the semidarkness of the car.

AT THE TOE, Arlie asked Jack to get the mail out of the rural box at the end of her driveway while she went inside and made peace with Caruso. "I know I'm late," she told the fussy cat, scooping her food into her bowl, "but it couldn't be helped. Have you been a good girl today?"

Caruso ignored her, going to the front door with her tail twitching.

"Well, fine. He'll be right in." Arlie shrugged at the cat's lack of loyalty and took bowls from the open cupboards above the counter. The chili smelled good and it had been a long time since she'd had a bologna sandwich at lunch.

"Your mail's a lot livelier than mine." Jack's voice came from inside the front door. Caruso meowed sternly.

"Not another frog, I hope—the neighborhood kids do that occasionally. It scares the mail carrier to death when she opens the mailbox." She set the table with soupspoons and cloth napkins that matched the quilted table runner then put a sleeve of crackers into a basket.

Jack came into the kitchen carrying a stack of mail in his right hand and something else in his left.

Something fuzzy that definitely wasn't a frog. Winding around her ankles like a blue-gray wool muffler, Caruso meowed again.

"What is it? I don't think I've ever gotten any mail I'd describe as 'lively,' unless you count the obscene birthday cards Holly sends me." Arlie came to where Jack stood. "Oh, it's a puppy. A teeny, teeny one. Look at its little white feet."

His eyes danced behind his glasses. They were standing so close she felt his breath against her temple. It was a warm feeling she didn't want to think too much about. "You get puppies in the mail here on the lake?" he asked. "It must be *really* interesting when someone has a baby. Do you deliver them after you deliver them?"

She crossed her eyes at him. "It's so little. I'll bet it's too young to be away from its mother. Where's your baby basket, Caruso?" Arlie went into the laundry room, scrabbling through the cupboard above the dryer until she found the old Easter basket Caruso had slept in until she figured out how to climb onto Arlie's bed.

"He's cold." Jack cuddled the puppy between his hands. "Do you want me to go get him some formula?"

"I made it when I found Caruso. It should be the same for a puppy, shouldn't it?" Arlie scrounged out the cloth diapers she'd used to keep Caruso warm when she was a kitten. "I'm afraid I'm going to be a hoarder—

I seem to keep way too many things." She wrapped the diaper around a rice bag, microwaved it and tucked it into the basket.

"You have room." Jack laid the whimpering puppy on the soft flannel bed and stroked his little fuzzy head with his index finger.

She foraged for the ingredients for homemade puppy formula. "Caruso was only a few weeks old when we found her," she explained, opening a can of evaporated milk and pouring some of it into a glass measuring cup. "Jesse taught me to do this stuff. He's a great vet." She added thick corn syrup and an egg yolk and poured in some distilled water, then whipped the mixture with a whisk. "You want to feed him while I brush the cobwebs out of my hair and finish getting dinner on the table?"

"Sure."

She handed him the cup of warmed formula along with an eyedropper and wondered for a heartbeat how Chris would have responded to that question. He was a good person—funny and smart and generous—but *nurturing* was so far down his list of attributes she thought it probably wasn't there.

Of course, she didn't think Chris had any secret children he hadn't mentioned, either.

A short time later, they put the snoozing puppy in the basket on the brick hearth in the living room. Freshly showered—the cobwebs had made her feel sticky all over—and with her hair once more in a towel, Arlie lit the gas fire, petted a curious Caruso and joined Jack at the table.

"So, what are you doing at Llewellyn's Lures?" she asked, laying a napkin across the lap of her favorite brown sweatpants.

"Getting ready to sell it."

She looked up in dismay. "Really?"

He shrugged. "Neither Tucker nor I are interested in running it. Most of my business concerns are in Vermont and his are in Tennessee."

"Llewellyn's has been here for a hundred years." Wasn't it enough that he walked away from things so easily? Did he have to be so cavalier about the nearly sixty employees whose jobs he was selling off?

"And I hope it stays. I truly do," he replied quickly. "We'll do everything we can to keep the status quo, to pass Llewellyn's on to someone who wants to keep it in business and run it the way it has been. After all, it's a profitable company." His expression didn't change, but his eyes did. They looked distant. Sad. And conflicted. "The truth—for me—is that Charlie lives in Vermont most of the time. I don't have custody. I don't even see him nearly as much as I should. But he's there, and I need to be there, too."

She couldn't argue that, though she'd have liked to. She'd have liked to throw things and shout at the top of her voice, *What about our baby? She'd be fifteen now.*

But he didn't know. Other than Gianna and Holly and herself, the only ones who knew were the medical staff who had attended her the night of the accident, the ones who told her the trauma was too much for the fragile life she'd carried.

Gianna had wanted her to tell Jack about the pregnancy, but Arlie had refused. It had been over nearly as soon as it began, one more loss added to a night already too full of them. He'd had enough on his plate, she thought, losing his father and dealing with the knowledge that Victor Llewellyn had caused the accident. She would tell him later, she'd promised her stepmother, when life was calmer. He would share her grief and make it easier to bear.

But by the time "later" came, Jack was gone from her life. Only in her heart did she know the lost baby had been a girl. Only in her heart had she nursed her, dressed her and taught her to sing. Only in her heart had she named her Sarah Angelina after her grandmother and the woman who'd been the only mother who mattered.

Most of the time, it was easy. As the nurses in the hospital had promised, time had healed the wounds of the accident—even the emotional ones. Grief had settled and smoothed and memories had dimmed. Delivering babies had provided healing and joy beyond what she'd been able to imagine even when she was training in midwifery.

"You're right." She felt as though she was speaking from the end of a tunnel, and she cleared her throat. "You need to be with him." She smiled, thinking of the boy with the beautiful eyes and shiny dark brown hair. "He's a sweet kid. Ornery. More like Tuck than you, I think."

"He is." Jack sounded surprised. "He looks like his mother and biological father, and he definitely got his mother's brain, but he does have a lot of Tuck in him."

Arlie frowned, not understanding. "Is he adopted?"

"Not exactly." He gestured with his spoon. "This is really good."

"Thank you." Arlie was glad he liked the chili, but wouldn't be diverted. "Would you want to explain 'not exactly'? I don't remember the term from my nursing or midwifery classes."

"Tracy was my study partner at Notre Dame from the beginning of freshman year. We dated some," he said. "Kind of like you in high school, she was good at things I wasn't and I needed all the help I could get. Her parents lived right there in South Bend—still do—but she lived in the dorm because she had an unbelievable course load. She also had an ex-boyfriend her parents hated. He drank, doped and gambled. When Tracy came up pregnant, she found out he had a wife at home."

"Oh, man." Arlie shook her head and offered him a half smile. "Her folks were upset?"

"She was afraid to tell them. Not that they were bad parents or mean or any of that, but they were older and very conservative. Bottom line was, she didn't want to hurt them. An abortion wasn't even a consideration. She was out of her mind with not knowing what to do. One night, it was really late and she still wasn't in from the library, which wasn't like her at all. I went looking and found her standing on the bridge over the St. Joe River. She swore she wasn't going to jump or do anything stupid, but she was feeling pretty desperate." He shrugged. "Scared the bejesus out of me."

It would have. His mother had taken her own life when he was a toddler. He had no memory of her, but Arlie knew Janice Taylor's mental illness haunted him—it always had.

"What did you do?"

"We talked about it. She was just so scared, and, you know—" He stopped for a moment, taking a drink and looking past her into the kitchen. She wondered where he'd gone, what memory was adding to the sadness in his eyes.

He set down his glass and took another bit of chili. "I felt like my life was a waste anyway. I'd survived the accident with no visible scars. I'd walked away from you. I'd even walked away from Tucker. I hated that my father went through life tossing other people's pain around like so many dry leaves, and yet I'd done the same thing. I thought if I helped her, it wouldn't cost me anything and maybe it would mean I wasn't a *complete* waste of space. So I offered to marry her and take care of her until the baby came. She wouldn't have to come clean with her parents and it wouldn't be a shock if a marriage between an eighteen-year-old genius and a nineteen-year-old loser didn't work out."

Arlie thought of Chris. If he asked her to marry him for the sake of convenience, she would probably do it, and she was thirty-three years old. It made the fact that two teenagers had done just that a very believable scenario.

"Pregnancy and going to school was a bear for Tracy. She was sick the whole time. We talked about what she was going to do when the baby was born. She wanted to be a corporate lawyer, not a mother. Finally, we made the decision together to give him up for adoption and then have our marriage annulled. Neither of us wanted to be parents and had no emotional or physical investment in the baby. I was just trying to be a nice guy for a while and she was just trying to get through the pregnancy without her whole life imploding."

Arlie put down her fork. "Then what happened?"

"Then he was born." The look of torment left Jack's eyes, replaced by the purest kind of joy. "Our marriage wasn't a physical one, but I was still her delivery coach, so I was there. They handed him to me, and I was so scared of breaking him. I was amazed at how tiny his fingers were and that his feet were so disproportionately huge. When I touched his hand, he clutched my finger. We became an instant television commercial. I just told Tracy he wasn't going anywhere. She said that was what she was thinking, too."

"But you're not married anymore?"

"No. We're still good friends, but we stuck with that part of the life plan. We finally told her parents everything. They weren't all that surprised, and they've been more than helpful with Charlie. Tracy travels even more than I do, so he sometimes spends months at a time with them."

"How did you end up in Vermont?"

"Tracy's home office is in Burlington. Llewellyn's has a plant close to there, so it seemed a good place to base out of. And it has been until now. I have a house there, a business I no longer own but still consult for."

"Can't you live and work in both places? Chris Granger spends half the year here and half in California."

"I probably could, and staying here wouldn't

be bad at all," he admitted. "I like it. I've always liked it. But you know what kind of scars the Llewellyn family has left on the whole community. Like it or not, it's my family. It's me."

"It is your family, but you didn't make the scars." *On anyone but me.* She got up. "Do you want more? There's dessert."

"Then I'll wait for that." Carrying his empty bowl, he followed her around the counter into the kitchen. "I did make scars, Arlie, when I walked away. You know that better than anyone." The pain was on his face, as stark and deep as it had been the week of the accident. "Because of my father, everyone in that car was hurt except me. Everyone."

Arlie took lemon meringue pie—made by Libby Worth at the tearoom—out of the refrigerator while he loaded their supper dishes into the dishwasher. "Do you think they hurt less because you left?" *Do you think I hurt less?*

"Maybe they did. Your mom didn't have to be reminded every time she saw my face. Holly and Jesse, Linda's folks—don't you think seeing me was a reminder that I walked away from that wreck?" He closed the dishwasher door and met Arlie's gaze, his eyes dark and tortured behind his glasses. "Holly lost a foot, Jesse his girlfriend, the Saylorses their only daughter. Libby and Tuck both had head injuries and I freaking walked away without a scratch. Yeah, I have to think my leaving was good for them."

Arlie didn't know what to do. Her hurt had eased over the years until days would actually go by without her thinking of what she'd lost. Her father and the baby she'd carried were beloved memories, she didn't notice Holly's foot and even singing had been replaced by other things. Being in Miniagua had been her saving grace, a luxury the boy she'd loved hadn't allowed himself.

Watching his face as he talked, seeing the pain come and go, she realized his leaving may have been better for some of the victims of the accident. But not for him. Never for him.

She set down the pie and lifted a hand to his lean face, feeling the soft brush of his beard against her palm. "You lost your father, Jack. I know you and he weren't close, but as long as you were both alive, you believed someday you might be. You may have walked away, but it wasn't unscathed. Everyone knows that." She thought of the cold shoulder he'd received from the community since he'd been back. "No, I can't speak for everyone, but I can say *I* know that. And I do."

CHAPTER FOUR

JACK AND TUCKER had been best friends their whole lives before the accident. They used to say that if you could combine them to form one person, you'd have a really fine specimen of humanity. Jack, ten months older, was quiet but funny, his wit the kind that caught you unawares and had you snickering before you knew what had hit you. Tucker, on the other hand, was always "on." He'd have you laughing the minute he walked into the room.

They were both athletic, though their skill sets in any given sport were different. Jack started wearing glasses in kindergarten, and Tucker's hearing in his right ear was compromised enough that he had a completely charming way of holding his head when you talked to him, as though whatever you were saying was the most important thing in the world at that moment.

Jack couldn't remember how old he was when they found out they had different mothers, only that their grandmother had taken great pains to tell them Jack had belonged to Janice, Tucker to Ellen.

Victor Llewellyn had been, by nearly everyone's estimation, a loser. Jack, after watching *Leave It to Beaver* reruns, had once referred to him as a modern-day Eddie Haskell. Tucker had responded by saying that was an insult to Eddie. Ellen had sent them to their rooms, making them write "I will be respectful" five hundred times each. She'd also called them Wally and the Beave the rest of the day.

Ellen had never spoken ill of Victor, no matter how much reason she had, but both boys had known early on that being his son was more of a cross to bear than a source of familial pride. Margaret's most scathing riposte to any disagreement from her grandsons had been "You're just like your father."

Sitting at the Anything Goes Grill, nursing the oatmeal stout the familiar-looking bartender had recommended, Jack wondered if they'd both ended up believing it. If that was why neither of them was married. The strongest relationship in Jack's life was with Charlie, a fact for which he was grateful. But he would like there to be more. He'd like to fall in love with someone, maybe even share a home sometime.

Jack felt more than heard Tucker's presence when his brother entered the bar. Even after they found out they were born of separate mothers, they'd referred to themselves as Irish twins because their birth dates were within a year of each other. Their empathy alarm system had been nearly infallible. They joked that they could never donate kidneys to each other because they'd both have failure at the same time.

Walking away from his brother, even though he'd thought it was the right thing to do, had been as hard as leaving Arlie. They'd spent more time together the past few days than they had in years—although Charlie spent summer weekends and the occasional spring break in Tennessee.

"What he's having."

Even the voice sounded like his own. Tucker's hands, where they rested on the mahogany bar, could have been his. Jack knew when he looked at the man who'd come to sit beside him, he'd see his own blue eyes and straight nose mirrored. Only their mouths were different. Tucker didn't wear glasses or a beard, either.

The stud in Tucker's left ear was a tiny gold wishbone. Jack had bought it for him for Christmas their senior year—a few weeks after they had got their left ears pierced—because Miniagua High School's football team had used the wishbone offense instead of the more common I formation.

"How's your mother?"

"Fine. She wants you to bring Charlie to England."

Maybe it had been long enough that Jack could give normal life a shot. Maybe the occasional depression and anger weren't signs that he shared his mother's mental illness after all. He'd never been truly angry with Charlie, had never wanted to hurt him, though he was still afraid to be alone with him that much.

Jack was ten years older than his mother had been when she died, driven by the demons of mental illness. What little he knew of her family history wasn't encouraging, and he'd feared the inheritance of manic depression his whole life. What if he'd been wrong? What if he'd exiled himself from everyone and everything he loved for no good reason at all?

That was more than he could bear to think about. "Maybe next summer."

"Good." There was humor in Tucker's voice, but it was dark. "I might even go with you. Take you right down into the remotest area of the Cotswolds and leave you there."

Jack turned and looked at his brother. Tucker's eyes were clear and smiling in a way Jack knew his own were not.

Tucker leaned on the bar and was silent a moment, looking down at his hands. "I get that you're afraid you'll inherit Janice's mental illness. I know... I've always known that was one of the reasons you left. You left because you thought it would be better for Arlie. For me. For all of Miniagua, for that matter." His gaze grabbed and held Jack's as surely as if there was a string of invisible glue between them. "I respected your wishes. I'm not doing that this time. If a scene is what you want, that's what you'll get, but I'm not leaving the lake until I have a brother again, and worthless as you are at it, you're the only one I want."

Jack looked away, focusing on the liquor bottles reflected in the mirror behind the bar. He had to try twice to speak. The words stuck in his throat, where they'd been for all the years since he'd walked away. "I can't be sure," he said, sounding as though he'd swallowed a handful of pea gravel from out on South Lake Road. He drank slowly, draining the glass, and then he set it down carefully because he was afraid he'd drop it. He turned it in a slow circle on the bar napkin, keeping it within the same round wet spot.

"Can't be sure of what?"

"That I don't have it, too. What if I'd married Arlie and then hurt her or any kids we had or offed myself? What if you got married and I decided I didn't like you or the girl you married anymore? What then? Charlie wasn't supposed to be part of my life at all, and instead he *is* my life and I'm scared out of my mind that I'll hurt him."

His throat closed. He wasn't sure if he could say the words that had to come next. "My mother took her own life, Tuck. She took enough pills to do the job three times over. Dad and I fought the night of the prom, the night he died, and he told me she tried to take me with her. She took me into the closed garage with her and started the car. He said it was too bad she'd failed at that. I knew even when he said it that he was drunk and didn't mean it, but I was mad. I didn't take the keys of the limo. Do you understand now? I could have stopped him from taking the car that night and I didn't. I didn't."

"YOU PROMISED."

Arlie followed Holly to Gianna's dinner table, carrying a platter full of garlic bread. "A good sister wouldn't hold me to it."

Holly set the silverware beside the plates with a clatter. "No, ma'am, you're right. A good sister would let you drive that van until it dies some night in a snowstorm out there in the cornfields between Miniagua and Sawyer. There you'd be with a dead cell phone and nothing in the car except cleaning rags and a mop bucket. We'd find you frozen stiff the next morning. You'd probably leave a note. You know, saying something like, 'You were right, Holly. I should have kept my promise.' There'd be tears frozen solid on your cold, hard cheeks." She smiled beatifically. "What do you think?"

Arlie stared at her. "What a flair you have for the dramatic and the absurd. It's no wonder you write books."

"And what an alarming capacity you have for burying your head in the sand. A replacement van, no more than three years old and with four good tires on it, or I'm going to announce to the whole world that your name is really Arletta Marquetta Brigetta."

"It's not!" Arlie threw a piece of bread at her. "Gianna, she's telling lies."

"You two need to straighten up." Gianna brought the chicken marsala to the table, laughter making her dark eyes twinkle. "But I'm with Holly on this one. I don't want you driving that van anymore. Worry's starting to give me lines and we're just not having that. Everyone knows you girls were born while I was still in elementary school."

Arlie poured ice water into glasses, deliberately sloshing Holly's over the top. "Can the business afford another van?"

"It can." Gianna's voice was firm. "And shame on me for not having seen to it before this."

"But I'm the only one who drives the old one. And it's just been so loyal. I hate to shuffle it off to the salvage yard like it was nothing but a corroded bunch of metal." Arlie put the water pitcher on the counter, holding it against Holly's arm to make her squeal.

"It *is* a corroded bunch of metal." Holly waited for Gianna to sit, then slid into her chair. "That hole in the driver's-side floor is big enough you could drag your foot on the ground to stop the car the next time the brakes quit on you."

"See?" Arlie pointed her fork at her. "That could really come in handy."

"Girls." With infinite patience, Gianna grabbed both their hands, nodded a stern and unspoken order for them to clasp each other's as well and bowed her head for grace.

"How's Chris?" Holly speared a chunk of tomato out of Arlie's salad. "Is he off to California for the winter pretty soon?"

"I think so."

"Does Jack know you and he are seeing each other?"

"I think he does. But why should he care?" Although Arlie had to admit—to herself, at least—that it would be kind of nice if he cared. There was nothing unnatural about that, was there? Didn't everyone want old boyfriends they hadn't seen in half their lifetimes to care about new boyfriends? Even if the new ones weren't quite the real thing.

"Mollie saw Jack and Tucker together when she was tending bar at Anything Goes yesterday. She said it looked a little tense, but there was no shouting or bloodshed. When they left, they hugged."

"Did she talk to them?" asked Arlie. She

was hungry—her growling stomach was proof of that—but she wasn't at all sure she could swallow food. Shades of adolescence, when being in love had completely decimated her appetite. She sipped from her water glass instead, sighing with pleasure at the taste of the fruit-infused liquid.

"Tucker talked for a while after Jack left. She said he was just as nice and funny as he always was. Jack was a big tipper—Mollie thought he left twice as much as the bar bill was." Holly lifted a hand to forestall Gianna's reproof. "I know, Mama. That comes down on the wrong side of snoopy, but there you go."

"He always was a big tipper," Arlie remembered. His grandmother had told him tipping was both unnecessary and a certain way to encourage "laborers" to work less and complain more, so he'd overcompensated for her parsimony. It was one of the things Arlie loved about him.

"I think we should invite them for Thanksgiving supper." Gianna put another helping of chicken on Arlie's plate even though she wasn't finished with the first one. There was a reason she was consistently twenty pounds overweight, and Gianna Gallagher was it. "We always have dinner at St. Paul's when we help with the community meal, but it would be kind of fun to have a supper party later in the day." Pink washed her cheeks. "I thought I'd invite Max."

Arlie exchanged an amused glance with Holly. Although Max Harrison, who was the high school principal, had been part of Gianna's life for several years, she'd always kept the relationship private. The girls had been invited to dinner at her house when he was there a few times, but that was as far as it had gone. They still called him Mr. Harrison and had great difficulty drinking wine in his presence.

"That would be nice," said Holly. "I'll call Tuck. You can ask Jack, Arlie."

"I won't be seeing him." Saying it sent regret skipping haphazardly across her thoughts. She laid down her fork. She was thirty-three years old, for heaven's sake. She was a registered nurse-midwife who owned her own home and even her own lawn mower—which, admittedly, she'd been unable to start by herself since the day she brought it home from Sam's Hardware. Regardless of that, she was in charge of her own destiny. "Well," she said, "maybe."

"I DID SOME looking around and found you one." The owner of the only automobile dealership in Sawyer sounded excited over the phone. "It's a great deal, Arlie. The business went under before the new-car smell was out of it. You won't even have to paint over anything."

"I'll come in and look at it tomorrow," she promised. "I'm waiting for deliveries today and can't get away till everything's here and arranged." It was one of the Rent-A-Wife jobs she liked least, because there was too much sit-and-wait time involved, but it was her day off at the hospital and she didn't want Gianna moving furniture and appliances.

Besides, the deliveries were for the Dower House and she liked being there. She'd cleaned it again after Penny Phillipy worked her magic and Jack repaired damaged wood trim and floorboards. The house smelled like fresh paint overlaid with lemon oil, paste wax and window cleaner. New carpet had been laid upstairs and area rugs had been put in place, ranging from room-size in the living room to a braided oval where the kitchen table and chairs would go.

Three boxes of books were open on the floor in the little library, and she and the puppy shelved them while they waited, although the puppy wasn't much help. Arlie dusted the volumes as she went, grinning because it was obvious Jack still loved reading Westerns. His Louis L'Amour collection was shabby, falling open to favorite places in the same manner as her own beloved copies of *Pride and Prejudice* and *Anne of Green Gables*. The Zane Grey books her father had given him were even worse, the book-club bindings long worn off the edges of the covers, the gilt titles faded away from the spines.

She'd lost track of how many rainy-day dates they'd spent sitting on the floor of the used book store in Sawyer. Jack's interest in carpentry had been born one Saturday when he helped the store's owner unpack a crate of books on woodworking.

"That will drive your grandmother crazy," Arlie had said when he purchased a stack of the almost-new volumes.

He'd shrugged. "She'll never see them. As long as we show up for dinner and don't wear jeans when she has company, she doesn't care what we do."

That was true. He and Tucker had spent as much time as they could in Ellen Curtis's little yellow rental house on the other side of the lake, but they'd lived in Llewellyn Hall with their grandparents and their father.

Jack still had the carpentry books, though they were much the worse for wear. Arlie placed them at eye level on the shelf.

The puppy, named Walter Mittens because his feet were all white but called Wally because Holly kept referring to him as "Holly's little Wally," wore himself out running to the front door every time he heard a noise. Since it was late autumn and the wind was blowing the last of the leaves from the sycamores, oaks and maples on the grounds of Llewellyn Hall, he heard many noises.

Arlie arranged the new living room furniture while the deliveryman assembled the beds in the master suite and the bedroom that would be Charlie's. It was telling that Jack bought everything new for the Dower House. Even lamps and tables came from a store in Kokomo. She hadn't asked him about it—she knew without him saying so that he wanted no part of the Llewellyn legacy.

The new furnishings were comfortable and warm. The couch and chairs were upholstered in pewter gray and navy, with sudden startling flashes of dark red lending vibrancy to the setting. The tables were walnut, with rounded corners and scooped drawer pulls. The dining table and its six chairs, she noted with a snort of laughter, exactly matched the ones she had at the Toe.

Although the appliances had worked, he'd replaced them all. The old ones had been transferred directly to the house Habitat for Humanity was refurbishing in Sawyer.

She wondered, although she didn't want to, how long he intended to stay. If Llewellyn's Lures or the Hall sold right away, this would all be a waste.

She'd just finished making the beds and was following Wally down the stairs when the puppy hurled himself down the last three steps and at the front door, yelping wildly.

"You know," she said mildly, bending to pick him up, "if you're going to be a yapper, we need to talk about it. Hasn't Caruso convinced you yet that hers is the only loud voice allowed in the house?"

The door opened then, and Wally leaped with neither caution nor compunction from her arms to Jack's.

"Whoa!" The case holding Jack's notebook computer slid to the floor as he caught Wally in flight. "Your mother has absolutely no control over you," he said, stroking the wiggling puppy. "I see obedience school in your future."

His attention went from Wally to Arlie. She felt warm, as though he was touching her. "Everything get delivered?"

She nodded. "I arranged what I could. The paperwork is on your desk."

"Including Gianna's invoice?"

"Yes."

"Thank you."

If they got any more polite, they would surely shatter from the stiffness of it. They stood in the foyer, neither of them moving. Jack's hair was windblown, falling toward his eyes. His teeth gleamed through his beard when he smiled, and she thought he was doing that more often than he had the first few days he was back. He stroked Wally's curly little head.

"What does Caruso think of him?" he asked, handing the puppy to her and taking off his leather jacket.

"She thinks he's her toy. When they go to sleep at night she curls around him. He snores, and she swats him with a paw."

She hadn't seen Jack in a week. He hadn't been there when she cleaned up after the painting and wood repair had been done. She'd left him an invoice and a note inviting him to Thanksgiving supper at Gianna's.

He'd left her a voice mail on her home phone accepting the invitation with thanks. His check had arrived in the next day's mail at the office. There had been a picture in the envelope, too, one he'd snapped with his phone that first night Jack had found Wally in the mailbox, of Caruso lying with a paw stretched over the puppy sleeping at her side. Gianna had put the photo on the front of her refrigerator. She was using the envelope, addressed in the scrawl that hadn't changed since high school days, as a bookmark. She hoped no one noticed.

"Does it look okay?" Arlie gestured with her arm. "I arranged things the way I liked them. If you want anything moved, I'll be glad to help."

"It looks great." He opened the entry closet, then closed it, turning back to her with his jacket still in his hand. "Can I take you home? And out to dinner? Not at your house, but out. We can go anywhere you like. I don't really know what's open other than Anything Goes."

She swiped ineffectually at the front of her sweatshirt. "I'd need to change and ask Caruso to babysit for Wally." What was she thinking?

"I'll wait."

She guessed thinking didn't have anything to do with it. Right this minute it was all about feeling, and she felt as though she wanted to be with him. "All right."

They rode to the Toe in near silence. Wally sat in Jack's lap under the steering wheel and ignored Arlie.

Her nerves jangled to the point that she felt as though she'd swallowed a tambourine. Was this a date? After sixteen years, was she actually going on a date with her high school boyfriend? No, this just couldn't happen. There had been enough drama in both their lives—they didn't need to look for more.

"Is this a date?" she blurted as he pulled into her driveway. "Jack, it's been sixteen years. You have a kid. What are we doing?"

"We're going out to eat. I've eaten cookies and chili at your house and I'll cook dinner for us at the Dower House sometime after I buy more groceries than a package of bologna and a loaf of bread. I don't know if it's a date or not." He traced her cheek with the tip of his forefinger, touching her hairline, the sparkling gold hoop and the tiny diamond stud she wore in her ear and the little dent the accident had placed just off center in her chin. "I know I want to see you. To spend time with you." He grinned. "I wouldn't even mind helping you pick out a new van. If that old one is any indicator of your taste in vehicles, you're not to be trusted."

"Oh, that reminds me." She beamed at him. "There's one at the dealership. If I hurry, we can run by and look at it and you can give me your vastly superior opinion on it." And then it wouldn't really be a date. And she wouldn't have to think about—or even admit—how much she wanted to see and spend time with him, too.

At least, not yet.

CHAPTER FIVE

THE VAN WAS RED. Its electric windows worked and it had a fully operational CD player. Arlie bought it on the spot. Jack laughed at her as they walked back to his SUV. "You didn't even look for dents." He opened the passenger door for her.

She had her seat belt buckled by the time he got behind the wheel. "No need. As soon as I back into the hitching rail at Sam's Hardware—which I realize has been there all our lives—there will be a nice new one. William Detwiler, the Amish bishop who bought my grandparents' farm between Sawyer and the lake, says I might be safer in a horse and buggy. Then he shakes his head and says he doesn't think it's fair to do that to a horse."

"The Amish community has grown a lot since I left here."

She nodded. "Gianna's best friend is Amish. They're both widows with daughters and they both like to cook and garden. Lovena Beiler's the one who taught me to quilt and got me started on my slight fabric addiction."

He grinned at her, pulling onto the two-lane highway that would take them away from Sawyer.

"How's it going at the factory?" she asked. "Have you found buyers?"

"There is a lot of interest. From Japan. From China. From Thailand. From Mexico. There's nothing wrong with that, except that we'd like to keep the business here, where it's always been, and it's hard to guarantee that."

Arlie was dismayed. She knew the fifty-some employees of Llewellyn's Lures. She'd worked summers there when she was in college. She was still the pathetically bad left fielder on their softball team. "No one in the United States wants it?"

"Actually, there is a large manufacturer in this country that would like to absorb Llewellyn's. They would even leave the Indiana and Tennessee plants mostly intact, though they'd bring in their own management teams to rearrange the processes and the administration. The biggest problem for me is that they want to close the one in Vermont and make the one in Michigan a warehouse-only concern. The Vermont plant is the smallest and the least profitable, but it means a lot to the area it's in. I live there—it means a lot to *me*." He looked thoughtful, coming to a stop at the four-lane highway that led toward Indianapolis or South Bend, depending on which way you turned. "Where are we going?"

"There's an Amish-style restaurant about six miles that way." Arlie pointed across the highway. "It has a huge buffet. Their pie and Gianna's pasta are the reasons I haven't retained my girlish figure." She looked down at herself. "I probably have retained it—I'm just keeping it hidden under the extra twenty pounds." She eyed him resentfully. "You still weigh the same as you did then, don't you?"

"No. I've gained twenty pounds, too."

"You have not."

"Yes, I have." His teeth glimmered white in a grin. "But I grew a beard and three inches after graduation. That helps."

"I *thought* you were taller. I'm glad to know I'm not just getting shorter." Which was what Holly had tried to convince her was happening. "What do the employees want to do? Have you talked to them about it?"

"Yes. We met with the management staff and the floor crew separately and then with everyone at once. There are fifty-nine employees altogether, and I'm pretty sure we amassed fifty-nine opinions. And that's not counting Tucker's or mine." He chuckled. "Sam's dad, Paul, who has worked there since the day he graduated from high school, called me a whippersnapper."

Arlie frowned. "Mr. Phillipy? That doesn't sound like him." He'd taught her how to swing a bat well enough that her teammates stopped dropping to their knees in supplication every time she stepped into the batter's box.

"The plant manager, a friend of my grandmother's who came from Somewhere Else—did you know those two words were capitalized, by the way?—well, he'd sell the whole place down the river in a New York minute. I think Mr. Phillipy thought I was headed down the same road."

Arlie knew the plant manager—he was an acquaintance of Chris's. She thought Jack's assessment was right on the money. "Has Mr. Phillipy changed his mind?"

"I hope so. Is that it?" He gestured toward a red barn sitting by itself on the left side of the road. Although there was no paved parking lot, the grassy area around the building was packed with cars. He pulled in, finding a space far away from the restaurant's entrance. "I hope you don't mind parking in the back forty."

She laughed, opening her own door as soon as he turned off the SUV's engine. "You're starting to talk as though you never left the lake. Do they have back forties in Vermont?"

"They probably do. No one's ever looked at me funny when I said it." He caught her hand as they walked. "At least, if they did, I didn't notice."

She was glad they'd parked in the very back of the parking area. By the time they entered the building, they'd discussed the buggies at the hitching rails, what they were going to eat for dinner and who was going to win the high school football game that night. It wasn't a home game, she explained, or that was where she'd be.

Arlie's arm was warm all the way to her shoulder. She was enjoying it more than she thought was going to be good for her in the long run.

When they had filled their plates at the buffet and were seated, Jack sipped his coffee, closing his eyes in enjoyment. "If I liked booze as much as I like coffee, I'd be in real trouble—" His expression grew thoughtful. "What's your favorite part of being a nurse?"

Arlie didn't have to think about that. "The part I'm not doing right now. The midwifery."

"That's right. You're a nurse-midwife, and I'll bet you were a good one. What made you leave that?"

She hesitated. "I lost a baby in delivery, and then I lost heart." It had been like losing her own all over again, though it shouldn't have been. But Jack couldn't know that.

"I'm sorry." He captured and held her gaze. "But I'm surprised, too, because you're not one to give up the first time you're knocked down."

Her eyes veered from his. She stared at a point beyond him, as though searching for words. "I couldn't deal with it when the baby died, and then Gianna had her heart attack, so I tendered my resignation and came back to Miniagua to lick my wounds and take care of Gianna's at the same time. I bought the house and was in the process of learning to use power tools and put in toilets that don't leak when Gianna came up with the idea for Rent-A-Wife."

"But you still miss 'birthing babies,' don't you?"

She closed her eyes for a few seconds, feeling pressure behind them that could become tears in a heartbeat. "I do. Every single day. And I keep my license up to date and stay current with all the changes. I even help the Amish midwife when I'm needed. But I didn't think a clinic could thrive here—the area's too small and the only gynecologist in Sawyer doesn't want to work with a midwife. And I'm not leaving here again. Not ever."

"I'm surprised you moved away in the first place." He chuckled, though he looked embarrassed. "Was it because I was such an idiot and left? Because I wasn't worth it—we both know that."

"I'd lived in a sort-of big town the whole time I was in college. Back then, I wasn't in a hurry to return to a place without fast food or a shopping mall." She laughed, too, shaking her head at him. "Besides, I've never known a seventeen-year-old yet whose heart doesn't get broken at some point. It healed." Her smile slipped away. "I had other boyfriends and other breakups. It was the accident I couldn't get over." The accident and the loss of their baby. Sadness pushed and she pushed back, though it was as persistent as the tears that had threatened only a moment ago. "Most of us couldn't, could we? At least, not completely."

She reached for his hand, pushing it up until they were palm to palm. He reached for her other hand, setting it against his own in the same position. "We were each other's mirrors," he recalled, his voice hardly above a whisper. "We had so much empathy going on Tuck used to call you 'the third twin.' Until the reflection broke."

She started to say something, but was interrupted by a male voice. Not derisive exactly, but not overly friendly, either. "Arlie? Are you playing patty-cakes or what?"

Chris's tone was as quiet as it always was, but there was a touch of arrogance in it when he spoke. Something faintly accusatory. Arlie stiffened in instant resentment. And she didn't let go of Jack's hands.

"Jack," she said. "You remember Chris Granger."

"Chris." Jack stood, still holding one of her hands as he extended his right one to Chris. "Long time."

"Yes."

Their handshake was short and brisk. Arlie had never known how quickly testosterone could take over a room. As an avid fan of

Regency-era romance novels, she wouldn't have been at all surprised if one of them had tried slapping the other around with a glove. Of course, it was only November and no one in Indiana was wearing gloves yet. "Would you like to join us?" she asked and managed not to squeal when Jack's fingers tightened around hers.

"No, thank you." Chris glowered at her even as he smiled regretfully. "I'm here with my folks."

"Oh." She gave him a commiserative smile. Chris's parents were nice, but they kept their only son and heir on a short leash during the months he lived on the lake. "Tell them hello. Enjoy your dinner."

He nodded. "I'll call you." With a nod and a clipped "Jack," he stalked away.

The silence he left behind was the first uncomfortable one Arlie and Jack had shared since the night she'd met Charlie.

Then Jack laughed.

"Really." She removed her hand from his and glared at him. "There is no possible way that was funny."

He traced a finger down her jawline, stopping at the dent in her chin. She could no more have pulled away than she could have flown.

"What?" She sounded like a petulant child, but there was no way to unsay the word.

"Arletta Marquetta Brigetta—" he grinned when she rolled her eyes at the hated nickname "—do you realize the scope of our conversation in the last couple of hours? We have talked about dating—as in each other—cars, the Amish, Charlie's homework and if he needs a haircut, food, football, your business, my business and midwifery. I have to admit, meeting the guy who's now your boyfriend—which I assume Granger is—makes this the most eclectic date I've ever had. How about you?"

"He's not my boyfriend. We just…see each other." Saying more would compromise the tacit agreement she and Chris shared. But it was as though the width of the table between Jack and herself had gone from a couple of feet to a space too wide to cross.

"For how long?" The beard hid so much of his expression she couldn't tell what he was thinking, but he wasn't smiling.

"A couple of years."

Jack raised his eyebrows. "No wonder he didn't like us holding hands. I wouldn't either if I were him."

"We're not exclusive." She knew that was

weak. And not exactly true. But exclusivity didn't always mean intimacy. Not even close. She'd felt more physical closeness walking across the restaurant parking lot with Jack than she'd ever felt with Chris.

It was time to talk about their "courtship." Time to change the rules. Or give them up entirely.

"What about you?" Not only did she resent Chris for acting like an outraged lover, she wasn't particularly fond of Jack's chilly demeanor. She didn't have to wait to talk to *him*—he was right there. "You don't have a social life outside of Miniagua? You don't date? You've been *married*."

"I do and I have." He caught her hand again. "I'm sorry. We were talking about when you decided to be a nurse-midwife and live in Indianapolis. I was shocked then, because even though I was the one who walked away, there was always this thought in the back of my mind that we'd be together someday. I know how wrong that was, and it was just as wrong tonight, but I felt the same way when the rich kid got a little possessive."

She shook her head. "Rich kid? Isn't that the pot calling the kettle black? You're both rich kids—that's how you were referred to in school."

"It probably is, though neither of us is a kid anymore." He smiled, though it didn't reach his eyes. "I'm sorry again. I'd like to stay friends, like we were before this conversation went south. Think we could do that?" The question, like the smile, was rueful.

So was the twisty little feeling in her heart.

"You're not my bodyguard, for heaven's sake." Arlie glowered across the counter that separated her kitchen from the dining area. She'd invited Chris over for a clearing-the-air breakfast on Friday morning, although she wasn't inclined to cook for him now that he was there.

He scowled back at her. "Aside from the fact that his father was responsible for your father's death and the crippling of your sister, he walked away from you when you were still an emotional wreck. He spent an evening with you and didn't bother telling you he had a kid and an ex-wife. Don't you think seeing him socially might possibly be a mistake?"

"What I think is that Daddy's been gone for sixteen years and that the boy who walked away from me was as heartbroken as I was. He didn't do the right thing, but—"

"Not even close," Chris interrupted.

"Did you hear what I said?" Arlie poured coffee for them both. Not that Chris deserved it—he was displaying all the least attractive traits of the back end of a horse. "He was eighteen and feeling guilty about every single thing that had happened both before and after the accident. How adult were you at eighteen? You were packing your brand-new convertible for the drive to Berkeley, weren't you?"

"Llewellyn's family has as much money as mine does. It wasn't like he had to work his way through Notre Dame." Chris accepted the cup. "Thank you."

"I'm not talking about money, Chris. It was never even a factor." She sipped her coffee, coming around to sit at the table with him. "There's no way I can explain to you what it was like for any of us after the accident. We all handled it differently, with varying degrees of terrible, depending on who it was and when it was."

"Arlie, you told me yourself he kept his son a secret. How can you possibly excuse that?"

"I can't answer that," she admitted, wishing she'd never confided in Chris how she'd come to meet Charlie, "because I don't fully understand it myself and because the truth is I'm still mad at him about that."

"So why open yourself up to having your heart broken again?"

She raised her eyebrows. "I don't know. Why are you waiting for a woman's husband to die so that you can go on with your life?"

His answer was immediate. "Because Heather *is* my life whether we ever have a real relationship or not. It wasn't her husband's fault he had a massive stroke that put him in a nursing home when he was thirty, nor was it hers or mine. Things just happen."

"Right. The accident wasn't Jack's fault, either." She eyed Chris. "Are you upset because you're afraid I might get hurt or because you know it's time for the whole pretend courtship between us to end?"

She hadn't known she was going to say it quite like that, but once the words were out she was glad she had. "We're friends," she went on, keeping her voice gentle, "and we hung out together anyway, so it was easy to pretend. To keep your parents and their friends from asking too many questions— though I'm pretty sure your mother will be glad to know I'm not going to be joining your family anytime soon. She likes me just fine as one of your little friends, but that was as far as she was able to go with that scenario."

He chuckled drily. "You think she's going to prefer that I'm in love with a married woman who has two kids, a mortgage and a Saint Bernard and is in all likelihood never going to love me back?"

"Heather's still not letting you help with that mortgage, huh?" Arlie had never met the woman Chris loved. She'd talked to her on the phone, though, and she liked her.

"No. Kind of reminds me of when I wanted to buy you a van so you'd quit driving that moving violation on wheels every time you worked for your stepmother. What good is having money if you can't help people you care about?" Chris got to his feet, taking his cup to the sink in the corner to rinse it out. "So, are we breaking up?"

"I think so. It was only in everyone else's eyes that we were ever a couple anyway." The assumption had been convenient for both of them. Chris hadn't liked being the lake's most eligible bachelor when in his heart he was neither a bachelor nor eligible. Arlie had been weary of saying "No, I'm not married yet" to the lake residents who returned every spring and "Yes, I hear it" to Gianna's friends who took every opportunity to mention her ticking biological clock.

He dried his cup and set it upside down on the dish drainer before coming back to the table. "Still friends? Even though you can't beat me at Scrabble?"

She rolled her eyes, getting up to walk him to the door. "Anyone can beat you at Scrabble, preppie. Wally probably could by now—he's almost housebroken—and we know Caruso can."

"You're heartless," he accused, laughing, and kissed her cheek before opening the door. "Lunch one day next week, since we seem to have never gotten around to eating breakfast?"

"Sure. Maybe Thursday. I'm working Monday through Wednesday." She started to close the door after him, then met Jack's frosty gaze from where he got out of the SUV he'd parked beside Chris's BMW. "Don't give me dirty looks," she cautioned, stepping onto the porch. "I just won one argument with an old boyfriend. I have no problem with winning another one."

"Old?" Chris squinted at her, then turned

toward Jack. "Winning is relative. Since I was never her boyfriend anyway, I don't think it counts."

"I was." Jack shrugged. "But I wasn't a good one, so she deserves to win, I guess. Did you say you never were?"

"She'll explain it to you." Chris hesitated, thumping his fingertips on the top of his car. "Be good to her, though, boyfriend or not. She's not bad once you get used to her."

The words were light, but his expression wasn't. Arlie felt a surge of affection for him. "Give my love to your mother, preppie."

He snorted. "Bet on it, laker. See you." With an almost-friendly nod at Jack, he got into his car.

Arlie turned her attention to Jack. Even though it was mid-November and the late-morning temperature was languishing in the low thirties, she felt warm in his presence. Almost uncomfortably so, but not quite.

Actually, it felt rather delicious.

"Did you need something?" What Jack *needed* was a haircut—he had as long as she'd known him. In high school, he'd kept it long to irritate his grandmother. Arlie had no idea why his hair was shaggy now, but she was pretty sure he hadn't come to her house this morning to discuss his coiffure.

"Actually, I thought if you'd like I'd take you to pick up the van. I was at the plant this morning but was invited to stay out of the way because they needed to get work done." His eyes sparkled with familiar laughter, and her breath hitched. "I need an ego boost, so if you'll just be nice to me, I'll even pay your way at the movies tonight."

Her eyes widened. "It's Friday. Have you lost your mind? We can't go to the movies."

"We can't?"

"It's high school football night and it's a home game. If your sister's the cheerleading coach, which mine is, and your mother's the assistant concession-stand manager, which mine is, and you're not working, which I'm not, you show up. You don't *see* the games, because you're selling nachos and popcorn and watery hot chocolate. When you're not doing that, you're digging out ice packs for cheerleaders with sore hamstrings. Sometimes, you're telling crying teenage girls that life really does go on after the right tailback acts like a jerk. But you still go."

"Oh, well, that was stupid of me. I should have remembered that, although I haven't been to a game since I was playing. I wasn't a jerk then, if you'll remember, because I was a halfback. Is Miniagua good this year?"

"I know a good way to find out."

CHAPTER SIX

ARLIE HADN'T BEEN EXAGGERATING. When you spent the game hawking concessions and trying to look over the heads of the customers, you didn't see much. Judging by the score—Jack *could* see the scoreboard—Miniagua's young Lakers were doing pretty well for a One-A team playing a Two-A conference foe. To put it mildly, most of the way through the second quarter, they were stomping their opponents into the fertile central Indiana dirt.

"The band director's wife is in labor and he had to leave right after we played the national anthem and the drum major is out sick." A senior clarinet player leaned over the counter just before the two-minute warning. "Please, Arlie. You helped choreograph the halftime show. You can direct it. Please?"

"I'm not a director." Arlie handed coffee to a customer and shook her head at the clarinet player. "I'd have you all marching through the Masts' cornfield playing Oak Hill High

School's fight song instead of our own. We could get tossed out of the school district, maybe the entire conference. Holly would do better than me."

"You're the closest we have. You were the drum major in high school. Your sister is the cheerleading coach, so she's already busy over there." A girl from the flag corps appeared beside the clarinetist. "The next best candidate is the kid who pulls the band trailer out to the field. His only qualification is that his mother plays the organ at St. Paul's."

Jack snorted and untied Arlie's apron. "Go. Some of the basketball team's coming to help out here during the last half anyway. Your mom and I will take pictures for future blackmail purposes."

"You won't have to," the girl with the flag promised. "We have good school photographers. They embarrass us all the time."

Jack nodded. He took a business card out of his wallet and handed it to her. "I'll want prints. Can you take care of that?"

Arlie gave him a scowl so sharp that he'd probably require stitches. "Have I told you I have a violent side and I don't mind indulging it? And that the next time I talk to Charlie, I'm telling him all kinds of stories?"

She was already running a hand through her hair and moving toward the access door to the concessions building. Gianna grabbed her arm and tucked the wild red curls up into one of the plastic clips she'd been carrying in her pockets ever since the girls were in elementary school. She pulled strands free in the back and around Arlie's face. "Your idea of violence is making Caruso eat dry food for an entire day." Gianna gave one of the loose tendrils a tug and her stepdaughter a quick hug. "Go on now. Don't forget to smile."

"The nice thing is that no one really sees the director. It's just the flag corps and the cheerleaders who need to smile." Arlie waved as she walked away between the two band members.

Jack stood at the access door and watched her go. She talked all the way to where the band stood in formation at the far goal. Near the fifty-yard line she waved to people she knew and stopped to hug the football coach and some of the players. She and the cheerleading coach did a little dance together, drawing applause and laughter from the crowd.

His heart felt as though it just might burst through his chest.

"It's just amazing, Gianna." The customer speaking worked at Llewellyn's Lures. "Even though they don't look the least bit alike, you never even remember that they're really not sisters."

"They're sisters in all the ways that count." Hostility lent stiffness and "mother alert" to Gianna's always-friendly voice.

The woman apparently didn't hear the note of warning. "I heard that Arlie and that Granger boy were breaking up because Jack Llewellyn's back on the lake. You might want to urge some caution on Arlie."

Mention of his name made Jack look over at Gianna with raised eyebrows. The Miniagua gossip lines were working fast.

"He won't stay," the woman went on, oblivious to his presence behind the access door. "That type never does. And he left her once. Doesn't she remember that?"

"That'll be three dollars." One of the basketball players interrupted the conversation by placing an order of nachos in front of the woman. "Mrs. Gallagher, if you and Mr. Llewellyn would like to take a break to watch the halftime show, we can handle this. Two more of the basketball team are coming to work halftime."

Jack couldn't see the woman's face because the tall ballplayer blocked his vision. It was tempting to go over and push him aside so he could see, but the truth was the kid had three inches on him and was a good sixteen or seventeen years younger. Jack probably shouldn't push him anywhere. Besides, he liked his attitude.

There was one thing, though. He pushed away from the door and set a hand on the kid's arm. "Call me Jack, okay?" He met the woman's shocked eyes across the counter. "I'll be around for a while, ma'am, but I'm sure Gianna appreciates the warning and the reminder of my past. She'd probably forgotten. Right, Ange?"

"Actually—" Gianna took his arm and accompanied him to the door "—I think I have."

"That was a nice thing to say," he said as they quick-stepped to the bleachers in time to see the marching band strut onto the field.

"I meant it." She patted his arm, then gave it a little squeeze. "But there is one more thing—you hurt my girl again, and it's me you'll deal with. I mean that, too."

STANDING ON THE raised podium the art class had painted to resemble a Miniagua Marching Lakers uniform was fun. She'd spent nearly as many hours with the high school band helping out on the choreography as she had when she played first chair clarinet. Chris teased her sometimes, saying she and Holly may have graduated, but they'd never actually left Miniagua High School.

There was truth to that. Neither she nor Holly could drive the first half of their senior year, due to the accident. Riding the school bus was not only demeaning—they were seniors, after all—but very difficult. This meant Gianna dropped them off and picked them up for every practice, game or meeting. When both girls would have liked to take a semester to let their injuries heal and grieve their losses, begging to be tutored at home rather than start school with their classmates, their mother pushed them back into activities.

It had been the hardest time of Arlie's life, even worse than when her mother left. Her father was dead. The baby she'd hardly known she was carrying was gone forever. Jack had left for Notre Dame and she'd known in her heart that if he came back, it wouldn't be as her boyfriend. There was very little left of the person she'd been and she wasn't sure she liked what remained.

But no one at school talked about the accident or Dave Gallagher or asked her how Jack liked Notre Dame. Linda Saylors's absence left a solemn, quiet spot in their class, but they were all diminished by it—it was never a lonely grief like the one for Arlie's father or for Jack and the unrealized dream that had been their baby.

Neither she nor Holly had wanted to go to the prom that year, and their class had decided unanimously not to have one. They'd told the juniors to go on without them if they wanted to, but that they'd go bowling and eat pizza in Sawyer—and that was what they'd done. In the end, the junior class had joined them, and there'd been no formal gowns or tuxedos at the lake that spring.

What there *had* been, she remembered, was a loud and impromptu version of the *Footloose* prom dance in the parking lot of the bowling alley. What the Miniagua students lacked in talent and grace, they made up for in laughing and off-key singing.

She'd known beyond all doubt that safety anywhere was only an illusion, but she'd felt safe on the lake. She still did.

She hadn't been able to play in the band her senior year, but she'd helped plan the

Marching Lakers' show, sitting on the bottom row of bleachers with Holly and counting steps just as she had this year. She'd made adjustments on the map and taken to the field to straighten lines. One time, she'd marched the flag corps right into the bleachers just to see if they'd go. They did.

Now, sixteen years later, Mr. Harrison approached the podium where she was trying to get her bearings. He shook a finger at her. "Not into the bleachers, Arlie. People are sitting there."

"I know," she said, laughing. "You'll tell my mom on me, right?"

"You bet." He grinned back at her. "Thanks for standing in for the director. He was trying to figure out the two-places-at-one-time thing, and his kid hasn't even been born yet."

She didn't have a baton—presumably the director's was on the way to the hospital with its owner—but Libby Worth handed her the empty cardboard cylinder from a roll of paper towels and it worked admirably. Arlie added exaggerated body language that drew laughter from the crowd.

When halftime was over and the band had gone into the school to store instruments and change clothes, Arlie returned to the concession stand. "That was *fun*." She kissed Gianna's cheek, two-stepped with one of the basketball players past the candy-bar display and ended up at the popcorn machine beside Jack. She knew her eyelashes were negligible even before the mascara wore off, but she fluttered them at him anyway. "Bet you didn't know I'd be such a cool date, did you?"

He grinned at her and put a decidedly proprietary arm around her waist. "Sure I did."

After the game, when they had helped Gianna neaten and close the concession stand and Arlie had accepted sweeping bows of acclamation from a rowdy group of band members, they walked across the semiempty parking lot to Jack's car. The air had grown colder, and Arlie shivered inside her fleece jacket. Jack's arm came around her shoulders, drawing her closer into the warmth of his side.

This was how sixteen had felt. She'd been safe and warm and loved, with laughter brimming close to the top and sweet music always in the background. It was nice, even for a little while, to feel the same way at thirty-three.

"Anything Goes has really good hot chocolate with a little of what the bartender calls 'warming agent' mixed in," she said. "What do you say?"

"Sounds good to me. Think we'll get carded?"

She laughed, sliding into the passenger seat when he opened the door. Apparently, she wasn't the only one reliving adolescent feelings. "Do you want to park at the Toe and walk to Anything Goes? That way, you can drink two cups of chocolate if you like."

He started the car. "A walk would feel good. I haven't been moving enough since I've been here."

"Holly would be glad to have you on the cheerleading squad. They move all the time."

"Nah. I don't have the right legs for a skirt, especially one of those short ones." He pulled onto the road. "Is there a bicycle shop on the lake anywhere or do you have to go to Break-away over in Peru?"

She eyed him in the glow of the dash lights. "Do I see an entrepreneurial gleam in your eye?"

He frowned at her. "I can't believe you just said that."

"Said what? It's what you do."

"It may be what I do, but it doesn't mean

I can pronounce it. I think I'm offended that you can."

She laughed. "Well, what do you call yourself? I didn't mean to offend you, though I don't really mind that I did. Entertainment's entertainment, no matter where it comes from. And you've probably noticed it's still lean here on the lake."

"Let me think about that for a minute." He drove past the community church, past the parsonage that appeared to be filled with more teenagers than it could safely hold. The Sea Chantey Convenience Store and Bait Shop— the owners couldn't find a Cole Porter title that really matched—and Through Thick and Thin Barber Shop were closed up tight. He maneuvered the SUV around the omnipresent potholes as though he'd never left the narrow graveled roads of Lake Miniagua, even missing the one the lakers had christened "the crater" in front of the quilt shop.

They parked at the Toe. Arlie checked on the animals, ignored her blinking answering machine and joined Jack for the half-mile walk to the restaurant. She started to pull gloves from her jacket pocket, then didn't. She wasn't cold even though the air was— she was enlivened.

"The lake sounds like winter," he commented. "The waves are crisp lapping up on the shore, like there's ice in them."

"Have you figured out what you call yourself yet?" she asked, waving at Mrs. Benteen and Mrs. Phillipy as they walked their matching dachshunds on the other side of the road.

He was silent for a minute or two, slowing to look at the For Sale sign in front of the old Miniagua Drugstore and Soda Fountain. "Remember when we'd go in there and get shakes and malts after ball games?"

"I do. Daddy used to take us there after church every Sunday, too. They'd have a buffet set up just for Sundays. Gianna loves to cook, but she enjoyed those days off, too." Arlie slapped his arm and didn't object when he stilled her hand by taking it in his own. "Avoiding the question?"

"Nope, just thinking. I'd say I'm Jack of several trades. I like working hard and I never want to be bored. Getting a business going well is hard work. You have to find the right personnel and help create the right working environment for everybody concerned. I like to work myself right out of a job, so when it looks as though the business is going to stay afloat, I get out."

"Have there been any failures?"

"Uh-huh. I bought a drive-in theater because there are so few of them left and I hated to see one more go down the tubes, but this one was in a growing, bustling area. They didn't *want* to spend weekend nights watching movies from their cars. I lost a bundle on it, but I sold it to the city and it became a much-needed park." He shrugged. "It was like a loss with benefits."

"Holly says that about her foot."

"What?" He stopped walking so suddenly she stumbled into him. And thought about staying there, with her cheek against his chest, her free hand at his waist, where the warmth of his skin sent a tingle through her palm.

But no. No. Feeling any kind of tingle with Jack Llewellyn was off-limits. She regained her balance, her hand still in his. "Her foot. It was awful that she lost it. No one knows that any better than her, but what it did toward making her the person she is can't be measured."

"So instead of feeling forever guilty about her foot, I should feel proud of myself and my family because she lost it?"

The bitter words surprised her. And disappointed her. She withdrew her hand, placing it on her hip. "Actually, Jack, it's not about you at all. It's about Holly. You had nothing to do with the accident, other than being in it and knowing enough first aid to help Gianna keep us alive till the ambulances got there. But Holly's the one who made herself strong—it had nothing to do with you."

He stared at her for a moment, his mouth just agape enough for her to see the laugh build before it burst out. He pulled her into his arms where they stood in the parking lot of the Anything Goes Grill and hugged her long and hard.

"Maybe I needed to come back to the lake to be told to get over myself." He spoke close to her ear, laughter still making his voice rock and tremble so that she felt the vibration of it. The tingle.

She hugged him back, inhaling the scent of him and enjoying the feel of his arms around her. She tried, unsuccessfully, to stop the thought that filled her head and her heart.

Maybe you needed to come back to me.

NATE BENTEEN, WEARING a Miniagua Lakers hat and a polo shirt with the logo of Feathermoor Golf Course stitched on its left front, was behind the bar. He waved when Arlie and Jack came in, and pointed to a partially filled long table near the huge stone fireplace. "I'll join you as soon as Mollie gets back," he called, referring to the regular bartender. "You want hot chocolate with stuff in it?"

Jack nodded, letting Arlie go ahead of him to the table. Tucker was there, he saw, and Sam and Penny Phillipy. Holly sat across from Tucker. Libby Worth was beside her. Jack had to control his shudder. It was like a prom-night reunion. The only ones missing who were still alive were Gianna, Cass Gentry and Jesse. No one seemed to know anything about Cass and Jesse didn't socialize much.

Holly waved at her sister. "There she is, the first person to ever direct the Marching Lakers with an empty paper-towel roll and more hip movement than I've ever seen outside of Zumba class."

Arlie slid into a chair beside her. "The real question of the night," she said, leaning forward to look at Libby, "is why you had the paper-towel roll in your purse to begin with."

"I changed the roll in the women's restroom on the way out of the tearoom. I put it in my purse to drop in the garbage can when

I went home. But I forgot, which was good for you."

Libby, whose smile transformed her plain face into something special, beamed at her. "If you'd done any more hip bumps out there, you might have been arrested."

"Hey, it worked." Tucker gestured in Arlie's direction. "She didn't march the flag corps into the bleachers."

"I couldn't. Mr. Harrison was going to tell Gianna on me if I did."

Nate brought over a tray of drinks and joined them, and they talked and laughed until midnight. Jack didn't say that much, nor did anyone say that much to him, but the ice with which he'd been greeted when he first came back to town seemed to have melted somewhat.

They exchanged memories, skirting around the painful ones, and talked some about the years between Then and Now. Jack found himself speaking in unison with his brother— something they'd done in the old empathetic Irish twin days—and exchanging wry grins with him.

The walk back to the Toe went more quickly than he wanted it to, but he had to admit he was tired. Arlie's quietness indicated she was, too. "I enjoyed the evening," he said, following her up the sidewalk to her front door.

"Me, too." She scrounged in her jacket pocket for her key—even in Miniagua people locked their doors anymore. "Be careful when we go in. Caruso will probably be mad because we left her to babysit for Wally."

But the big cat and the puppy were both asleep on the hearth. Jack noted with a grin that the Easter basket had been replaced by a bed big enough to accommodate both animals.

"Caruso used to sleep with me." Arlie hung her jacket in the entry closet. "Now she stays down here with her baby—he can't climb stairs yet and if I take him up with me, he cries to come down. Do you want some coffee?"

Jack looked at the curved-top clock on the mantel, remembering it from when they were teenagers. "No, I better not. It's been long enough since the hot chocolate that I'm okay anyway." He gestured toward the blinking answering machine. "You must have been popular while we were gone."

"It was already blinking when we left." She grinned, reaching to push the play button. "I didn't want to buy any insurance."

Her smile faded the instant she heard the voice on the machine. It took Jack a moment to recognize it. When he did, he reached for Arlie's hand automatically, thinking—as he often had when they were kids—that he might be able to protect her this time.

"Arliss?" The word was clipped. "It's your mother, Arliss. I'll call you back."

CHAPTER SEVEN

ARLIE FROWNED AT the answering machine, then pushed the delete button a little harder than was strictly necessary. "It's not even Christmas." She went to the fireplace, turning on the gas and standing still in front of it before the heat even began to radiate from the logs. The temperature in the house wasn't cold, but she was. The sound of her mother's voice sent chills rippling down her spine and settling in the pit of her stomach. Hot chocolate that had tasted so good and been so warming a short time ago didn't seem like such a good idea now.

"Will you call her back?"

"No. She'll call again." Arlie sat on the love seat, pulling the lap quilt off the back and wrapping it around her. "You should go, Jack. I don't deal well with her."

He knelt in front of her, tucking the blanket around her legs. "Is this the part of the conversation when I ask you if you have any brandy? I'm pretty sure you don't, but do you want some coffee or something instead?"

Don't be nice to me. Don't stay with me. I needed that Then, not now.

Who was she kidding—she needed it now, too. She didn't want to be alone. "I wouldn't mind if you heated up the cider in the fridge. Could you drink some?" Comfort was what she wanted, that was all, but a part of her realized she wanted it as much from the man as from the drink.

When the cider was hot, he brought it into the room and took a seat beside her.

She sipped from the aromatic liquid slowly, letting it melt the ice inside. "Did you feel betrayed by your mother when you were little?"

He hesitated. "Not betrayed exactly. At least, not until much later."

Her short laugh hurt her throat. "If I hadn't had Gianna, I'd still be blaming myself. Thinking if I'd been a better little girl, my mother wouldn't have left me and Daddy would still be alive. Guilt isn't a very nice gift to receive from parents."

"I don't think it's meant to be nice." He set his cup on the table at the end of the couch. "Why does she call you, Arlie?"

She shook her head. "I don't know. I used

to think she wanted to tell me she was sorry, but she didn't know how. Now that I've pretty much accepted that there is no Easter Bunny or Santa Claus, I've kind of gotten over thinking that. Then I thought she wanted money, because Dad's insurance money went to Gianna and Holly and me—she didn't get any. She hinted sometimes, like when I bought the house, but never came right out and asked. She called Gianna my 'wicked stepmother' and Holly my 'ugly stepsister' once, and I hung up on her and wouldn't pick up when she called back, so she never mentions them now." Warmed by the cider and his concern, Arlie took the blanket off and pushed it aside.

"Do you ever see her, or is it always just a phone call?" He folded the blanket and laid it on the arm of the couch.

"When I lived in Indianapolis, she came to the clinic once a year or so and we would go to lunch. I think she lives somewhere in Indy, but I don't know for sure. I asked her, but she never answered."

"Was it comfortable, spending time with her?"

Arlie shook her head again. "Not at all. Even after a few times. I have trouble looking at her. When I do, I can see that I look like her, and that makes me mad."

"You haven't seen her since you lived in Indy?"

Arlie laughed aloud. "The spring I first came back to the lake, she came to the Toe. It was a shambles. I was putting the hardwood floor in the living room. Penny was painting the kitchen. Nate was planting perennials in the flower beds. The neighbor kids had made the refrigerator box into a lemonade stand in the yard and were charging a nickel a glass."

"What did she do?"

Arlie heard the sympathy in his voice. Frowning, she tried to remember accurately.

"She stood here and said this was all I'd ever have, just a little house on the lake and a cat. That I'd never be anybody." Arlie met Jack's eyes. "She was right, in a way. I'll never be rich and I'll never make great strides in my profession, but I don't feel any great need to *be* somebody." She did feel a need to practice midwifery again, but she'd deal with that later.

"Because you already are somebody."

"I suppose." Although even when she talked about it, it didn't concern her. She supposed lack of ambition wasn't necessarily a good thing, but she was comfortable with it.

And tired.

"You need to go home," she said. "I am such an unexciting date that I'm going to fall asleep sitting here sometime in the next two minutes."

He got up, pulling her to her feet. "Doesn't that mean I'm the boring one if you can't even stay awake? Come on and lock the door after me."

"It was fun." She followed him to the door, Caruso and Wally tumbling out of their bed to go along, no doubt hoping for a midnight walk. "It's been a long time since I've been a drum major and had a date with the cutest guy in school on the same day."

"Don't forget, you also got to unstop one of the toilets in the women's restroom and have a nachos-eating contest with a basketball player. What were you thinking when you did that, anyway? Don't you know all a teenage guy has to do is inhale and food just disappears?"

"I do now." She shook her head, bending to lift the puppy, who was leaping at her shins in a repetitive request to be picked up *now*. "I don't know. I guess I just went a little crazy. I was so impressed with myself for fixing the toilet I thought I was invincible."

"Pride goeth before——"

"Don't even go there," she warned, laughing and opening the door. "Be careful going home. If you talk to Charlie, tell him I'll email him tomorrow."

Jack took a moment to scratch Caruso's cheek and pat Wally's head. "I will. Want to pick up the van in the morning?"

"I can get a ride. It's okay."

"I'm *offering* a ride."

"Oh." Depending on him wasn't a good idea. Even though they'd both grown up and she at least had no intention of going the boyfriend-girlfriend route again, Arlie had no doubt she would be hurt when he left Miniagua again. It would be better for both of them if they established boundaries and saw each other less instead of more.

Soon. They would do that soon.

"I'll fix breakfast," she counteroffered.

"Sounds good." He touched her cheek. "Remember to lock the door."

"The kids want a little walk first, then I will. Promise."

He got into his car, but didn't drive away until Caruso and Wally had made mad dashes around the perimeter of the front yard and returned to the porch where Arlie waited. She waved to him and went inside, locking the door behind her.

She was a big girl. She'd lived alone since the week she graduated from college. She changed her own tires, plunged her own toilets—and a few others besides—and emptied her own mousetraps, with Caruso's close supervision. She hadn't needed to be taken care of in a very long time. Still didn't.

But it felt kind of good.

JACK FOLLOWED ARLIE and the new van back to the Rent-A-Wife office the next morning, pulling in behind her on the narrow street.

"It's amazing!" Arlie climbed out and stood back to beam at the red vehicle. Wally's head bobbed as he perched on her arm and looked around with shiny eyes. "The heater worked without me thumping the dash. The radio played on more than one station. I didn't rip my pants on that spring thing on the seat. I didn't have to get out at a traffic light in Sawyer to close the hatch because it popped open. We should have done this years ago!"

"Gee, why didn't I think of that?" Holly, who was standing on the sidewalk in front of the office, put her hands on her hips.

"I don't know. I'm so disappointed in you."

Arlie gave her a laughing hug. "I thought you were on your way to that writers' thing you're speaking at this afternoon."

Holly kissed Wally's head. "I'm heading there now. I left a jump drive in the office I needed—it has my PowerPoint on it." She flashed a sidewise grin at Jack. "Mama or I would have taken you to pick up the van if you'd said something."

Arlie blushed and gave her sister a push. "Drive carefully and have a good time. See you tomorrow?"

Holly nodded. With a final wave to Jack, she sprinted to her car, scarcely a hitch in her step.

When Arlie and Jack were in the SUV, preparing to go to the Toe, Wally leaped to Jack's lap, gazing adoringly up at him.

"Do you work weekends at the hospital?" Jack patted the puppy and handed him to Arlie.

"Two a month. I work three twelve-hour shifts a week—some nights and some days— which took me forever to get used to. A few times at first, I had to pull off the road and take a nap on the way home. I just work at Rent-A-Wife whenever Gianna needs me.

She has a good enough crew that usually it's not that often."

He put the SUV in gear and headed toward the Toe, slowing to a crawl as he passed the deserted storefront of the Miniagua Drugstore and Soda Fountain. It sat near the end of the street, with the miniature branch of Sawyer's library on one side and the It's De-Lovely Beauty Salon and Day Spa on the other. Anything Goes Grill was across the street. The empty two-story redbrick building had good bones, Jack noted, and plenty of parking—which was seldom the case in Miniagua's two-block commercial area. He wasn't sure of the square footage, but it seemed ample for whatever enterprise insisted on presenting itself. More than ample. There would be space for at least one rental unit on the second floor.

"You're thinking," Arlie accused.

"I am," he admitted. "Can't help it. It's an old habit."

"Anything you want to talk about? I'll be glad to tell you if you're wrong."

He snorted laughter. "What if I'm right?"

"I'll have to consider that." She smirked at him. "Doesn't happen often. Got plans for the weekend, now that you've rescued me?"

He sped up, swerving around the washed-out basin in the road in front of the quilt shop. "Tucker, Sam, Nate and I are going to Indianapolis to watch the Colts play tomorrow."

"That will be fun."

"I hope so. At least Sam and Nate are talking to me now." He held up a hand. "I'm sorry I said that. I deserve any treatment I've gotten since I came back." He seemed to physically pull away from the direction the conversation had taken and returned her smirk. "Did you want to go along and direct the music?"

She stared at him for a second, gauging the seriousness of the question, then burst into laughter so loud Wally barked a stern rebuke. "I can't go," she said. "I'm sewing tomorrow, with Gianna, Holly, Penny and Libby. Kind of like you guys at the football game only we're not as well dressed and we have a better vocabulary."

He parked at the Toe. "We don't really dress that well."

She laughed again, and Wally nipped her chin. "Thanks for the ride this morning."

"Thank you for the breakfast."

For a moment, their eyes met. Clashed. Arlie didn't know what to say or do. "Well."

She reached for the door handle. "I guess I'll see you later."

"Yeah. Thursday at your mom's if not before."

"Right." She smiled, feeling unaccountably nervous. She also wasn't ready for him to leave. "Want a cup of coffee before you go?"

"You bet."

They went into the house together. Arlie put Wally down and watched him run to where Caruso slept in a patch of sunlight splattering the floor in the kitchen. The puppy yipped all the way, sliding into Caruso's prone body when his paws couldn't gain purchase on the wood floor. The cat gave a bored yawn and proceeded to wash her little charge with a sandpapery tongue. Wally wriggled under her ministrations, beside himself with joy.

"Where do you quilt?" asked Jack, accepting the cup she handed him. He looked around the compact kitchen area. "Doesn't it take up a lot of space?"

"It does, although it would take up less if I were neater. Come on. I'll show you." She led him through the breezeway into the garage. "When I moved in here and was moaning about not having enough room, Lovena's husband—who is a contractor—suggested we add an upstairs to the garage. It made my mortgage considerably bigger than I'd intended, but I love my sewing room."

Jack stopped at the bottom of the wide staircase against the garage's back wall, staring at the red Mini Cooper parked neatly beside Arlie's bicycle. "I didn't even realize you had a car."

"It's how I get to work. Other than that, I don't drive it much—it seems like I'm always in the company van or walking. I thought about selling it when I moved back to the lake but Gianna pointed out that it was paid for and was there if I needed it. She was right, because when I got a job, it was in Sawyer. A nice ride on a bicycle, but not when it's cold or raining."

"She's always right, isn't she?"

"Yes, but we don't like to tell her that."

The sewing room was big, the same size as the two-and-a-half-car garage on the building's first floor. It had a hardwood floor, great lighting and built-in storage in every nook and cranny. A small bathroom, complete with a shower, took up one corner, a collapsible cutting table another, with room on every side of it to work from. A sewing machine and another machine he couldn't identify sat on expandable tables. Quilts hung everywhere. The center of the room was bare.

"Wow." Jack looked around. "I had no idea. How could I not have known how artistic you are?"

She shrugged. "That's easy. I'm not. I just learned to read directions and became fearless about putting colors together. Oh, and the most important thing of all—I've mastered sewing with a scant quarter-inch seam. Makes all the difference between a quilter and a hack."

He frowned, his gaze continuing its circuit of the room. "You're kidding, right?"

"Yes, I am." She grinned at him. "I sew quilts for children in hospitals, and no one's ever brought a warm and cuddly blanket back because of a crooked seam."

He gestured toward the long center of the room. "So, what's this, the dance floor? You and that ballplayer were doing a pretty convincing two-step last night."

"It's where the frame sits when we quilt, which we'll do Monday. Lovena and some of her daughters will come then, too. They can't on Sundays—it's either church services or visiting days for them. When we're just sewing, everyone else brings their tables and machines and sets them up there."

He nodded and sipped his coffee, looking thoughtful. "I always thought of quilting as something people's grandmothers did."

"They do." She led the way down the stairs, flipping off the panel of light switches at the bottom and going through the breezeway into the kitchen. "But so do their daughters and granddaughters. I'm not much of a hobby person, but I love quilting."

"You made scrapbooks, a lot of them."

"It was therapeutic. Gianna couldn't keep Holly and me in counseling—we wouldn't go—so she got me started on scrapbooking and Holly on journaling. Once I got to the end of the tunnel and saw there really was light all over the place out there, I didn't scrapbook much anymore. Just once in a while. I don't know if Holly still journals or not."

He rinsed his cup and set it upside down in the dish drainer. "Thanks for the coffee and the tour."

"You're welcome." She walked to the front door with him, glad he felt comfortable in her house. "You guys have a good time tomorrow."

"You, too." He opened the door, then hesitated. "Did she call back?"

Arlie frowned. "Who?"

"Your mother."

She probably had. The answering machine had been blinking again when they came from picking up the van, but Arlie hadn't bothered listening to the messages. They could wait.

"No," she said, thinking it wasn't quite a lie, since she wasn't positive whose messages were on the machine in the living room. "She didn't."

When Jack had left, Arlie let Wally take a lap around the yard, then went inside. She put away the breakfast dishes and prepared another pot of coffee. She wiped down already-clean counters and gave Wally fetch lessons long enough to make him crawl tiredly onto the bed on the hearth. Caruso settled herself around him, giving her mistress a stern frown—apparently because Arlie had tired the cat's baby.

Frowning, Arlie went to the CD player on the shelf above the scrapbooks and below the one that held all of Holly's books. She didn't have to search the CD's menu for what she needed. It was always right there at the touch of her finger. Her anthem and her psalm.

When the music to "Dancing Queen" began to play, she pushed the message button on the answering machine.

CHAPTER EIGHT

"I WANT TO see you, Arliss. I'd rather not come to the lake, but I will if you insist. I'd appreciate it if you'd call back, but if you don't, I'll call again."

Click.

That pretty well summed up her relationship with her mother.

Arlie had been five years and two months old the day Glennis Gallagher set her on the couch in the living room with her Cabbage Patch doll, a plastic bag of Goldfish crackers and a glass of chocolate milk and told her to not move until Daddy got home. She had kissed Arlie's forehead, leaving a fresh lipstick mark, and left without looking back. Glennis carried a suitcase and a big purse. The leather coat she'd got for her birthday squeaked when she walked. The scent of musk perfume drifted through the air. The locks clicked when the door closed behind her.

Arlie had been a very obedient little girl. By the time Dave got home from a twelve-hour shift at his job at the automotive plant in Kokomo, his daughter had wet herself and was sobbing quietly into a sofa pillow. The crackers and milk were long gone and she was hungry and scared, but mostly she was embarrassed because big girls never had accidents on their mothers' good furniture.

Even now, as she sat on her own couch in the same room, which was unrecognizable compared to that day long ago, tears slipped silent and hot down Arlie's cheeks for the little girl she'd been. She remembered the sounds of leather and clicking locks, the feel of Glennis's cool lips against her forehead. She could still conjure the scent of musk in her consciousness.

It made her gag.

Her father had hugged her close, bathed her and put her into pink flannel pajamas. He'd set her at the kitchen table and made her an egg sandwich, bragging that no one made egg sandwiches like superdads did. He gave her more chocolate milk and a Twinkie, then tucked her into bed without making her brush her teeth again. He read *Goodnight Moon* to her even though she was a big girl of five and she'd heard it so often she knew the words by heart.

"Please don't tell Mommy," she begged when he kissed her good-night. "She'll be mad about the couch."

"I won't tell," he promised, "but you need to remember something, Arletta Marquetta Brigetta."

"What's that?" she whispered.

He smiled at her, then kissed her again, tucking her blanket in close. "Couches don't matter. You matter."

And now Glennis wanted to see her. It had been over three years since the last time, long enough for the latest set of wounds to heal.

Caruso came and snuggled in next to her thigh. Wally followed, turning around three times before collapsing in her lap, exhausted by the effort. Arlie wiped her tears away, jarred by the thought that her mother still had the power to hurt her at all.

The music ended, leaving the room silent except for the rumble of Caruso's purr. "What do you kids think?" Arlie scratched the cat's sail-like ears. "Should I call her back?"

She almost called Gianna to ask her what to do, but there was something intrinsically wrong with asking her stepmother how to deal with her mother.

With a sigh, she reached for the phone. "This is Arlie," she said when Glennis answered.

"Oh, Arliss. Thank you for calling back."

Arlie bit back irritation. The only time anyone used her full name was if they'd been watching or reading *Old Yeller*. Then they would refer to her as Little Arliss until she convinced them it hadn't even been funny the first time, much less the past two hundred.

"Was there something you wanted?" she asked, pure effort keeping her voice even. The swipe of Wally's tongue across her chin told her she hadn't been wholly successful.

"I need you to have your blood tested." The voice Arlie had heard so seldom she'd never grown used to it was even more unfamiliar than usual. It was high-pitched and nervous. Strain danced along the connection.

Arlie didn't think she'd heard correctly. "What?"

"I need—" Glennis hesitated. "I need a stem-cell transplant."

"Oh." A piece of memory niggled at the back of Arlie's mind, but she couldn't grasp what it was. "I'm sorry."

"It's my second bout with breast cancer and I'm running out of treatment options." Her voice wavered. "It's a treatment they don't like to give, but I've found an oncologist who's willing if a match can be found. You're my greatest hope."

Breast cancer? Second bout? Shouldn't Arlie have known about that? Even though Glennis hadn't raised her, they were genetically linked. Why hadn't— The elusive memory clicked into place. "Didn't your mother have that, too?"

"Yes. And my aunt and my grandmother. They were all dead before their fortieth birthdays." Glennis's dry chuckle sent chills down Arlie's back. "I'm a survivor. I'll be forty-eight next year."

No, you won't. You'll be fifty-five. Won't people think it's odd that you're only forty-seven but you have a thirty-three-year-old daughter?

Of course they wouldn't—probably no one away from the lake knew Glennis had a daughter at all.

"I made you an appointment at a lab in Indianapolis on Tuesday. Do you have a pen? I'll give you the address."

Arlie reached automatically for the pad and

pen beside the phone. "This Tuesday?" What was she doing Tuesday? "I'm working. Can't I do it in the hospital in Sawyer?"

"The appointment's already made. Surely you can change your schedule. You're not the only midwife around, are you?"

Good grief. Glennis didn't even know Arlie worked in the hospital, that she only did midwifery in emergency situations. "I can change it." It made it difficult for the staffing supervisor, but Arlie had never asked before; they would cut her a break. "Give me the address. What time is the appointment? Is it a fasting blood test?"

She stopped writing halfway through the address—it was in the building where she'd worked, the same lab the clinic had used.

Glennis answered her questions, still in that strange voice, and then she said, "Arliss, my husband doesn't know about you."

Well, how about that? I didn't know about him, either.

"I don't understand."

"If you meet him during this…ordeal, I don't want you to tell him who you are."

Arlie almost laughed, but stopped herself just in time. "I think I look like you."

"What color is your hair?"

"It's still red, like Daddy's." Glennis's had been strawberry blonde, and she always kept a rinse on it to lighten away the red. Arlie's, like her father's, was the color of the cherry cabinets in the kitchen.

"I look different now. Very different. He won't notice."

"Will you be at the appointment?"

"No." That hesitancy again. "I know you don't owe me anything, Arliss."

Then why are you asking? Why do you keep showing up in my life and giving it the hiccups?

"I wanted to be beautiful and rich and socialize with other people who were beautiful and rich. That wasn't going to happen on a lake in Indiana. A way out presented itself and I took it."

Arlie waited. *Are you sorry? Do you have regrets? Do you think leaving a five-year-old alone was the right thing to do?* She wanted to ask the questions but somehow couldn't. "Did you get what you wanted?" was as close as she could come.

"Yes. Yes, I did."

There seemed to be nothing more to say. The silence between them was even more awkward than the conversation had been.

Glennis finally broke it. "Well, all right, then. Goodbye, Arliss."

Arlie dialed the number of the saltbox at Christensen's Cove. Gianna's answering machine picked up. After the beep, Arlie said, "I love you, Gianna. Talk to you soon."

The day loomed long and dreary ahead of her when she hung up. Although she was looking forward to sewing with her friends tomorrow, she had no plans for today. Usually this was an unexpected treat because life was busy, and she didn't mind her own company. She was seldom lonely.

But today she was.

She got another cup of coffee and read for a while, finding comfort and entertainment in an anthology of romantic Christmas stories. When she went into the breezeway to check the animals' food and water, she noticed the totes stacked beside the garage door in readiness for how she always spent the Friday after Thanksgiving.

She opened the top tote and found the village of ceramic houses that would decorate the mantel until after New Year's. Probably, she reflected, the sky would not fall if she decorated the Toe for Christmas a couple of weeks ahead of schedule.

As she had hoped, setting out the decorations and putting up the artificial trees—she had three—made her feel better. She was able to put the conversation with her mother out of her mind—mostly.

When all the decorating was done inside the house, right down to Christmas towels being hung in the bathrooms and her Mrs. Claus apron on the hook in the utility closet, she took the last totes outside.

She twined the lights around the porch rails, humming Christmas songs as she worked. Knowing Gianna would wring her stepdaughter's neck if she caught her, Arlie hung the big wreath over the dormer windows upstairs, standing on the top rung of the ladder. She didn't look down—cleaning second-story windows had taught her that as long as she kept her eyes forward, she could pretend she wasn't afraid of heights. She was stringing the last strand of lights on the blue spruce tree in the front yard when Jack's SUV pulled into the driveway.

"Great timing," she said when he got out and approached the tree. "As soon as I finish these, I'm done."

"I waited around the corner for two hours

before coming over." He grinned at her and began stacking the empty totes.

She plugged the thick green extension cords into the outlets on the side of the house and stood with her hands clasped together, looking around at the decorations. "I am positively one of the best elves Santa ever had," she bragged. "Doesn't it look great?"

"Yes."

But he was looking at her, not the decorations. His expression made her feel less certain than ever about their relationship, but it went a long way toward melting the icy place left by the conversation with her mother.

"I've written up some proposals about the plant," he said. "I may know more about business than you do, but you know more about lakers in general and the employees specifically than I do. I wondered if you'd take a look."

She nodded, pleased by being asked. "If Mr. Phillipy looked at it and said you're all wrong, he's probably right."

Jack sighed, an exaggerated sound that should have shaken the last of the leaves from the maple tree in the yard. "He hasn't seen it yet. If you go through it and find problems, I'll tell him it was all your idea."

Arlie scowled. "You are a corrupt human being."

"Only mildly. And I'll pay for the pizza."

"Oh, well, then, a little corruption never hurts. I like supreme, with black olives added."

"You always did. Bread sticks?"

"You bet. What's pizza without bread sticks?"

"Good. It's all in the car."

She burst into laughter. "Taking a little bit for granted there, weren't you?"

"Maybe a little." He lifted the stack of totes. "Garage?"

"Yes." She ran to open the door for him. "I need to take pictures of the decorations and send them to Charlie."

"He'll drive his mother crazy wanting to do the same thing at their house."

Arlie frowned. "That would be bad?"

He laughed. "Only if Tracy tries doing it herself. But she has a personal assistant with the patience of Job, so it might work out."

They sat at the kitchen table with the food, mugs of spiced cider and printouts of Jack's business plan for Llewellyn's Lures.

Arlie was fascinated by the sheer comprehensiveness of the ideas.

"Chalkboards in the restrooms?" she asked

at one point, looking over at him with raised eyebrows. "And colored chalk?"

"Summer labor, high school and college kids, are good workers. They're fun to have there and they kind of, like Mr. Phillipy says, 'get the joint jumpin'.' They also put more graffiti on the walls in three months than the rest of the work force does all year long, so September always means having the restrooms painted. I've put the chalkboards up in other places and it's helped a lot. We'll see."

She grinned at him. "That's taking business away from Penny."

"Actually, I talked to her about that." Jack took another slice of pizza. "She rolled her eyes and said even though she just hated the idea of not being able to paint the men's rooms at Llewellyn's Lures every single September, she thought she could learn to live with it."

Arlie felt her smile fade. "You're serious." He really had done that. She could tell by the lack of guile in his expression.

Jack nodded, forking pieces of black olives onto her plate. "The last thing you want to do when you go into a business with the idea of making changes is screw things up for anyone else. I didn't know if Penny really counted on painting the restrooms every fall."

Arlie read on, making suggestions here and there, all of which he noted on his copy of the plan, his red Sharpie lending importance to her ideas. When she got to the last page, she read it. Then read it again. "Really?" she asked. "Weren't he and your grandmother friends?"

Jack hesitated. "They were, but as a plant manager, he's done nothing but take the company on a downward spiral. His business practices are terrible, bordering on unethical. He harassed a few of the women, though none brought charges." He sighed. "I'm not as naive as that sounds—I know it happens all the time—but it shouldn't."

"So." She set down her mug, wiped her lips on the linen napkin that had apples embroidered on it and smirked at Jack. "Are you thinking of staying here after all, Mr. Llewellyn?"

JACK'S FIRST IMPULSE when Arlie asked the question was to say no. Of course not. Why would he stay in a place that was a thousand miles from Charlie? Not only that, Miniagua wasn't going to grow. Its year-round population was virtually the same as it had been sixteen years ago even though several new businesses had been added. Sawyer, where the plant was located, had progressed quite a bit, but he had no interest in living there.

Besides, he missed Vermont, missed seeing Wish Mountain when he drank his coffee in the morning. He would be thinking about skiing if he was there—Opening Day on the mountain was looming large. He'd ride his bike with Charlie in the Tim McGuffey Memorial Ride instead of sending a check. He'd eat soup at McGuffey's Tavern and buy books from Louisa's Garret on Alcott Street. Charlie would be just an hour away.

But if he stayed in Vermont, he wouldn't be just across the family compound from his brother. They were still wary around each other, but they were closer than they'd been since high school. He and Sam were becoming friends again. He'd even spent time with Nate and Jesse.

And if he stayed in Vermont, he wouldn't be sitting across the table from Arlie Gallagher.

Jack didn't mind being alone. Really he didn't. When he wasn't in contact with people he cared about, he worried less about the mental illness that ran in his family suddenly surfacing. He hardly ever worried about anger rising up and crippling his decision-making. But *not* being alone—drinking coffee with old friends, spending time with people at the plant, with his brother, with Arlie—it was… It was a life-changer.

"I've been here two weeks," he said, tamping down regret. "I don't think that's enough time to decide to apply for an Indiana driver's license." He nodded toward the proposal. "So, overall, what do you think?"

"I think it's wonderful. The wages and benefits package you're suggesting is a lot more generous than they've ever had." Arlie's smile was approving. "Can the company afford that?"

He shuffled through the pages. "Price increases. I know no one likes them, but the truth is Llewellyn's hasn't raised either wholesale prices or shipping fees in a long time. That's nice for the customers, but it's not reasonable—you can bet the purchasers haven't kept the retail prices the same, nor should they have."

"I can't wait to hear what Mr. Phillipy says, especially if he likes everything and believes I thought of all of it."

Jack slid the copies of the plan into a folder. "Oh, didn't I tell you? If he likes it, I'll tell him I thought of everything. It's only if he *doesn't* like it that your name will come up."

She beamed at him. "You're such a hero."

"That's what I thought." He pushed the folder aside and captured her gaze across the table. "Did you call your mother back? Is that why you had that deer-in-the-headlights look when I got here?"

"I did call her." Arlie got up and went to make fresh coffee. She kept her back to him. "You want some apple crisp with this?"

He followed her into the kitchen, bringing their empty pizza plates and putting them in the dishwasher. He gazed admiringly at the dessert she took out of the refrigerator. "Are you going to force me to eat it whether I want it or not?"

"Oh, probably."

"Then I'll just go down without a fight."

"There's that hero thing again." Her voice was light, but it sounded forced. She heated the crisp in the microwave above the stove. He met her eyes in their reflection in the glass.

"Arlie."

She turned and handed him the warm dessert plates, smiling brightly. "What? Do you want whipped cream?"

He looked at the apple crisp. "With this? That's just sick."

"That's what I thought, too, but you've lived off in the wilds of Somewhere Else for so long I thought maybe you'd taken up bad habits."

He laughed. "There are those capital letters again. I can hear them."

She followed him back to the table, carrying their cups. "She's ill and needs a stem-cell transplant. I'm going Tuesday for blood tests to see if I'm a viable donor."

Jack waited until she looked at him to speak. "I'm not sure what to say. You don't owe her anything."

Her smile was slight, but it was there. "It's not like it's a kidney. It's a minor inconvenience for me. I can't do less for her than I'd do for anyone else."

Jack thought she'd probably have given a kidney, too, but he didn't say so.

CHAPTER NINE

"Do you think I was wrong to do it?" Arlie had vacillated all day Sunday about whether or not to tell Gianna about Glennis's request, but in the end had decided to go with the truth. She'd asked her stepmother to come over early on Monday, before the other quilters arrived. "Jack thinks I don't owe her anything."

Gianna poured tea and snuggled the quilted cozy that had been one of Arlie's first projects over the china pot. "I don't think you do, either. Jack's right about that." She stirred cream into her cup. "I, on the other hand, owe her a lot. It may not have been her intent, but she gave me you, for which I will forever be grateful. I'm not naive enough to believe she stayed out of your life for altruistic purposes, but the truth is our lives as a family were better because she didn't interfere. Don't you think?"

"Probably." Arlie sipped her pumpkin spice

tea. "But you're not helping me here. Am I doing the right thing?"

"Does it feel right?"

"Yes."

"Well, then." Gianna looked at her watch, a gift from Arlie's dad. "All right if I go with you? I'll bet if I call, they'll be willing to test my blood, too. I said I owed her a lot, so I guess that's the least I can do. Even if I don't match her, I'll be on the registry."

Against her will, Arlie remembered the night of the accident, when Glennis had been too upset and too far away to come to the trauma unit in Sawyer's small hospital to donate blood for her daughter. Gianna, sharing her desperate concern with the janitor waxing the hallways, had found blood Arlie needed when he told her he was A-negative and would be glad to help. He was working overtime and wouldn't normally have been there in the middle of the night, but that time he was. He was a perfect match and had saved Arlie's life.

He'd retired to Florida, but they still wrote letters to each other and she'd given the first quilt she ever made to him and his wife. Later, when she'd got better at quilting, she offered them a prettier, better-made one.

They told her to forget it—they loved the imperfect stitches of the cover they had and wouldn't give it up for the world.

As she so often did, Gianna knew what Arlie was thinking. "When I lectured you girls on letting go, I was talking to myself, too." She poured the rest of the tea into their cups and set the kettle to heat for more. "I doubt I'll ever truly forgive her for not coming that night when you needed her blood, but I try not to think of what might have been. All of Dave's girls survived, and he'd be so proud of us."

"He would. Do you still miss him, Gianna?"

"Every day. Do you?"

"Yes, though not like I used to. I always think the baby is with him and he's taking care of her." Arlie smiled, though tears threatened the corners of her eyes. "I think of him when I play 'Dancing Queen,' but it doesn't make me sad. Just makes me think of you two together and what good lives you gave Holly and me. We were pretty lucky there for a while."

"So were your dad and I." Gianna looked past Arlie, her expression wistful. "I like Max Harrison. Actually, I more than like him, but I keep wanting to feel about him the way I did about Dave. It's not happening."

Arlie nodded. She still wanted to feel about someone the way she had her high school boyfriend. That wasn't looking real hopeful, either. She thought Jack could still make her heart sing if she gave in to it, but she'd never be sure he wouldn't walk away again. Letting go was one thing—letting go without a net was something else entirely.

She met Gianna's dark eyes, holding her gaze. "You do understand, don't you, why I still call you by your first name?"

Arlie's question was abrupt and obscure, but her stepmother got it—it wasn't the first time she'd asked it. Gianna reached to stroke a hand down the curve of Arlie's cheek, touching the dent in her chin and pausing at a long, thin scar on her neck. "You know I do. *Mom* and *mama* aren't happy words for you." Her smile slipped into its usual warm place in Arlie's heart. "We belong together, you and me."

"Good afternoon, favorite people in the world." Holly came in the door, snagging her cup from the shelf and coming to the table. "Got enough for me?"

"That's the best thing about this family."

Arlie got up and gave her a hug. "We always have enough to go around." She looked at the clock. "You're early."

"I know. Mama texted me about your appointment, so I came by early to tell you I'd come along and toss in some more family blood." Holly shrugged. "I donated my whole left foot and ankle to the world of medicine—a few stem cells shouldn't be a problem if I'm a match for someone." She smiled at the small Christmas tree on the counter. "Did I tell you yesterday your decorations look good? Since you got them up early, you can come help with mine. I live in an apartment, so I don't have nearly so many."

Arlie raised an eyebrow at her. "Not so many? You live in half a house, and you decorate the whole thing right down to the mailboxes."

"Because my neighbor's in a wheelchair. She doesn't climb ladders well."

The sound of horses' hooves brought them all to their feet. "It's Lovena and two of her daughters," said Arlie, opening the breezeway door to wave at Lovena's son-in-law as he turned his buggy back toward the road. "Hello. We're so glad you're here." She held the door open for the women.

"We brought cookies," said Miriam Hershberger, Lovena's elder daughter. "To add sweetness to the quilting."

"Thank you." Arlie took the container of snickerdoodles. "We'll take these up to the sewing room with us." She eyed Miriam, noting her advanced pregnancy and the pallor of her already-fair skin. "Are you all right?" Arlie kept her voice low—the local Amish, while not exactly standoffish, were nevertheless not forthcoming when it came to health matters.

"Ja." Miriam smiled. "Just a little tired. I'm looking forward to the quilting."

"Are you seeing Hannah Detwiler?" Hannah was the local Amish midwife. Arlie had learned much from her and even taught her a few things, but Hannah was, in her own words, "getting too much old." Babies, even very well-behaved ones, had a tendency to be born in the middle of the night, and Hannah was past the point of being at her best then.

Miriam nodded. "There is no one else if we don't want to go to the hospital in Sawyer, and I don't."

"Be careful going up," Arlie cautioned. She frowned as Miriam moved slowly up the stairs. The woman was five years or so younger than Arlie and this was her fifth child, not unusual in Amish families, but Arlie suspected there was more to her lack of color than being "just a little tired."

Miriam stopped halfway up, meeting her eyes. "If I need you in a few weeks, will you come?"

"Yes. Just have Caleb call from the phone in his shop. You have my numbers?"

"I do."

"We're good, then."

If binding a quilt was Arlie's least favorite part of making one—and it definitely was—quilting it by hand with a group of friends was her favorite. She'd read recommendations that a single quilter should do all the stitching on a project to give it artistic perfection, but she'd never finished one alone. Nor did she want to.

"The last quilt we did together went to the women's shelter in Kokomo. This one should be auctioned for the Amish school," said Holly, threading needles with the stiff thread used for quilting. "Isn't there a fish fry next week, Lovena?"

"*Ja.* The building is done, but the scholars need more books." The older woman nodded. She began to stitch, her hand flying over the quilt's surface. "The quilts bring *gut* earnings." Her soft blue eyes twinkled behind rimless glasses. "The English sometimes spend foolish at the auction and it's good for the Amish."

Gianna laughed across at her friend. "Shame on you."

Sarah, the youngest of Lovena's seven children, had been married for a year. When Arlie set a platter of ham salad sandwiches beside the plate of cookies and a thermal carafe of coffee on the cutting table, the young woman's complexion took on a distinct greenish hue. She got up and hurried to the bathroom.

"Ah," said Libby Worth softly, meeting Arlie's glance across the expanse of the quilt. "How many grandbabies will this make for you, Lovena?"

"An even dozen." Lovena smiled. "Such blessings."

"One day, I hope to have some blessings of my own." Gianna sighed deeply, casting dramatically woeful looks at her daughters. "I hope."

"The Llewellyn boys are back on the lake, we've heard." Miriam's eyes sparkled much as her mother's had. "Are you walking out with Jack, Arlie?"

Arlie frowned down at the quilt, at her stitches that weren't even close to being as fine as Lovena's, then raised her gaze back up to meet Miriam's. "Did you really just ask me that?"

"Ja." Miriam nodded, chuckling. "But I didn't expect you to answer."

Arlie joined the laughter at her expense, and she didn't answer the question.

But she thought of little else the rest of the afternoon.

ARLIE, HOLLY AND GIANNA took the new van to Indianapolis, talking nonstop as they always did. They had their blood drawn at the lab first, with the girls laughing at their mother's squeamishness.

Sitting in the leather chair with her arm immobilized, Arlie watched her blood fill the glass tubes and knew without any doubt that her cells would be a match for Glennis's. She wasn't intuitive by nature, but this went beyond intuition to unquestioning knowledge.

How odd would it be to go full circle in that way—to give life back to the woman who had given it to her? All without love from either side of the equation. The thought both chilled and elated her.

Afterward, Arlie went upstairs to the suite marked A Woman's Place while her family delivered child-size quilts to the nearby children's hospital.

The gynecological clinic had been her place of employment for more than seven years. She'd loved her job, but hadn't liked living in the city no matter how much more exciting it was than the lake.

She'd never regretted returning to Miniagua, and she still enjoyed nursing, but walking into the clinic reminded her of just how much she missed her specialty.

Not only was most of the staff the same, one of the patients in the waiting room had been hers. The woman was pregnant again and had a whole string of pictures of her four-year-old on her phone. Arlie looked at all of them. "Well," she said, "it's obvious I delivered him. Look how cute he is!"

"Go on into the lounge and grab a cup of coffee," suggested the receptionist, opening the window between her and the patients. "It'll give everyone a chance to see you while you're here."

Arlie went down the hall and into the

cramped employees' lounge at its end. She talked to everyone and was preparing to leave when her old boss came in. "When are you coming back?" Kari Ross, the gynecologist whose clinic it was, gave her a hug, then stood back with her arms crossed over her chest.

"To Indy? Never. You saw me trying to live in the city—it didn't work." Arlie rolled her eyes.

Dr. Ross shook her head. "To delivering babies. To caring for women when they need it. It's what you were made for, Arlie. You can do that anywhere."

"I have a job, and the local gynecologist didn't want to work with a midwife." *And I have an Amish friend I'm worried about, whose baby I'd love to catch for her. But what if it happens again and we're too far from the hospital to get help? What if Dr. Creepface in Sawyer is right and midwifery should be returned to the past? What if?*

Kari's dark eyes were serious. "I'm sure you're a boon to the hospital, but it's not where your heart is." The doctor nodded when the nurse stuck her head in. "I'm coming." She gave Arlie another hug. "Come back and see us."

"I will." Her phone dinged with a text message, and she looked at its screen. "Gianna and Holly are here to get me. We're off to lunch and a shopping spree at Quilt Quarters."

Kari smiled at her. "When you open your clinic, let me come and help you set it up. It can be A Woman's Place on the Lake. Sound good?"

It did sound good.

No, it sounded wonderful.

CHAPTER TEN

HEARING FROM A faceless voice over the phone that Arlie was a match for Glennis came as no surprise. The stem-cell donation was scheduled for a Friday morning in mid-November. She'd received injections for the past four days to increase her bone marrow's production of the cells, leaving her aching and tired and more worried about the procedure than was warranted. Not looking forward to spending the evening before it alone, she'd volunteered to do the books for Rent-A-Wife just to keep her mind occupied.

She'd just logged on to the accounting program when the office door opened. Holly, carrying cups of coffee from the Silver Moon and a bag of potato chips under her arm, came into the room. Her dark hair, always sleek and shining, was in a messy bun with a pencil through it. Her reading glasses were on top of her head and she wore her writing uniform of flannel pajama pants and an ancient Miniagua Lakers sweatshirt.

She set a cup in front of Arlie and tore open the bag of chips, pouring half of them on an invoice for a new vacuum cleaner. "If you tell Mama I wore these pants in public, I'm telling her you use spaghetti sauce from a jar."

"She already knows. She borrowed a jar from me for that lasagna you ate fourteen helpings of the other night. What are you doing here?"

"I came to do the books. If you do payroll and I do the rest of it, it won't take us long and you can get some good sleep before tomorrow. Is Mama taking you to Indy?"

"No." Arlie knew she was blushing, but she chose to blame it on all those extra stem cells. "Jack is."

Holly didn't say anything, just set her coffee on the other desk and tossed her coat onto a client chair. "Have you done the entries yet?"

"No." Arlie pointed at the tidy stack of papers on the corner of her desk. "Someday we need to get Gianna to enter daily data on the computer instead of on ledger sheets. Or to hire an accountant."

"I'm for that." Holly booted up her computer. "Arlie?"

Arlie hit Print for the first paycheck. "Hmm?"

"Be careful, okay?"

There was no question what her sister meant. "I will."

"I don't want you to be hurt."

"I know." Arlie moved to the next file and hit Print again. "Same goes."

"What?" Holly looked up, her glasses already sliding down her nose.

"I don't want you to be hurt, either. I want one of your romantic novels to be an autobiography."

Holly laughed, though there was a hitch in it. "Someday."

As close as they were, they each respected that the other had skeletons in her personal closet, and Arlie wondered if one of Holly's secrets was bothering her. "Do you want to come for a sleepover? We can order a pizza. I don't have to start fasting until midnight."

"Yeah, that would be good."

They finished in record time. Arlie rode to the Toe with Holly, dropping the envelopes for invoices sent and bills paid into the collection box in front of Miniagua's miniature post office. The office was open only two hours a day, but everyone on the lake went to it as often as they could in the hope of keeping it open—they didn't want to drive five miles to Sawyer to mail a package.

By the time they called to order pizza, the Toe's doorbell had rung twice. "I was lonesome," said Libby, entering after the first ring. The second guest, a few minutes later, was Penny Phillipy.

"Sam's playing poker and I didn't want to sit home by myself and think about paint. I think about paint too much. Can I stay awhile?"

It wasn't until she went to bed at ten thirty, when Penny and Libby had left, Holly was asleep down the hall, and Wally and Caruso were both snuggled behind her knees, that Arlie realized there'd been nothing coincidental about everyone showing up tonight. Her sister and her friends didn't exactly understand why she had to do this thing for her mother, but they were going to be there for her whether they understood or not.

She'd been concerned about whether she'd be able to sleep or not.

She shouldn't have worried.

"IT WILL TAKE most of the day. Are you sure you don't want to just drop me off?" Arlie slung her purse over her shoulder.

Jack hit the remote lock on his car and joined her for the walk into the hospital, his laptop under his arm. "Are you kidding? I have a travel Scrabble game in my coat pocket and this time Charlie's not here to destroy me on it. How much more excitement could a guy stand?"

"No offense to Charlie, but I've read the dictionary cover to cover. You don't have a prayer against skill like that." Her bragging was completely untrue and without conscience. She enjoyed it.

He followed her through the first set of automatic doors. "Do hospitals bother you?"

She looked around the high-ceilinged entrance lobby. "Good grief, no—I work in one, remember? They're the reason I became a nurse-midwife to start with. I was hurt outside the hospital—I was saved on the inside." She led the way down one hall, turning right at its end. "The nursing part was a no-brainer—I thought all you had to do was write numbers on charts and smile at people."

The African-American nurse standing at the desk they approached nodded agreement.

"That's what I thought, too, plus I'd get to wear a nice uniform and a cool cap with a black stripe on it." She gestured at her scrubs. "Wrong."

Arlie smiled at her, recognizing the casual nursespeak calculated to ease patients' tension. "You get to walk around with a stethoscope in your pocket," said Jack. "That's got to be good for something."

The nurse, whose name tag read Leo Grant, RN, laughed. "Makes me look like I know what I'm doing, right? You all set, young lady?"

"I am."

Jack waited in the procedure room while Arlie changed into a hospital gown and a pair of socks that went halfway to her knees. He grinned at her when she shuffled from the changing room to the bed. "I knew that's why I fell so hard for you when we were kids. It was how you looked in one of those gowns."

"Humph." The nurse laughed again. "I went to all the trouble of getting you those nice socks and he doesn't even notice."

"Hey, I'm not a foot man," Jack protested.

"Okay. If she's buyin' it, it works for me." Leo booted up the computer screen in the room. "Says here you have little veins, Miss Gallagher. Do you know what that means?"

"Central line instead of IV. You're gonna sedate me first, though, right? I'm a chicken with needles anywhere, but there's something about up there around my neck that makes it hard to swallow. It also makes me think of the kind of movies I wasn't allowed to watch when I was a kid."

"Scary ones, huh?" The nurse nodded seriously, coming to the bed and starting the vitals process. "Been there."

Arlie looked over at where Jack sat. "I'm going to get seriously sleepy. Why don't you go have some coffee? If you'll tell them at A Woman's Place that I sent you, they'll give you a really good cup and maybe even a doughnut." She fluttered her lashes at him. "The patients will think you're cute, too."

"A Woman's Place? Do you work there?" Leo was pushing equipment into position when the door opened and a tall man in a lab coat stepped into the room.

"I used to. I was a nurse-midwife. Now I'm just a nurse." She mentioned the hospital in Sawyer.

"Ah." The nurse nodded. "You're still a

midwife, honey. It doesn't go away just because you try and run from it for a while."

"Leo knows about running away from things," said the doctor, approaching the bed. He introduced himself and shook hands with Arlie and Jack. "She keeps mentioning retirement and we keep talking her down with those very words she just said to you."

Jack got to his feet. "Okay, I'll go find coffee. And a doughnut. Two doughnuts—I'll eat one for you, too. I'll be back, so don't start off on foot without me."

Arlie shook her head, her curls bouncing on the white pillow. "It's seventy-eight miles home. Even with all the old railroad beds turned into walking and biking trails, I'm not up for that."

Jack went to A Woman's Place as Arlie suggested. It was a cheerful office suite, staffed by smiling women in jeans. "We donate to a different cause every month to pay for Friday's denim privilege," the receptionist explained. "I keep offering to give more if I can wear my pajamas instead, but so far it's not working. Let me take you back. We're all friendly, really. And most of us are sane."

Jack told her who he was and why he was there. She burst into laughter when he mentioned doughnuts. "Kari will want to see you. She's been worried about Arlie."

By the time he was led into Kari Ross's office, Jack had met all the staff who had worked with Arlie and been given a steaming cup of coffee and a huge pastry.

The doctor was probably forty, with glossy dark hair and laughing brown eyes that reminded him of Gianna and Holly. "Do you mind if I ride back to the hospital with you?" she asked. "My car is already there—having two physicians in one household often means our vehicles are in unexpected places. I have a couple of post-ops to see, plus I'd like to talk to Arlie."

Jack knew Arlie liked and trusted the gynecologist who had been her boss. By the time he pulled his car into a parking place at the hospital, he liked her, too.

"She misses all of you," he said, as they walked across the bridge that connected the parking garage to the hospital.

"I'd love for her to come back. I'd never ask her to leave the lake, but midwifery is what she should be doing all the time." Kari veered off in another direction. "Tell her I'll be in to see her in a little bit."

Jack nodded agreement and went toward

the room where Arlie was, frowning when he saw a woman entering without knocking. She wasn't wearing scrubs, and the doctor who'd been in earlier was an Indian man, not an attractive older woman in high heels.

It was ridiculous to think he should know everyone Arlie did, especially after sixteen years of no contact, but the anxiety he felt when the stranger entered the room was both instant and intense. He broke into a sprint, avoiding other people in the hall, and tapped on the door of the room before opening it. "Arlie?"

SHE FELT ALONE.

The room was oddly noiseless despite the soft swishing sound of the machine that took Arlie's blood, emptied it of stem cells and delivered it back to her. A nurse or technician was in the room all the time, but they worked and moved quietly. Arlie had dozed most of the time since she'd been sedated, waking only at sudden sounds. She wasn't in pain or even discomfort. She just felt strange. She wondered hazily if this was what was meant by out-of-body, because she was nearly positive she was no longer attached to hers.

The clock on the wall indicated that Jack

had been gone less than an hour. It seemed longer, even though she'd slept. She moved her hands restlessly and the nurse glanced sharply at her. "You doing okay?"

"Fine." And she was. She wasn't the first medical professional who was uncomfortable on the other side of the treatment spectrum from what she was used to. She felt unnerved in the room with only the quiet nurse and the whooshing machine for company.

Then she smelled the musk perfume.

She stiffened, and the nurse came over to her, glancing and nodding at the woman who'd entered the room but keeping her attention on Arlie. "Are you sure you're all right, Miss Gallagher?"

"Yes."

Glennis's lush blond hair had to be a wig. She wore heavy makeup that didn't completely disguise her pallor or the thinness of her face. Her sweater and slacks were elegant and expensive—Arlie could almost feel the softness of the cashmere even though Glennis didn't come close enough for her to touch.

"My husband suggested I stop and see you."

Arlie frowned. "I thought he didn't know about me."

"He thinks you're a distant relative. I had to tell him something."

"Well, that was accurate." She almost laughed, but not quite.

"Don't be unkind, Arliss."

Arlie knew that before the accident, her own voice had been like her mother's, sweet and clear. She had mourned the loss of that personal music when she was alone, but had never said much about it to anyone else because it had seemed like such a small thing in the face of all the other horrors of that night.

For the first time—and what she was certain would be the last—she was grateful for the huskiness of her voice. She didn't want to sound like Glennis. There wasn't much that was more bitter than sweetness feigned.

"Arlie?" Jack's voice eased the crackle in the air as he came in and approached the bed. "Your mom called to see how you were doing. She said to remind you that it was lasagna night and I'm invited, too." He bent over Arlie, acting for all the world as though he didn't know Glennis was in the room, and kissed her forehead. "I might have made that last part up. But I told her you were fine. She sent you this." He kissed her cheek that time, his lips warm on her skin.

She smiled at him and blinked against the tears that welled onto her lashes. "Jack Llewellyn, this is Glennis Hancock."

She didn't specify who Glennis Hancock was, but she didn't have to—his blue eyes communicated to her as articulately now as they had in high school. He knew who the woman standing arrow-straight just behind him was.

"Ma'am." He nodded in her direction.

"Jack." Glennis stepped closer to the bed and met Arlie's eyes. "You think of her as your mother?"

Arlie wished she could sit up straight, but she couldn't, so she held her birth mother's gaze and said, "She's loved and taken care of me for twenty-six years. So, yes, I guess you'd say I consider her my mother. She chose to be, just as you chose not to be."

Glennis flinched and drew in a deep breath. "As I said, my husband suggested I stop and see you. To thank you and to see if there was anything you needed. I assume there is not?"

"No." Arlie had needed something from her birth mother when she'd been that little girl left on the couch. Not now. Not ever again.

"Actually, there is." Jack's voice was pleasant, but not one that invited argument.

They both looked at him. Even the nurse looked at him, and Arlie almost laughed again.

When he went on, his voice was still firm. He looked professorial and unyielding. And handsome. "As well as being sorry, Arlie was really surprised to learn of your illness. She knows her father's family health history. It might be helpful if she knew yours."

"Oh, well, yes, I suppose so." Glennis nodded shortly, looking offended.

"Since she hasn't known where you were most of her life, why don't you leave her your email and physical addresses in case you forget to get the information to her?"

"She has my phone number." Glennis frowned at him. "I keep in touch."

Her selfishness didn't surprise Arlie—she'd had a lifetime to grow used to it—but Jack's intervention made her realize it was up to her to set limits on it. "Don't talk about me as though I'm not here." She captured and held her mother's defensive gaze. "You 'keep in touch' every few years, whenever it suits your purpose, and that's fine with me. I knew where I stood with you when you left me on the couch. But Jack's right—it's important for me to know your medical history. It's my history, too."

"Fine. I'll call you later with the information." Glennis didn't sound as though it was fine at all.

Jack got his phone out of his jacket pocket. "Go ahead and give the addresses to me," he suggested. "I'll text them on to Arlie. She can't really get to her phone now because she can't move. If you give it to me, we'll know it went through." He stood very straight beside the bed, one hand on Arlie's upper arm, and there wasn't even a hint of pleasantness in his expression now. His voice was clipped and icy. "In case you need reminding, she's donating stem cells to supplement your treatment, whereas you were unwilling to donate blood sixteen years ago to save her life. Giving her family medical statistics is the very least you can do."

Glennis gave him the information. "I'll be going now." She started toward the door, then turned. "You were a good child, Arliss. A pretty child. Even I knew I was terrible at being a mother, just as your grandmother was before me. I went about it wrong, leaving you the way I did, but you were better off with your father than you would have been with me." Before Arlie could ask, she shook her head. "Staying was out of the question."

"When I needed blood—why wouldn't you come?"

Unexpectedly, tears shone in the golden-brown eyes Arlie knew were the mirror image of her own. "When Gianna sent the police to find me, I couldn't be found in time because I knew how to hide from what I didn't want to face. And then there's the other little part of that medical history you were talking about—I'm an alcoholic. I've been sober for a good many years, but I was far from it that night. Just like your father, Jack, only I was lucky enough not to drive a car. I don't expect or deserve forgiveness for that." She opened the door. She stopped again and went on without turning back. "For what it's worth, I've never forgiven myself, either. Goodbye."

Arlie and Jack were silent for a moment after she'd gone. His hand still lay on her arm. The apheresis machine whirred and swished. The nurse came to the side of the bed where Glennis had stood. "You're still all right?"

"Yes." And she was. Or she would be soon.

"You're almost done. Was it explained to

you that you might be asked to come back in case she needs more?"

Please no. "Yes."

Kari Ross came in when the procedure was finished. She smiled at Jack. "If you want to go ahead and get the car, I'll bring her to the front door. She's probably still achy and tired."

"And hungry," said Arlie, deciding to ignore that she was once again being talked about as though she wasn't there. "That wasn't the machine making noise the last half hour—it was my stomach."

Jack pulled on his coat and tucked the laptop he'd hardly used under his arm. "Gianna's lasagna is calling your name."

He left, closing the door behind him, and Kari helped Arlie get dressed—she actually *was* achy and tired. "He's really nice, isn't he?" said Kari.

"He is." Arlie shook her head at her old boss and started ticking off on her fingers. "He's also leaving the lake as soon as he can. He has a twelve-year-old son who needs to take priority. My mother's medical and maternal track records are excellent reasons I shouldn't have thoughts of permanency with anyone, much less Jack. Okay?"

"No, not okay, but we're both tired. I'll tell you later how off base you are." Kari gave her a hug. "Let's go."

"We're having a craft party Sunday, making Christmas ornaments. You want to come up? Bring your embroidery hoop and make us all look bad."

"I'd like that." Kari grinned at her and led the way to the door. "Especially the making-you-look-bad part."

CHAPTER ELEVEN

"I'M STARVED AND I was noble today, so I get the first helping." Arlie snatched the lasagna pan from Holly's hands.

Holly looked down her perky nose at her sister. "I was passing it to Jack. He's company."

"No, he's not. He's Jack." Gianna passed the bread sticks. "You girls behave yourselves."

"Tell us about it," Holly said when they'd said grace and Arlie's mouth was full. "What was it like?"

Jack saw the concern in Gianna's expression. He winked at Holly. "She was brave. Hardly cried at all."

Holly nodded solemn assent. "That's good. Usually she throws such a fit."

Arlie swallowed visibly. "I do not." The look she gave Jack should have seared off his eyebrows. "It was all right. I was drowsy most of the time."

She told them what she remembered. Jack filled in what she didn't, and Holly ad-libbed just to keep things entertaining.

"There was a great nurse there, named Leo." Arlie helped herself to more lasagna. "If I ever went back to midwifery, I'd like to work with her."

Something in her voice, an eagerness that was more than likely unconscious, slipped under Jack's skin. He looked at Gianna and Holly and realized he wasn't the only one who'd heard it.

"You want to do that, don't you?" Holly skipped a second helping of lasagna but took two bread sticks—one of them straight from her sister's plate.

"No." But it was still there. That itch in her voice that made Jack think of the look in her eyes when she told him about A Woman's Place. She said it again, her voice firmer. "No." She took back her bread stick.

He wondered who she was trying to convince. Unless it was herself, he didn't think it was working.

"Glennis came in after the procedure." Arlie wiped her lips and met her stepmother's eyes across the table.

Gianna laid down her fork. "She did?"

"You never told me she was drunk the night of the accident."

Gianna hesitated, then nodded. "I know."

"It was bad enough she couldn't come because she was too upset and too far away. But drunk?" There was an underlying tremor in her voice now.

"I never thought she'd tell you, and I didn't think you needed anything to make matters worse." Gianna took her time speaking, rubbing the tines of her fork over and over with her napkin. "I didn't think you knowing she was drunk that night would help you in any way. It doesn't make it right that I didn't tell you, but in my mind you'd been my child for ten years. I didn't care at all what happened to her. Except for the fact that she gave birth to you, I probably still don't."

"But she's an alcoholic." Arlie lifted despairing hands. "One more wonderful branch on the family tree."

"That occurred to me," Gianna admitted. "Later on, anyway. I've been critical of her for not telling you about the breast cancer in her family, but I should have made you aware that drinking might be a problem, too. Not that you ever drink much, Arlie, but I suppose the tendency might be there. It sounds ridiculous, but alcoholism is something we haven't given much consideration to." Her look at Jack was apologetic. "I'm sorry. I don't mean to make light of it. I know it's something that hangs over you and Tucker."

Jack shook his head. "Only its results. We got the eyes and the hair, but I think the addictive part passed us both by." He hoped so, anyway.

"If the tendency was there," Holly ventured, "it was probably there that night in college when that party got raided."

Arlie flinched. "You mean the night we found out Long Island Iced Tea didn't have all that much to do with Earl Grey or chamomile?"

"Yeah, that one. When we ended up sitting in the police station in Hartford City." Holly shuddered.

"Gianna came steaming in wearing silk pajamas and Daddy's letter jacket from Miniagua High School and kept us from being arrested and spending the night in jail." Arlie grinned at Jack. "You should have seen her, Jack. All she needed was a tiara to have looked like royalty."

"Then she brought us home and never

stopped yelling all the way." Holly cast her mother an admiring look. "How did you do that without drawing breath, Mama? I'm sure it was a record of some kind."

Gianna blushed. "It probably wasn't one of my finer moments. Neither was making you girls scrub and wax every inch of hardwood floor in this house on your hands and knees while I read you your study notes. But I was so mad and so scared I didn't know what else to do."

Jack couldn't imagine what it would have been like to have someone care that much about him. He didn't think even Ellen, as kind as she'd always been, would have gone to those lengths.

"Blisters," said Holly with a dramatic sigh. "We had blisters."

Arlie spoke into the laughter. "We did, and we got over it, and we didn't drink like that anymore. Ever. We even passed the test you read us the notes on. You always did the right thing by both of us, Mama. Every time."

Jack had always known that none of the Gallagher women cried alone, so when they became a weeping circle around Gianna's chair, he put his arms around all three of them.

"YOU MADE HER DAY, calling her Mama," said Jack. "Made her cry, too."

He had parked his rental car at the Dower House when they left Gianna's and was walking Arlie back to the Toe. He'd intended to drive her straight home, but she'd wanted the walk. Wanted the crackling cold air off the lake to clear away the medication-induced fog that was still coming and going in her head. This meant taking the long way around the lake, making a ten-minute walk more like forty-five.

Pleasure curled in her heart at his comment, and she lifted her face to the cloudy sky. She smiled when the snow drifted down. "It made mine, too. She's always been my mother in my heart, but I could never say the word. It had a bad flavor."

"I know that one." He shrugged, his gaze lingering on the lake. "Neither Janice nor my father were ever like real parents anyway, and you don't miss what you never had."

Arlie didn't think that was necessarily true, but she wasn't going to argue the point. Dave and Gianna Gallagher had been the best parents anyone could ever have, creating a family dynamic that, perfect though it was, ended too soon.

They reached Miniagua's downtown section. Main Street was one area in Miniagua that was actually paved, but there was so much gravel on the surface you could hardly tell it. "I put a bid on it." Jack gestured at the Miniagua Drugstore and Soda Fountain.

Arlie looked at the building, remembering the days when its lower level rang with laughter, clinking china and music from a jukebox filled with songs her parents remembered and loved. "What are you going to do with it?" she asked.

"I don't know," he admitted. "I just know it bothers me having it sit there empty."

"You never talk about what you did after you went away," she said. "I know you went to college and married Tracy and had Charlie. I know you became Jack-of-all-kinds-of-trades. I know you live in Vermont, but where else have you lived? What about your personal life after you and Tracy separated? You've seen me in a hospital gown, after all, so it's your turn to share. Have you been engaged?" She met his eyes in the dim light of the street lamps. "Have you been married again?"

That was a ridiculous question, wasn't it?

Surely he would have said. Well, no, he hadn't mentioned Charlie, had he?

"Not married again. I was engaged for a while after college, till the day we were picking out wedding invitations. Everything she liked, I didn't, and vice versa. We looked at each other and realized it was all wrong."

"Doesn't it get lonely?" Arlie thought of Chris and their pseudo relationship. It had filled a lot of hours she'd have been alone otherwise.

"Not really. I miss Charlie when I don't see him for a while, but I like being by myself, just like you do. I have friends where I live. I date. I just don't have serious relationships." He smiled at her, but his eyes were dark and grim behind his glasses. "My mother's mental illness was more than just a little chemical imbalance—she killed herself. I'm not going to get over being afraid it's genetic, that it might happen to me and consequently to everyone around me. It's why I don't see Charlie more. I know he can't inherit it, per se, but what about environment? Will something from my psyche osmose onto him?"

Arlie thought of her mother's alcoholism, of the family's history of breast cancer. She had always wanted children, had always planned to have them, but it was looking less and less like a good idea. Maybe Jack was right. Maybe some people were just meant to be alone.

CHAPTER TWELVE

MAX STOOD BESIDE Gianna behind the island in the kitchen late Thanksgiving afternoon and pointed a stern finger at Arlie and Holly. "If you two call me Mr. Harrison one more time, I'm going to tell your mother about the thing with the beer."

Gianna's dark eyes narrowed. "What thing with what beer?"

The high school principal eyed the carving knife in her hand and edged away from her. Just a little. "I don't know yet. I'm making it up as I go along."

Arlie and Holly exchanged glances. "I can't think making up stories about us is a good way to get us all on a first-name basis," said Holly gravely, shaking her head. She reached across the island to where a strip of dark meat was ready to fall off the edge of the platter. She almost had the sliver of turkey before her mother slapped her fingers.

"I don't know, sis." Arlie leaned closer to

her and spoke in a stage whisper. "So far, the stories he's making up aren't as bad as the real thing." She looked disdainfully at the fingers Holly was clutching in terrible pseudo pain. "You should have known she'd get you. She has eyes in the back of her head—whatever made you think swiping something right in front of her face would work?"

"I don't know. I guess I thought having Mr. Harri…Max here would draw her attention away from us," Holly muttered. "Okay, Max. Do you like to play board games?"

"I do."

Holly held up a finger. "Do you like to win them?"

"I do."

She held up another finger. "Do you get mad when you don't? Arlie does."

"I do not." Arlie smacked her arm.

Holly smiled at Max. "She has tantrums and throws game pieces in the fireplace—when there's a fire in it. If that's not getting mad, I don't know what is."

"I don't get mad." Max accepted the full platter from Gianna and carried it into the dining room. When he came back, he was chewing busily, nodding approval to Gianna.

"Excellent turkey, Widow Gallagher. And, no, I don't get mad—I get even."

Holly slapped her forehead in disbelief. Arlie gasped theatrically and asked, "Mama, does he really call you that?"

Her stepmother waved a dismissive hand. "Only when he's trying to get a reaction from my daughters." She tilted her head. "There's the doorbell. Somebody make sure Wally doesn't chew anyone's pant legs."

Jack, Charlie and Tuck arrived together, Tuck carrying two bottles of wine and Jack a fall-colored gift bag. Charlie was taking off his jacket when his uncle caught him in a half nelson. "Look! I brought the turkey!"

Wally barked as threateningly as something weighing only two pounds could. "Go get him, slugger," said Jack, bending to pick up the puppy. "Oh, hey." He straightened as Max entered the foyer. "Mr. Harrison. Nice to see you." He elbowed Tuck, then extended his hand. "Arlie told me you'd be here, but I forgot. Whatever you remember, it was all Tuck's fault. This is my son, Charlie. It might be his fault, too."

Arlie snorted, taking their coats to hang them in the entry closet. "At least you're not blaming me."

"Give him time," Tuck said, laughter in his blue eyes.

"Since you're being neat, Arletta Marquetta Brigetta," suggested Gianna, coming in and hugging the Llewellyns, "why don't you hang up you girls' coats, too? I know neither of you ever has, but it would just look nice since we have company."

"So, who's company?" demanded Holly. "Even Mr. Harrison isn't—"

"Like I was saying," Max interrupted, "there was this thing with the beer. I didn't want to tell you, Widow Gallagher, but your youngest here is forcing me into it. It's Max, Holly."

"Well, Max." Tucker approached, his hand outstretched. "It's so nice to see you."

Max shook hands. "It might still be Mr. Harrison to you, Tuck. I think there really *was* a thing with you and some beer."

"Yes, there probably was." Tucker sighed. "Let that be a lesson to you, Charlie. Even if you turn into a completely wonderful adult, you'll forever have to pay the piper for your past transgressions. Including the ones people make up. Anything I can do to help, Gianna?"

"You can come and pour the wine you

brought, dear." Gianna reached up to pat his head. "And we're letting go this year, so all is forgiven. Right, Max?"

"Oh, I suppose." Max thumped Tuck's shoulder. "Come on, everybody. I never got a chance to eat dinner at the church. Oh." He stopped halfway into the dining room. "It was great Llewellyn's Lures supplied all the turkeys. Thank you so much from all the organizers." He shook hands with Jack and Tuck again. "It saved the combined churches enough money they'll be able to have another community meal on Christmas without begging on street corners for funding. There aren't many homeless around here, but we have as much poverty as anywhere else. A holiday meal makes it easier on a lot of people."

Jack and Tuck exchanged looks as they went into the dining room. "We can donate the meat for the Christmas meal, too," said Jack. "The community's supported Llewellyn's for a hundred years or so. It's time the factory paid a little of that back."

"Oh." Gianna looked at the gift bag Jack carried. "Is that for me? Not that I'm greedy or anything, but I do love presents."

He handed her the gift. "I did it in a hurry,

so it's kind of rough, and I'm more of a crafts-man than an artist."

Gianna stared at the carving she withdrew from the bag, tears sliding instantly down the curves of her cheeks. "Oh, Jack. This is from the ball game, when Holly and Arlie were both there by the football field acting silly. How did you do it so fast?"

Jack flushed. "By having really good tools and by not doing it all that well. The school photographer took the picture of them. It was in the prints he gave me."

The dark walnut carving was abstract, but anyone who knew Arlie and Holly could see them in the wavy shape of two girls dancing together. Carved in the base were the words *Gianna's Dancing Queens* along with the year.

"Oh, my goodness." Gianna hugged him hard, then hugged everyone else, too, saving her dancing queens for last. "What a beau-tiful gift."

Arlie linked arms with Holly. "Do you think she means the carving or us?"

Holly gestured at where the men were fighting over who was going to pull Gianna's chair out for her. "Probably not us."

Max sat where Dave used to sit, at the foot

of the table, and Arlie remembered her father and Gianna arguing over that at their first family Thanksgiving. "You are the head of the family," Gianna had said. "You should sit at the head of the table."

"You are the family's heart. Right, girls?" Dave had grinned at Arlie and Holly, sitting wide-eyed on either side of the laden table, and pulled out the chair at its head. "You will sit at the head."

And she always had.

The family wasn't so sentimental that no one had sat in Dave's chair since he died, but it was different when Max occupied it, as though the air in the room was electrically charged. Chill bumps chased each other up Arlie's arms. Meeting her stepsister's gaze across the table before they said grace told her Holly felt the change, too.

More letting go.

"HE CHEATS!" ARLIE INSISTED. "He's a high school principal and he cheats at Scrabble." She gestured toward Charlie. "In front of an innocent child. Isn't that illegal?"

Jack started to answer, but Gianna beat him to it.

"No, sweetheart." She straightened her letter tiles calmly. "It's immoral and unethical, but I don't think it's illegal." She frowned across the kitchen table they'd retired to for board games—the food was closer than if they'd stayed in the dining room. "And if you throw your tiles into the fire, you're grounded. This is my game. You gave it to me for Christmas after you—"

"I know," Arlie interrupted sulkily.

"And don't pout." Gianna shook a finger at her and nodded toward Charlie. "Don't forget the innocent child here."

"I didn't cheat," said Max. "You had the right to challenge."

"You were an English teacher before you were a principal. I assumed you had enough respect for the language you wouldn't make up lies about it."

The comment was so ludicrous that even Arlie joined in the laughter at her expense. "I'm going to make coffee," she said, rising from her seat beside Tucker. "I'm so far down on the score sheet I think I just fell off the bottom. Who wants some?"

"Does it come with pie?" asked Jack, busily laying tiles adjacent to the last word Max had "created."

"I don't know. What kind of pie? Someone ate all the pecan."

Jack thought of the piece he'd eaten for dessert. Then the other piece he'd had while he and Tucker loaded the dishwasher. "It was Wally. I saw him."

The puppy, hearing his name, rushed in from the living room to put his front paws on Gianna's leg and whimper piteously, begging to be picked up. She lifted him to her lap. "I don't need grandchildren when I have you, do I, precious?" She held the tiny mutt close to her cheek.

Holly stared down at Jack's word on the Scrabble board. "I'm challenging that. It doesn't even have any vowels in it."

"Sure it does. The blank tile is a *U*." Jack frowned at the board. "And an *I*. Yes, it's a *U* and an *I*. I should get double points for that, right?"

Arlie wandered back to the table to look. "Even if that were allowed—which we all know it's not—what exactly is a *quisp*?"

"Well, you all know Tuck's mom, Ellen, is from England, right? So when we were little, we called potato chips 'crisps' because she did," Jack explained seriously, though a grin quivered in his cheeks. "Except that Tuck couldn't pronounce *R*s until he was at least fourteen, so he called them 'quisps.'"

Tuck buried his head in his hands. "I'm so sorry, but he's absolutely right. I could pronounce them by the time I went to kindergarten—I just didn't because it was a surefire way of irritating Grandmother."

"Oh, fine." Holly slumped dramatically in her chair. "What a day of discovery. Max cheats and isn't above telling lies about sweet young girls to their mother. Arlie and I don't have to have children because Mama loves Wally. *Quisp* is a real word. Wally ate the pecan pie. The speech impediment that made me feel sorry for Tucker in high school wasn't a problem at all. What else will we find out today?"

"I skipped third grade," Charlie volunteered, "because I could read at college level. Dad and Tracy have always been very proactive in the development of my vocabulary. Unfortunately, I was the only kid in fourth grade who couldn't tie my shoes."

"You *could*," Jack corrected, "but you *wouldn't*. It was much like Tucker's lisp, only it was me you were irritating." He exchanged grins with his son. "It worked, too."

Arlie smirked at Holly, the expression

marred by the whipped cream on her chin. "We're out of pumpkin pie, too. I think Max ate it."

After they helped finish off the already-decimated desserts, Jack and Tuck announced it was time for them to leave. Arlie and Holly, exchanging eye-rolling nods toward their mother and Max, followed suit. "They want to be alone," Arlie whispered loudly enough to have been heard next door.

Holly grinned. "You're right. Gross, isn't it?"

"Be careful going home," Gianna admonished. She turned on the porch light and peered through the front door's sidelights. "Oh, my goodness, it's snowing. Arlie, did you walk over this afternoon?"

"I brought food, remember? I came in the Mini Cooper, so I'm good to go." Outside, they swept off all the cars, laughing and slipping a little on the dusting of snow. Arlie hugged Holly and Tuck and waved them off.

She may have been good to go, but the little red car wasn't. The battery she'd had to charge earlier in the day had died again. "It's no problem," she said. "I can walk home. It's been a long time since I had a nice walk in the snow, and Wally could stand to run off some of that pie he ate today."

"Hold on." Jack pulled his SUV up beside the Mini. "I've got jumper cables."

Before he got the hatch of his car open, Arlie's phone rang from her purse. "Probably Chris. He usually calls from California on Thanksgiving night to tell me he's spent the day swimming or something."

But it wasn't Chris. After a short, terse conversation, Arlie disconnected and pushed the phone back into her purse. "It was Caleb Hershberger. It's Miriam. I need to go."

She got out of her car, slamming the door shut. "Jack, can you take me home so I can get my bag, then drive me out to the Hershbergers' farm? It's right next to the Detwilers'." She smiled at Gianna, wrapped in a shawl and waiting anxiously on the porch. "Lovena's going to be a grandma again, so can your grandpuppy stay with you tonight? He does okay with Caruso, but I'm not sure how long I'll be gone."

"Of course. Leave Charlie here, too. He'll keep Max honest if we play Scrabble again." Gianna stroked the boy's hair back from his face. "Is that okay with you and your dad? I guess I should have asked that first."

"Is it okay, Dad?" Not that Charlie cared. He stepped off the porch to take the wiggly puppy from Arlie.

"Call us if you need anything." Max nodded at Jack. "Keep her safe. Her mother worries."

Jack heard Arlie gasp. He opened the passenger door for her, then went around to climb behind the wheel. "You remember, too?"

"It's what Daddy said every time Holly or I left for a date, though everyone knew he was the chief worrier." Arlie's voice trembled. She buckled her seat belt. "Thanks for the ride. If you like, you can drop me off at the office and I can take the van."

"No sense in that. I'll talk to Caleb while you and Miriam are…busy." Jack didn't know why the subject of childbirth was embarrassing to him, but it was. He knew how private their Amish friends were, and talking about Caleb and Miriam's forthcoming child made him feel as if he was invading that privacy. "I'll pick his woodworker's brain. He's a whole lot better than I am." He drove carefully in the snow. There wasn't much, but what was there was slick.

"I don't know." Arlie smiled over at him.

"That carving you made for Mama was pretty perfect."

By the time they arrived at Caleb and Miriam's farm, nearly a half hour had passed from when Caleb called. Jack drove straight to the back door of the farmhouse, sliding a little on the snow. "Go ahead in. I'll park and bring your bag."

She pushed her door open. "You can leave the car here."

"No. If something goes wrong, the emergency vehicle needs to be able to get close to the house."

"Good point, but I need my bag right away."

By the time Jack parked his car near the barn and went to the house, Caleb was pouring coffee from the pot on the stove. "I was in there," he said, "and they told me I wasn't necessary for a while."

They talked quietly. About wood and the working of it. About all the crops being harvested on time. About it being early for such a sticking snow. Caleb went up the stairs when Miriam wanted him and came back down when she shooed him away.

Jack remembered the night Charlie was born. Tracy hadn't had a long labor. She'd had some kind of pain block so that as labors went, at least according to the gynecologist, hers was a piece of cake. Even the delivery had been uneventful. At least till the eight-pound little boy with watchful eyes and a shock of silky hair greeted his mother and her temporary husband and their lives were changed forever.

Jack thought how hard it was for men like Caleb—and himself—to wait instead of do. If there had been a way the quiet Amish carpenter could have taken his wife's place in labor rather than wait in supportive silence, he would have done so.

If it had been Arlie who labored, who suffered what he'd heard referred to as "love's greatest pain," Jack thought he'd have felt the same way.

"WHAT IS TAKING so long?"

It was five o'clock in the morning and Miriam had been having contractions since right after supper the night before. She had rested between the pains, even falling asleep occasionally, but she was tired.

"She's a lazy one is all." The bedroom Miriam and Caleb shared was austere by English standards, but still warm and comfortable. A rocking chair was in the corner. A well-used cradle sat beside it, all ready to receive a new occupant. The light was dim but enough. Arlie carried a battery lamp to provide additional illumination when she needed it.

Miriam looked doubtful. "She?"

"Or he. I'm just getting a girl vibe. What would you rather have?"

Miriam's lips tightened perceptibly, an expression that meant she was in intense pain. "Either is *gut*." She smiled, the effort of it making her chin quiver. "Caleb won't like if it's a lazy boy."

"Ah, Caleb's a soft touch. He'll like whatever you have." Arlie listened to Miriam's heartbeat, then the fetal one, frowning in concentration. "No ultrasound, right?"

Miriam breathed through a contraction, her eyes closed and her fist clutching the pillow beside her, before answering. "No. It's been easy up to the past week or so when I have been so tired."

Arlie listened again. "You're getting close. I'm going to check you. Okay?"

"Ja."

Arlie washed her hands again and put on new gloves, then examined Miriam, massaging to ease the baby's way. "Do you need to push?"

"Almost." The word was little more than an exhalation.

"Do you want Caleb?"

"Please. Yes."

Arlie straightened the kerchief Miriam wore before she stepped out of the bedroom and hurried down the stairs to the kitchen. "Caleb? Time."

Caleb came silently, smiling briefly at Arlie as he passed her at the bottom of the staircase. Arlie met Jack's eyes when he looked up from where he whittled on a piece of wood. His gaze was warm and encouraging. "Go get a baby," he said softly. "I'll wait."

The sun was peeking weakly over the horizon when Arlie stepped back into the hallway. She went down the stairs as quietly as she could, carrying a dark plastic trash bag filled with towels and bedding to wash so Miriam wouldn't have to deal with it. The children were sitting at the table with Jack, eating bacon, eggs and toast. Gloria, who at two had just lost her status as the baby of the family, was on Jack's lap. They were sharing a plate.

Isaac, the eldest of the three boys, looked up when Arlie came in. "Is *Mamm* all right?"

"She is. She'd like to see you all as soon as you finish your breakfast and wash your hands."

David, six, got up from the table and gave Arlie a shrewd look. "You brought another baby with you in that bag you carry, didn't you? It's just like the one Hannah Detwiler brought Gloria in." He frowned at the little blonde charmer on Jack's lap. "I hope it's not another girl."

When the four stair-step-aged children had taken their plates to the sink and washed their hands, they went up to their mother as quietly as Arlie had come down.

She sat down and Jack got up. He poured a cup of coffee and brought it to her. "Caleb made it. It's strong enough to walk right out of the cup, but it's good anyway. Is Miriam all right? The baby?"

The coffee was robust, to put it kindly, and it lent Arlie renewed strength. She smiled at Jack. "Babies. Hannah had heard two heartbeats, but she thought it was an echo—happens sometimes. I heard two when I got here, but I wasn't sure enough at that point to spring it on Miriam while she was in labor. They're wee ones, a girl and a boy—one right at five pounds and the other a pat of butter's worth under, but they're healthy and so is their *mamm*."

Arlie had finished her paperwork and was washing the breakfast dishes for Jack to dry when the back door opened. Lovena came in, shivering in her black cape and bonnet. She was carrying a Dutch oven that she set on the gas stove. "Salads are in the buggy," she said. "Jack, will you bring them in while I unhitch my horse?"

"Of course." He got his jacket and followed her toward the door. "I'd like to unhitch for you, but I don't know how. I'm afraid the horse would be to Kokomo before we caught him."

Arlie made more coffee, then went upstairs to check on her patients and get her bag. "I know it's useless to tell you to rest, but your *mamm* is here, so I'm leaving you in good hands." She smiled at Miriam after Caleb shooed the children out ahead of him, then looked down at the two tiny babies in the cradle that now sat beside the bed. "You know to keep them warm, and it wouldn't hurt to have the doctor look them over, but I'll come by tomorrow. What are their names?"

"Daniel and Rebekah." Miriam smiled

back at her, looking better than she had a few days ago when they had spent the afternoon quilting. "*Danki* for coming."

"You're so welcome." After another look at the babies and a wave at Miriam, Arlie left the room.

Already carrying the plastic sack of bedding, Jack met her halfway up the stairs and took her bag from her. "Wait in the house with Lovena while I bring the car to the door. If you fall asleep walking across the yard, I can't carry you."

"Are you referring to the extra twenty pounds I really don't like talking about?"

He grinned at her. "No, I'm referring to the fact that I'm already carrying these bags."

Standing still in the big warm kitchen with her hands hanging loosely at her sides, she watched through the window in the back door as he walked across the yard. The children were running around in the snow. One of the boys threw a snowball that ended in a splatter on the back of Jack's leather jacket. He set Arlie's things in the back of his SUV, then closed the hatch and knelt to scrape up snow, shape it and return fire. Caleb came out of the barn and joined the battle on Jack's side.

Behind her, Lovena chuckled and said something in Pennsylvania German.

Arlie smiled over her shoulder. "Do I even want to know what you said?"

"Nie." Lovena shook her head, still chuckling. "Your *mamm* and I—we will talk."

We need to talk, too.

As though he'd heard her thoughts, Jack met her gaze through the glass, his smile warming her right to the cold tips of her fingers. It was time to have the conversation they hadn't had over sixteen years ago.

Soon.

CHAPTER THIRTEEN

By the Thursday after Thanksgiving, both the first snow and the one that had followed it had melted and the sun had made a timid appearance in its wake. Since no suitable buyer had appeared, Jack and Tucker had completed their proposal for the immediate future of Llewellyn's Lures.

They presented it to the board of directors and then to the management team at the facility, the plant manager conspicuously absent. "We will find a new one," said Jack from his uncomfortable seat at the head of the conference table, "and we will need you to help hire him or her. Applications from present company will be accepted." He met Paul Phillipy's eyes. "In fact, they are encouraged."

Paul cleared his throat and fingered the collar of his shirt. Although it was a dress shirt and he always wore a tie, his discomfort was a visible reminder that he preferred to be a blue-collar employee.

Jack and Tucker grinned at each other. "Until such time as a new manager is found, Tucker and I will share the position. We have obligations and homes in Tennessee and Vermont, so there will undoubtedly be times when neither of us is here. We're pretty confident we won't be missed."

A surprised ripple of laughter followed that announcement. Even Paul smiled.

"Do you have questions?"

The comptroller spoke from her seat on Tuck's right. "Is the plant still for sale?"

Jack hesitated, meeting his brother's eyes. *Do you want to take this one?*

Tucker nodded imperceptibly. "Officially," he said, "it is, although we're not going to have a sign planted on the front lawn. The word is out in the business community and we receive daily inquiries. However, there's no hurry. We are not interested in selling to a conglomerate and becoming the fishing-equipment capital of the world. There are fifty-nine employees here—actually, there are sixty, since Charlie charged us for sweeping floors while he was here."

Everyone laughed again. "He did a good job. You boys did, too, when you'd come in here with your granddad."

"Yeah, but, Paul—" Jack cringed "—the kid was talking about profit sharing and paid vacation. Tucker and I didn't do that."

"Sure you did. Just took you two twenty-some years to collect is all."

"We aren't collecting that yet." Tucker straightened the papers in front of him. "But, as I was saying, there are sixty employees here. We're not going to sell the plant unless their jobs are protected. Since that doesn't seem to be a popular stipulation with most buyers, I'd say sale is a moot point. For the time being, at least, we're here."

Jack stood to end the meeting, shaking hands with all who had attended. When the room was empty except for Tucker and himself, he turned off the lights and stood at the window that overlooked the plant's front lawn. *I want to be here. I don't want to leave the lake. I want to complete the reconnection with Tuck. I'm not ready to say goodbye to Arlie. I want to take her to deliver babies and have her fall asleep when I drive her home. I want to have snowball fights with other people's kids because I'm never going to have more of my own and Charlie's never going to live with me.*

He hadn't been able to tell Arlie goodbye

sixteen years ago. He didn't think he could now, either.

"They didn't ask about the satellite plants," Tucker observed from behind him. "What do you think?"

"They're small. The Michigan one is little more than a shipping point. We could easily bring most of the work from the other plants here. Miniagua would welcome the expansion. But do we need to?"

"Not now, I don't think, but it could happen eventually."

They left the plant together, locking doors and setting alarms automatically. They waved at the night watchman and crossed the parking lot.

Tucker spoke. "You want to have dinner somewhere? Maybe play some poker if we can find anyone to play with?"

"Sure." It got easier every time they were together. They hadn't talked about the years of near silence between them and neither of them was completely comfortable with the other—at least, Jack wasn't—but it was enough that they talked. And remembered good things. And sometimes laughed.

ARLIE'S SEWING ROOM was always a mess between Thanksgiving and Christmas, and this year was no exception. Gianna stacked fat quarters of fabric neatly in a clear plastic tote and tsked. "How do you find anything in here?"

"Easy." Arlie beamed at her. "My mother always gets here early and cleans up after me. Do you want some tea?"

"Yes."

They sat in chairs beside each other, a small table between them holding their steaming cups. Arlie crocheted slowly while Gianna's fingers flew, the sparkly white thread forming an angel.

When Gianna tied off her finished project, Arlie squinted at the partially finished body she was working on. "Are you sure I have the right hook?"

Gianna looked over her glasses at the hook in Arlie's hand. "You do, but you need to loosen your grip a bit—it won't fight back—and next time you need to practice once or twice before we start doing Christmas ornaments. It's hard to get good at it when you only do it one day a year."

Holly came up the stairs and flung her coat at the row of hooks on the wall. "It's so cold out there I think it's time to consider moving south." She filled her cup and came to sit with them, kneeling to rub her leg. "Makes the stump ache."

"We can't move south." Gianna sipped her tea. "The Grangers and the Llewellyns own that whole end of the lake."

"When's Max retiring, Mama?" Arlie's fingers slowed. She looked at her stepmother, noticing signs of aging she normally overlooked. There were crow's-feet around Gianna's dark eyes and lines carving parentheses around her mouth. Her always-gentle features were softening.

Gianna was only fifty-six, but she wasn't as active as she used to be. Well, she was, but she chose her activities more carefully—she'd given up riding roller coasters and had refused to go parasailing with Arlie and Holly. Her annual trip to the cardiologist usually coincided with a spa and shopping weekend.

Passing time wasn't something Arlie had given much thought to. As her grandfather used to say—often—it was what it was. He had also urged everyone within hearing not to waste a minute of it. Grief had taught the Gallaghers how right he was.

But retirement? Was Gianna ready to give up the Rent-A-Wife business? Would she marry Max? Would they leave the lake for places that didn't freeze over in the winter?

"Max? Another five years, I think, when he's sixty-two." Gianna took Arlie's hook and angel from her hand and tied it off. "There you go." She went back to her own project. "What about you? Are you and Jack getting serious again?"

"No." Although it hurt Arlie to say the word. "He'll leave. I'll stay."

"Why?" Holly reached for the tin of cookies she'd brought and opened it. "Neither of you has to stay where you are. Why are you letting location create a stumbling block?"

"It's not." Arlie glared at her. "There's more to it than that."

"I figured there was, so why don't you just come out and say it?" Holly handed her a cookie. "Here. Don't be mad at me."

"I'm not." The cookie was a snickerdoodle, Arlie's favorite. She chewed thoughtfully. "But the past is too big. I know you said to let it go, Mama, and we have, I think, but there's still a ton of baggage that doesn't go away just because someone flaps a scarf and says 'alakazam.'" She waved her crochet hook and the ball of thread rolled off her lap and across the floor.

Caruso caught it and swatted it back to her with her paws. Arlie stared at the cat in amazement. "Did you see that? She just fetched. Is that not the smartest cat in the world?"

"Is there anything you won't do to change the subject?" Holly picked up the thread and tossed it to Arlie, then lifted Caruso and the ever-attendant Wally into her lap.

"Very little, and having a talented cat helps. You're so jealous because you don't have one."

Gianna sighed. "Girls."

Arlie smiled a rueful apology at her mother. "Okay, look at the way things are. Jack's mother was mentally ill. His father was... well, what he was. Neither he nor Janice ever lived outside their own wants and needs. Because of them, because he's afraid he's inherited all their worst traits, Jack won't enter into any kind of serious relationship and I don't blame him. I really don't." She crocheted with jerky fingers. "As for me, I come from a biologically appalling line. You've taught me to cook like you do, Mama, and my hair's the same color as Daddy's, but that doesn't undo what Glennis handed down."

"You're grasping for straws, sister dear."

Holly opened a bag of craft sticks. "Everyone has things in their past they have to get around."

"Then there's Charlie."

"Oh." Holly and Gianna both stopped what they were doing.

"It's not as though he has a terrible mother—he doesn't. Vermont is his home—and Jack's—as much as the lake is mine. We were always first with you and Daddy, and that's what Charlie needs to be with his parents." Arlie picked her hook back up. "Jack and I are friends. Beginning and end of story."

Even as she talked, as she willed her fingers to relax around the hook and the thread, she remembered Jack's hand on her arm when Glennis came into the hospital room. Remembered him looking around inside the Toe when he'd walked her home Friday to discover she'd left the door unlocked that morning. She remembered her first thought when he'd mentioned buying the old drugstore building. *Does that mean you'll stay?* She recalled the surge of hope that had leaped in her chest.

It wasn't until she'd gone to bed that night, the animals in place beside her, that she'd allowed herself to think of it again. *So what if he does stay? There's no future for us because there's too much past.* She thought of scary-smart Charlie, with his silky hair and shining eyes. *And there's too much present.*

"Hello? Is my favorite nurse-midwife here or am I breaking and entering?" Kari's voice floated up the stairs.

Arlie laughed. "Come on up."

It was an enjoyable afternoon. Ten women filled the room, and by the time the shadows deepened into evening and the snacks were all gone, they'd made enough Christmas ornaments to decorate the community tree in the clubhouse and disburse to every patient at the nursing home between Miniagua and Sawyer.

Kari and Penny embroidered and two friends of Gianna's knit. Gianna crocheted. Holly and Libby painted and attached tiny bells and wreaths to sleds they made with craft sticks and a coping saw. Arlie—after crocheting half an angel in the time it took Gianna to complete two—gave up and went to the sewing machine. She sewed miniature patchwork Christmas stockings and stars. Mollie, the bartender at Anything Goes, stuffed things, starched and pressed others, and kept everyone's cups full of tea or coffee. "That's the only craft I'm good at," she said and made everyone laugh.

Kari had been the first friend to arrive and was the last to leave. "I'll tell you," she said, placing her embroidery tools in a quilted tote bag to take home, "I love my family more than anything on earth, but there's nothing like a day with girlfriends to clear the cobwebs from my brain." She said goodbye to Gianna and Holly, then hugged Arlie. "Thanks for asking me. When are you coming back to work?"

The words fell into a silence broken only by the soothing tones of Gianna's beloved Kenny G Christmas CD floating from the CD player.

"Tomorrow. I'm going back to work tomorrow," said Arlie. "I'm working half a shift at the hospital, and in the afternoon, I'm administering flu shots at the clubhouse." She looked sternly at her mother and sister, who waved dismissively at her and started down the stairs with trays of cups and plates. "Even though everyone should already have theirs, they don't."

Kari linked arms with Arlie and followed them down the stairs. "You know what I mean. You should be catching babies."

"I know." Arlie pushed open the garage door for her. "Be careful going back. It's really dark tonight and snow's coming."

Kari put her things in the backseat of her car and turned back to Arlie, hugging herself against the cold wind off the lake. "You belong here," she admitted.

"I do." Arlie smiled into the breeze. "It's not that I couldn't be happy anywhere else— I'm sure I could. But I want to stay here. I want to be around my family and the people I grew up with."

Kari nodded acquiescence. "But, at the risk of repeating myself yet again, you need to be delivering babies." Her smile faded. "We all lose them, Arlie. You don't forget. You go over the delivery a gazillion times in your mind trying to think if there was something you should have done differently even when you know there wasn't. But you don't quit. You don't try to stop being what you are. What is it your mother says? You have to let it go."

The wind gusted so fiercely Arlie had to

close her eyes to keep them from tearing. "I know," she said. "But letting go of the other things that have happened was almost easier. They were beyond my control. I should have known with Meg's baby. I should have known."

"You couldn't have. If I'd been seeing her, I couldn't have, either." Kari hugged her hard and stood back. "Do you have privileges at the hospital in Sawyer?"

Arlie nodded. "I did get that far in opening my own practice, despite the gynecology department head's disapproval. I have them in Kokomo and Peru, too."

"Keep it in mind." Shivering, the gynecologist got into her car. The window went down as soon as she started the engine. "Or, for that matter, I know a good place in Indy that's just crying out for a good nurse-midwife."

"Go!" Laughing, Arlie waved her off.

Inside, Arlie gave Caruso and Wally snacks and poured herself a cup of coffee. She turned on the fire and bent in front of the bookcase, searching through the scrapbooks for the last one, the one she hadn't looked at since she'd finished it. It was on the bottom, and she pulled it out carefully so as not to dislodge the ones stacked on top of it.

There had been so many mothers and babies in the seven years she'd practiced. Little Josie Sturdivant had been the first baby for both her mother and for Arlie. It had been a textbook pregnancy and delivery. Arlie remembered feeling like such an idiot for crying, but she'd cried anyway, and so had Josie's mother, father and both her grandmothers. Josie's brother and sister were in the scrapbook, too, born two years and four years later. Arlie sent them birthday cards. She sent them *all* birthday cards.

Except Meg Delancey's baby, stillborn of his single mother in the middle of the proverbial dark and stormy night. He had been the only baby she had lost, though certainly not the only birth she'd called a physician in to attend. The doctor, who'd taken two hours to get five miles to the hospital, had been scathing in his repudiation of midwives in general and Arlie in particular. He'd never forgiven her. She'd never truly forgiven herself, even though she knew she hadn't caused the baby's death.

She didn't send Meg cards, though she and Kari had attended the baby's funeral, but she cherished one Meg had sent her. *I will never forget you. You did everything you could.*

But had she? Had she really? If so, why hadn't it been enough?

CHAPTER FOURTEEN

"THAT'S AMAZING." Jack had come to Caleb Hershberger's furniture-building shop to get some input on the table he was making and was admiring the finished rocking chair near the front of the store. He reached out to touch the silken wood, feeling its warmth. "Your work is beautiful."

Caleb's already-ruddy cheeks reddened. "My Miriam—she says I feel the working of the wood in my heart. She reads too many of Holly Gallagher's romantic books, I'm thinking. But other times, she says I have wood chips in my brain, so maybe I shouldn't complain about the reading." He grinned. "Can I help you with something?"

Jack knelt in front of the rocker, moving it gently and running his hands over its body-shaped curves. "Well, I came to talk about the finish on that side table I built to fit those old postal drawers I found in the attic at Dower

House. But now I want to build a chair like this."

Caleb shrugged. "You have the feel for the wood. You will make a fine chair." He grinned. "Just run it through the heart and don't get the wood chips lodged in the brain."

"Cherry, you think?" Jack was already planning a trip to the lumber yard.

"*Ja.* Cherry would be fine. Warm." Caleb nodded approvingly. "You want some of that stain I have for the table?"

"Yeah, if you've got it to spare. And I brought you a couple of those drawers."

"*Gut.* Back here."

After he left Caleb's, Jack stopped at the Sea Chantey to put gas in his car. It had been a strange kind of day. Things had been one step forward, two steps back at Llewellyn's Lures. He and Tucker had shut themselves in the front office and had a loud disagreement about what to do with the Michigan plant. His next-door neighbor in Vermont, who watched the house for him whenever he was gone, had called. She said someone had come by and offered an extravagant amount of money to rent the small farm for the year and a half he and his wife would be teaching at the nearby college.

Eighteen months? What would Jack do for that long if they found a plant manager and he returned to Vermont? He didn't have a business lined up to purchase and make over. Where would he stay when he went back to see Charlie? Jack and Tracy were friendly, but staying at her house wasn't a solution. He needed a place where they could just be guys, as Charlie said, and Tracy's Burlington town house certainly wasn't that.

He did like the idea of his redbrick farmhouse being lived in, its vista of the Green Mountains enjoyed. Maybe the tenants would even like and take care of his raised-bed garden.

He put the fuel hose back into the pump and looked at the display of Christmas trees beside the convenience store. "Who's selling the trees?" he asked the clerk when he went inside to buy a loaf of bread to replace the green mold in his bread drawer.

"Senior class. They're working to pay for prom and a class trip—they're wanting to go to New York City this year."

Jack laughed. "We sold magazine subscriptions and had car washes."

The clerk grinned back. "So do they."

Outside, he pulled his SUV over close to

the trees and the shivering salespeople and got back out of the car. "You got any Fraser firs? About eight feet?"

"You bet, though you missed the best ones over Thanksgiving weekend." He remembered the senior from the football game— she'd been the one who got the pictures to him. "Need a door wreath to go with that?" she asked, leading the way to the trees. "And how about a nice Charlie Brown tree for the kitchen?"

Not the kitchen, but it would look pretty shining through the window over the desk in the library. Maybe Arlie would take pity on him and decorate the wreath.

"Okay." When he'd made his choices— well, accepted the ones the girl made for him—he smiled at her and nodded thanks to the boys who tied the tree onto the roof of his car. "How much?"

She counted feet and checked the cardboard price list before giving him the total. "And the Charlie Brown tree is free because we know who fattened up the concession-stand cash drawer when you helped work."

"Thank you." He gave her twice what she'd asked for. "Have a good prom and trip. Stay safe."

Her face softened, and he knew she remembered the story of what had happened after their prom. Arlie had told him Linda Saylors's picture still graced the hallway wall at the high school. The commemorative crosses still stood sentinel at the side of the road where the accident had happened.

In the car again, he called Arlie's cell phone. "Do I sound pathetic?" he said when she answered. "I mean to. I just bought two trees and a wreath and I don't have decorations. Do you want to go with me to get some and then help me put the stuff up? I'll buy pizza."

She laughed, and he thought he heard relief in the sound. "Order the pizza and I'll be right over. I have enough lights and stuff to decorate the whole lake. I've never met a garage sale I didn't like. Do you have Christmas tree stands?"

"No, but the little tree will fit in a flowerpot—there are some of them here."

"See you soon."

Within an hour, the tall Fraser was standing in front of the big windows in the Dower House's living room. It was decorated with hundreds of tiny twinkle lights and Jack and Arlie were sitting on the floor in front of the fireplace going through boxes of ornaments.

"I have to ask," he said, rejecting a plastic palm tree.

"Ask what?" She reached for her glass on the table behind her and sipped, the jewel-toned wine seeming to lend its color to the paleness of her cheeks.

"Here are all these ornaments. Enough for at least three trees, and you already have yours up. Yet you and your friends and family spent all day yesterday making *new* ornaments none of you needed. I don't get it."

"That's easy. You said all the magic words there—*family and friends*, *new* and *need*. We all got to spend the afternoon together, having a great time. We put new ornaments on the community tree every year. Then the kids get to take the ornaments home with them. We take the others to the nursing home because so many of the residents' families and friends have either died or they just don't come around. Everyone who celebrates Christmas needs something to celebrate the season *with*, even if it's only a crooked angel I crocheted." She clinked her glass gently against his. "It's one of the joys of living on the lake." She looked at the watch on his wrist. "So is waiting for pizza delivery. Did you call?"

"I did."

As if on signal, the doorbell rang. "Sorry," said the shivering driver, "had a flat tire."

They ate pizza and bread sticks as they put the ornaments on the big tree. Then they set the little one up in the library and covered it with multicolored lights and hand-painted balsa wood Santa Clauses and snowmen. While Arlie attached stars and glittery bulbs to the wreath, Jack made and poured hot chocolate.

"How was your day?" he asked, putting unused items back into the boxes.

"Busy. I worked at the hospital this morning. Then I ate too much lunch with Libby, then gave flu shots at the clubhouse this afternoon. After that, I helped Mrs. Benteen put her tree up. It's twelve feet high and I swear it takes a thousand ornaments. I stood on a ladder and she handed them to me. I was there when you called." She sipped her chocolate, smiling with the pleasure of it, then opened her eyes. "It was a good day, but I was unsettled anyway, though I can't really explain why. What about you? How was your day?"

He told her, sitting beside her in the twinkling, fluttering light from the Christmas tree and the fireplace. She finished the wreath and set it aside as he talked. He put his arm around her, not meaning to exactly, but relieved when she didn't pull away, and they leaned against the front of the couch to drink their chocolate.

"Do you remember that hymn 'It Is Well with My Soul'?" she asked.

He nodded, the tune and words slipping immediately into his mind.

"The man who wrote it... He suffered the most awful losses, but he still found peace." Arlie smiled into Jack's eyes. "Sometimes, like here and now, I feel that way. I didn't last night, and I may not again tomorrow, but right now I do. Thanks, Jack."

He loved her face. He wasn't *in* love with her—he'd withheld himself from that emotion for so long he didn't think he had it in him—but that didn't mean he couldn't still love her, couldn't still care more for her than anyone, couldn't still ache to hold her.

When he touched her, trailing his forefinger down the sweet line of her face, he was surprised at the strength of his emotional response. He wanted to be Rhett Butler or Mr. Darcy or at least one of Louis L'Amour's Sacketts and take her in his arms. Maybe carry her up a flight of stairs since the Dower

House had such a nice wide one. This wasn't a book and he was definitely no hero, but he wanted to protect her from all harm, to lend peace to her soul tomorrow and tomorrow and tomorrow.

Regret worked its way inexorably into his thoughts. Regret because they didn't have tomorrows.

But they did have now. He lowered his mouth to hers, keeping the kiss light and fresh, almost friendly. But more. He held her face between his hands and lengthened and deepened the kiss, giving it every shred of tenderness he had in him and taking what she gave in return.

For now, sitting in front of the flickering fire with the lights from the tree dancing silent and soft across their faces, it was enough. It was well with their souls.

"It's Sarah. Will you come?"

The hushed, desperate words over the telephone brought Arlie wide-awake as surely as if they'd been shouted. "Of course." She swung her legs over the side of the bed.

"It's too soon," she whispered to the caller, a man she'd never met, Sarah Mast's young husband, Aaron.

"I know." Grief lent weight and age to his voice. "I know."

"I'll be there as soon as I can."

"Gut."

She was dressed and in the car with her bag in a matter of minutes, thankful for the new battery that meant the engine caught instantly. Snow lay on the ground but the sky was clear of clouds, the stars lending a touch of blue to the silent surroundings as she made the drive through the night to the Mast farm.

Arlie hated attending miscarriages. Not only because it made her remember her own, but because she didn't usually have any answers. Saying "Sometimes it happens" wasn't good enough for either her or the woman with an empty womb. Sometimes finding out the reason for the loss was even worse.

Sarah and Aaron lived in the main house on the farm next to Jesse Worth's. When Arlie turned into the driveway, Aaron waited on the porch.

Arlie was surprised Lovena wasn't there yet. *"I don't know how they know, but they always do,"* a lecturer on Amish midwifery had said once about the mothers of women in delivery mode. In Arlie's limited experience, she'd found that to be true. The prospective grandmothers were often there before she was and almost always before she left.

She sat with Sarah through the next few hours, easing the physical and emotional pain any way she could.

Tears dripped down the young woman's pale face. "Will this always happen? It was my second one already." Her voice was soft, lilting with the slight accent of Pennsylvania German that always sounded like music to Arlie. "I lost the other one when I hardly even knew it was there."

But you'll never be able to forget that it was. "Give it time," Arlie suggested. "Give *yourself* time. I want you to get an ultrasound, all right? We'll know what to do then."

Sarah nodded agreement. "Will you stay awhile?"

"I'll stay."

"Tell Aaron to get some sleep. He must go to work in Kokomo early."

"In Kokomo?" That was twenty-five miles one way, and where did the horse and buggy stay while he worked?

"Ja." Sarah smiled at her. "He gets a ride with someone English. He doesn't take the buggy to Kokomo every day."

"Ah. I'll go tell him."

She urged Aaron to get some sleep, then made tea for Sarah and herself. Although the worst of the physical stress was over, the young Amish woman's emotional pain was still raw. Arlie would sit with her, talk with her, lend her strength until she could bear the weight of the grief on her own.

This was what had drawn Arlie to midwifery: the connection with families. When she trained as a nurse, she loved the "happy floor" that was obstetrics, but wanted more family contact than time permitted with a hospital delivery. As a midwife, she never had to hurry away, never watched the clock unless another patient was waiting, especially at home births.

While it hadn't been the same in the city, where virtually all births had taken place in the hospital, it hadn't been entirely different, either. Laughter and joy still lasted beyond the adrenaline rush offered by delivery. She didn't forget the names of the mothers and babies when she left work and made many additions to her birthday-card list.

"You should do this all the time," said Sarah. "You make me feel as though tomorrow is a new day. Hannah is tired, and there is no one in the Amish community to replace her right now. We can go to doctors and hospitals like most of the English do, but many of us don't want to."

"I think about it," Arlie admitted. She took Sarah's empty cup from her. "Try to sleep a little." She smiled, blinking back tears of sympathy when the other woman began to weep silently. "There will be joy in the morning."

Sarah sniffed. "*Ja*. There always is." She looked toward the still-dark window as though trying to gather herself. "It is wicked, isn't it, that sometimes I am jealous of Miriam and my other sisters because they have children so easily?"

"Oh, I don't know." Arlie leaned forward to give her a hug. "I pretty much hate Holly because she has great hair. That's not wicked, is it?"

Sarah's laughter was soft, punctuated with a hiccup, and Arlie smiled, satisfied. "You'll sleep now?"

"I will rest."

Aaron had left for work and day was breaking when Lovena came up the stairs to the bedroom. Her face was soft and gentle with acceptance, but grief darkened her eyes behind her rimless glasses when she looked at her daughter. "She sleeps?"

Arlie nodded. She'd done her paperwork while Sarah rested; she was ready to go. "You'll call me if I'm needed?"

"Ja." Lovena hugged her. "Be safe going home."

Jack was just getting out of his car when Arlie pulled into the parking lot of Llewellyn's Lures. She rolled down her car window when he approached. "I need to talk to you," she said. "Will you have some time later today?"

"IT SEEMS TO ME," said Tucker, leaning back in the client chair across the desk from Jack, "you're overlooking the most likely candidate."

"Paul Phillipy? I agree, but when I started mumbling around about it, he laughed in my face. I believe that was one of the days he used the term 'whippersnapper.' If we close Michigan, we could ask Tahne Monahan to come down here, but I don't think she'll accept. Her whole family's in Marquette." Jack smiled ruefully, leaning forward to fill both their cups from the thermos he'd brought from home. "Besides, I'm pretty sure I lost the battle yesterday on consolidating Michigan with Vermont."

"You're the oldest, Jack. It's one thing Grandmother did that made sense, setting it up so you have final authority in case of disagreement. You can override me." Tucker leaned across the desk for the sack of cookies from Libby's tearoom. He took a handful out of the bag. "Thought I didn't see them, didn't you?"

"I could always hope." Jack snatched the sack before his brother could empty it. "You took the last of those peanut butter things."

"Sorry about that." Tucker didn't look sorry, though—he looked pleased with himself. "I'm talking about you."

"Me?" Jack's hand came out empty.

"Yeah. You're good at managing the plant. You like it. You love it here at the lake. Why not stay? I know it would make it trickier spending time with Charlie, but you're on the road half the time anyway."

"The same things could be said about you. You're great at it."

"I think you have something stronger than Llewellyn's Lures keeping you here."

Jack hesitated, remembering the conversation with Arlie in the parking lot that morning. She'd been quiet but urgent, requesting time with him as though she needed an appointment. He had thought about little else since she'd left. Her eyes, always lit from within, had whispered of sadness when she rolled up her window and waved goodbye. Maybe this time she was going to walk away from him.

But it was another hour before he would see her. He needed to concentrate on business for right now.

Even after buying and selling an entire handful of businesses, he didn't know what he wanted to do. The idea of running the plant was appealing, but for how long? Would springtime find him yearning for something different, some*where* different? He liked to fish, but it wasn't even in the top five things he liked to do for entertainment—how could he get passionate about a manufacturing facility that made artificial bait?

The same way, he reminded himself, he'd come to care about party favors when he bought the tiny factory in Ohio. Or about sleds and toy wagons in Idaho. He'd even assembled a few guitars in a refurbished barn in southern Indiana. He had put a terrible price on Strings because he didn't really want to sell it in a hurry, but a buyer had shown up almost immediately with a generous checkbook and a boatload of excitement and Jack had let it go.

He loved the Chain and Sprocket, the bicycle shop in Vermont, but the born-and-raised Northeast Kingdom natives who'd helped run it had loved it more. He'd sold it to them on contract—they'd never missed a payment.

And from the first day he'd walked in, he'd been impassioned about the furniture-building factory, also in Vermont; he'd maintained a financial and emotional interest in it when he left.

"For the sake of argument, let's say I take the job. What happens in six months or a year when I decide I want to go to Maine and become a lobsterman?"

Tucker sat quiet for a moment, holding his gaze. "You forget," he said, "I know you get seasick. You'd never become a lobsterman." He leaned forward again. "I know something else, too. You left Arlie once—I don't see you leaving her again."

"ARE YOU OKAY?" Jack handed Arlie a takeout cup of hot chocolate and bent to pick up the puppy trying to scratch strips off his pant legs. "I see obedience school in your future, little guy. We'll send you and Charlie together. And maybe Tucker."

"I'm fine." Arlie hung his jacket in the entry closet, breathing in the scent of him. She could remember Gianna doing that when Dave came home. Even after she'd given all his clothes away other than things the girls wanted to keep, she'd left his coat in the closet at the Cove. Years later, Arlie discovered that was where her mother went to cry.

She shook off the memory and closed the closet door. "Hungry? I made sandwiches." Although she hoped he *wasn't* hungry; she wanted to get this over with.

"I am." He caught her hand when she started toward the kitchen. "But you've got something on your mind. I'd rather talk first, if it's okay."

She nodded and switched directions. When they were side by side on the love seat, she asked, "Do you remember that I used to keep a diary?"

"The one Holly used to say she was going to read and you would threaten to kill her?"

"That's the one." She reached for the book on the table beside her, running her fingers over its cover, a laminated picture of Holly and herself sitting by the lake. "She gave me this one for Christmas our junior year—it was my favorite one ever." She opened it. "This was the entry one day shortly before the accident." Her hands shook when she handed him the book, and she put them in her lap to still the tremor. "I'd like for you to read it."

He read the entry quickly, then again more slowly. As he read, he took her hand and held it tightly. When he'd finished he laid the journal down and folded her into his arms.

She hugged him back, and they held each other for a long time.

She had wondered, in those grieving days so long ago, what Jack's reaction would be if she told him. Would he mourn the loss of their baby or would he be relieved that the problem of an unplanned pregnancy had been solved?

Would he have left her if he'd known?

"Sometimes," she said, her voice splintery, "I feel righteous. I think it was better that I didn't tell you, because then you'd have stayed here out of obligation and it would have been awful for both of us. Or you'd have left anyway and I'd have hated you. Other times, I'm sure it wasn't fair that I didn't tell you. I never gave you the chance to decide."

"I wouldn't have put much stock in my decision-making abilities back then." He sounded as shaky as she felt. He lifted his hands to her face and held her gaze. "Will you tell me about it? I wasn't here then, but I'm here now."

She hesitated. She hadn't talked about it in more years than she could recount, other than a passing comment to Gianna or Holly. But maybe it was time to rip off the scab. "They didn't tell me I'd miscarried," she said, "until physical evidence made it obvious."

"Those days when you wouldn't see anyone," he remembered. "Gianna said you were trying to make your own peace with the accident and wanted to do it alone—that was when you found out, wasn't it?"

"I thought I was being brave, but stupid was probably more like it." Arlie went on to share the details of discovering she was pregnant, telling Gianna and making a doctor's appointment with a gynecologist. "I was going to tell you after that, but I didn't get to go to the appointment." The accident had happened instead.

"In truth, I know we were too young to be parents. But it was one more loss on top of too many. Then when you left—and I think we both knew you weren't coming back that day at the lake before you went away to college— it was the last straw. A part of me shut down and has never come back." She smiled at him even as the sadness flowed between them. "For you, too?"

"For me, too. But I have Charlie, which made all the difference in the world. Finding out about him was hard for you, wasn't it?"

"It was," she admitted, getting to her feet. "I'd been jealous *over* you before, but it was the first time I was ever jealous *of you*."

"I'm so sorry." He stood and held her still in front of him. "I know I've said it before and probably will again, but I'm so sorry I left. I thought I had good reasons, but they weren't good enough."

"And I'm sorry I didn't tell you about the baby when it happened. I'd like to say it was noble, but it wasn't—it was childish. I didn't think of her as our responsibility, but as mine. I was going to be everything to her that our mothers hadn't been to us. You'd have been a superdad like my father was, but I never even gave you the chance."

She led the way into the kitchen, uncovering the plate of ham salad sandwiches and setting them on the table. She wasn't sure she could eat yet, but she needed to do something with her hands. She expected Jack did, too.

He got potato chips out of the bread drawer. "I don't know about that. I'd have had the same fears then I have now. Will I pass on mental illness like my mother had? Will I get too angry the way my father did? I might be closer to a superdad if I could let go of those issues, but so far it hasn't happened."

"Well, hey." She set her cup of cooling chocolate at her plate and got a beer out for him. "As my mama says, this is the winter of letting go. Maybe we can work on that."

CHAPTER FIFTEEN

"WHAT DO YOU THINK?" Arlie had spelled out her hastily made plans to Gianna and Holly over tacos and Mexican rice. Sheets of yellow legal paper lay all across her kitchen table, a few of them decorated with drops of taco sauce. "The gynecologist in Sawyer still doesn't want me on board, but he doesn't run the hospital, thank goodness. He can't rescind my privileges. The clinic will be on part-time hours to start with, till I build up clientele. I'll have to continue working at the hospital until it picks up." She grinned, unable to hold back her excitement. "Caruso and Wally want to eat."

"What staff will you need?" Holly squinted at the graph-paper drawings.

"Another midwife, in time. A receptionist who doesn't mind keeping the books and watching older siblings while their mom's in the exam room. A doula—that's a birthing coach. Another nurse. It's hard to be sure. To start with, I just need me."

"And maybe a sister to do the office work and scheduling? I can still help Mama if she needs me, but I'd so love to be a part of this."

Arlie almost burst into tears. Instead, she squeezed Holly's hand. "I can't ask you to do it. I don't know how much I can pay. I don't even know if I'll succeed."

"You can deliver your first niece or nephew for free." Holly sniffed and waved her free hand. "I just got a good royalties check—I can live at least until the end of February as long as I eat at your house or Mama's a few times a week."

Gianna gathered the papers, looking thoughtful. "I think you need to quit your job."

"I don't think you mean that, Mama." Arlie pointed at the bottom line on the finance sheet. "I'd not only be eating at your house, I'd be living there."

"What I mean," said her mother firmly, "is that the young woman who came back to the lake three years ago wasn't the Arlie I knew. You know, the one who thought catching babies was the greatest job in the world."

"It was." Arlie put lettuce and onions on

her taco. "It is. But it's a fighting kind of job sometimes. Some doctors don't respect us or like it when patients want to use us. Patients' mothers and husbands sometimes get in the middle and make what should be a joyous experience into a power struggle." She bit into her taco, looking heavenward in bliss. She loved tacos. "When I came back, I needed to work and I needed the lake. The hospital was an answer to that."

"You forgot the other part, that I needed you after I had heart surgery." Gianna looked sorrowful. "I feel as though I interfered in your life. I didn't mind that when you were a teenager—it was my job—but I mind it now."

"I needed you, too," said Holly. "I was having big-time hip trouble that year, remember? You took care of Mama and me both."

"Neither of you needed me any more than I needed to be here," said Arlie briskly. "Living in the city is fun and exciting and so not for me. I'm a laker born and bred."

"You know," said Gianna, helping herself to another tortilla and slapping Holly's hand away from the meat sauce, "there is money. I know you girls finally accepted some of it to make down payments on your houses. We've used some off and on for medical bills and unexpected expenses, but there's still plenty more. I'm sure your dad would like for you to use it."

Arlie met Holly's eyes across the table and they both burst into laughter. "Daddy was the best man in the world," said Arlie, "but he was so tight he squeaked. His idea of either of us using that money would be moving it from one bank account to another that pays better interest." She felt her face soften and saw her own expression reflected on Holly's face. "Besides, it's yours. What you gave us for our houses… That was great and we both appreciate it, but we know our shares of whatever money there was after he died went for our educations. Even with scholarships, having both of us in school at once was a drain."

Holly nodded. "Especially since Arlie flunked anatomy."

"I didn't flunk it." Arlie threw a napkin at her. "I got a C minus, so I took it again. Twice."

After dinner and loading the dishwasher, the three of them went up to the sewing room and quilted. They were quiet, taking short, fast stitches on the flower garden quilt that would be a baby gift for one of the women who worked at Rent-A-Wife. They drank tea and watched a Christmas movie.

They were all people who would never have to wonder if they were loved, because even if the love never extended beyond the boundaries of their triad, it was a powerful thing. Arlie thought she could live forever without catching another baby if she could always have that love. Not all dreams were meant to come true.

They were together. Nothing had changed.

"YOU'RE PICKING UP WHAT?" Jack couldn't have heard right, could he? He held the cell phone away from his ear for an instant, looking at it in consternation.

Arlie laughed. "Oysters."

He grimaced, then wondered why he did that when no one was there to see the expression. "Why on earth would you want to pick up oysters? Everybody *hates* oysters. Where did you say you were going to get them again?"

"I'm meeting Chris in Alabama. He's in Mobile on business this week and is getting the oysters for us. Oyster stew is one of the biggies at the Christmas party in the clubhouse, which if you'll remember is Friday night. Mama cooks it. Sometimes we have trouble getting fresh ones, and this year is one of those times."

"You're *driving*?"

"Yes. I don't know if it's quite legal to carry oysters across state lines, but I'd rather risk that than try flying with them in a cooler in my lap. Holly was going to go with me, but she had to take Mrs. Benteen on an emergency trip to her sister's in South Bend. Nate's off making a bid on redesigning a golf course somewhere in North Carolina."

Jack knew about that. He'd recommended Nate to a friend, who'd used the designer's services and passed the word on to someone else.

"When are you going?" He checked the alarm system and left the building, jogging across the parking lot in the biting wind.

"Tonight. Well, in about ten minutes, actually. Mama's going to feed and water Caruso and Wally while I'm gone."

"Where are you staying?" he asked, starting the SUV and trying not to shiver. He jumped when the hands-free in the car came on and her answer came through the radio speakers.

"Oh, I'm not." Her voice was breezy. "I'll have breakfast with Chris if there's anywhere open where we are—it'll be the middle of the night—and head back home."

Jack rolled his eyes. She would do just exactly that, too. "Put a couple of pillows in the car," he said, "and a blanket. I'll go with you. What are you driving?"

"The Mini."

He rolled his eyes again, grateful she couldn't see him—that wasn't a gesture most women responded to favorably. Although they *did* respond—always. "How about we go in the SUV?" he suggested. "We can both drive and we can both be more comfortable."

"Jack, you don't need to go. I'll be fine and so will my car."

"I know. But I'm positive you'll be better with two drivers and a car with all-wheel drive." And he'd be better if she wasn't having breakfast alone in the middle of the night with Chris Granger.

Not that he was jealous or anything. Of course not. He and Arlie were not a couple, nor would they ever be.

"Don't you need to be at the plant tomorrow?" she asked.

"Tucker will cover." He drove past the Mast farm and remembered. "Have you ever caught up with the sleep you lost Monday night?"

She laughed. "You don't catch up with sleep."

"Okay." He looked at the clock on the dash. "I'm going home to change. I'll pick you up in a half hour, okay? Do you know where we're going?"

"Not exactly, but I know it's in northern Alabama somewhere right off the interstate, and I have Chris's phone number. I'll fix you a thermos."

She hung up before he could ask any more questions, and he smiled. Then he called Tucker and put up with five minutes of abuse before his brother told him to be careful, finishing with "you kids have a good time."

Jack hung up on him, but they were both laughing when he did. A lot of things felt good back at the lake, but few of them were better than laughing with his Irish twin.

Arlie was ready when Jack got to the Toe. She had two pillows complete with embroidered cases, an often-washed quilt, and two thermoses of coffee on the table by the door. A cooler on the floor held sandwiches, cheese and fruit. "We have to eat it all, too," she said, "to make room for the oysters."

"I forgot to ask." He pulled her to him, noting with satisfaction how well they fit together. "Since I'm being Sir Drives-A-Lot here, are you going to be my date at the party?"

She fluttered her eyelashes at him, and he grinned at her. They tended to be stubby even when their mascara was fresh, which it wasn't at this time of day—it was mostly gone. "Will you eat my mama's oyster stew?"

"No, ma'am, I will not. Unless she makes me, that is. If she gets insistent and says I can't have lasagna if I don't eat oysters, then, yeah, I'm eating oysters." He patted her shoulder. "But I'll leave plenty for you. I promise."

"Oh, you're all heart, you are." She leaned back in his arm, and their eyes met, a warm and exciting fusion that made him think he didn't want to go anywhere. He wanted to stay right here with her. "I'd like to go to the party with you."

"Good." He leaned in to kiss her lightly. *Keep it casual. Don't scare her off. Don't scare yourself off.* "We'd better go."

Her eyes looked a little foggy, and it took her a few seconds to answer. "Yes."

He checked the locks while she administered "Mommy will be home soon" assurances to Caruso and Wally. "Are you a backseat driver?" she asked.

"I don't think so. Are you?" He opened the driver's door, waiting while she took off her coat and put it and her purse in the backseat. "Why don't you drive first so you can get used to the vehicle before dark?" He squinted at the sky with its rolling gray early-December clouds. "You've got about ten minutes."

"Holly accuses me of backseat driving." Arlie got behind the wheel, adjusting the seat and the mirrors while Jack put his coat with hers and arranged their travel mugs. The car immediately filled with the scent of coffee. "But she drives like a demon, so what does she know?" After settling in, Arlie backed out of the driveway. "I love road trips. Once upon a time, I thought about becoming a trucker."

"You did not." He sipped coffee and stared across the seat at her, trying to gauge the truth in what she said.

"I did, too. I was only eight, I'll admit, but Daddy and Mama had just taken us on a trip. We were gone for ten days, and what we did was go as far as we could for three days, then get up on the fourth day and head back toward home. We stopped and looked at so many things and did so much national-park stuff that we didn't make it all that far, but it was fun." She chuckled, and he saw her expression soften. "Daddy got a little panicky when I said I wanted to grow up to drive an 18-wheeler. He wasn't sexist, but the idea of one of his little girls hanging out at truck stops scared him some. Mama told him not to worry—I'd probably change my mind at least once by the time I got out of school."

Jack laughed. "Tucker and I were going to run away to Alaska and go on the TV show *Northern Exposure* just because we liked it. We got the idea in warm weather. But when winter came along, we knew it was time for a change of plans."

Arlie nodded. She pulled onto the state road and reached for her coffee. "On another vacation a year or two later, Mama put all the cash into two envelopes. When the first envelope was empty, we had to head back. We had two whole weeks, but Daddy figured we'd be back by the first weekend, because the route was taking us past a couple of cool amusement parks. Holly and I had smartened up some, though. We made it to Oregon and didn't get back until midnight the day before Daddy had to go back to work."

Jack laughed. "I'll bet your dad knew not to underestimate you two again." He tilted his seat back to get more comfortable. "When I got a job in Florida after Tracy and I broke up, I drove there," Jack remembered. "I'd already walked away from you and from Tucker, and I was getting ready to leave Tracy and Charlie. When I went to Pensacola, I intended it to be forever. I'd fly back once a month to see Charlie, but I knew even then I wasn't cut out to be a hands-on dad."

He took a deep breath. Even this long after the fact, it was hard to talk about. "A year or so later, I got mad at a guy on the beach. We were at a weekend wind-down party because the place we worked had a high-stress atmosphere. He was drunk and hit the woman he was with. So I hit him." He hesitated. "That would have been all right, I guess—he was quite a bit bigger than me. I'd have been a real hero. But I hit him often and hard enough that my friends pulled me off him."

Arlie spoke into the silence that fell between them, her voice quiet and unruffled. "What happened then?"

"The story made it back to the office, which

shouldn't have surprised me since most of us at the lower and midmanagement level were at the party. Come to find out, the guy I hit was the nephew of the CEO."

"Uh-oh."

Jack chuckled, though there wasn't any humor in the dry sound. "Not that kind of *uh-oh*. The CEO knew what his nephew was up to, but couldn't just allow me to go around hitting people who ticked me off. So he asked if I'd see a therapist about anger management. I did. I think it was helpful. I've never lost it to that extent again. It didn't make me unafraid, exactly, because I'm still cautious with Charlie. I know what our dad's anger did to Tucker and me—I'd sooner die than do the same thing to a child."

"How about the nephew?"

His chuckle deepened into a laugh. "The next person who didn't like him hitting a woman wasn't a guy, and it wasn't just one person. A *bunch* of women in a nightclub had him wishing he'd never been born, and the bouncer took his time about breaking things up. I wasn't there, but I did hear that it was a good-for-the-soul time."

They talked about music then, singing the songs they'd loved in high school and laughing hard at themselves because they'd forgotten so many of the words. Jack loved Arlie's husky singing voice, though it was very different than what it had been when they were young. She didn't like it at all.

"It sounds like I'm Olivia Newton-John trying to be Bonnie Raitt. It doesn't work," she said when he told her he liked it. But she smiled. And kept singing.

"What was your favorite dance?" she asked after they'd completely butchered the Notre Dame fight song. "I know you won't remember."

"Of course I do. It was that one the DJ said was the 'last one of the evening, folks.' I knew there was no getting out of that one, but after that we got to go parking out on Launch Road."

"Noooo!" He could hear the blush in her voice. "It was when we'd do that line dance. All the guys said they hated it but you all did it, too. Remember?"

"I do." But he hadn't loved it. He'd loved that *she* loved it. "Holly was so good at that." Grief and guilt were sharp and sudden, and he fell silent.

"She still is," Arlie said. "She had to work at it but she still dances better than most people." She eyed him for a few seconds, then turned her attention back to the road. "No guilt, Jack." She smiled. "We didn't do so well on the biological-parents front, other than Superdad, but it wasn't our fault, right?"

"Right." But it wasn't always easy to believe. Even after sixteen years. Even after the trip through anger management with the therapist who tried to convince him one bout of unreasonable anger didn't mean he'd inherited his father's unfortunate tendencies.

"How long did you stay in Pensacola?"

"A couple of years. I liked it there—I still have a condo on the beach that stays rented most of the time because I never seem to get down there. But the company ran like clockwork. I liked the job okay—I did fine at it, but I was bored out of my skull." He sat sideways so he could watch her expressions. "Do you need more coffee yet?"

"I do. And I need something to eat. You ready to drive at the next rest area? It's coming up in a mile, the sign says."

"You bet." He smirked at her. "I'm a guy. I can eat a sandwich and drive at the same time."

After they'd changed drivers and both of

them were well into their second sandwiches, Arlie asked, "Where did you go next?"

"I was going up to see Charlie and drove through a big Amish community in Pennsylvania to see how much it resembled the one here. There was this little party-favors factory that was for sale. It was an old poultry house—and it was during working hours, so I stopped. I looked around and got ahold of the bank the next day."

"It was that simple?" She grinned at him and handed him half a banana. "Sometimes it pays to be the rich kid from the south end of the lake, huh?"

"It did then. My grandmother and my dad went ballistic, but my grandfather offered to loan me start-up at no interest. I was able to pay him back quickly, *with* some interest, and that's how I became Jack of several trades."

Arlie looked skeptical. "I have a hard time seeing you assembling party favors."

He laughed aloud. "Most of the assemblers there were women, and they thought it was pretty funny that I wanted to learn their jobs. They had all kinds of pictures of me in there in my shirt and tie messing with glue and cardboard and making a general mess. They told me if I hired myself to work on the line, we'd be out of business in no time, and they were right."

Arlie dozed off halfway between Louisville and Nashville. Jack turned the radio on low and drove and thought. He sipped the last of his coffee and considered pulling off at a truck stop to refill their thermoses, but he didn't want to wake her.

He'd always liked road trips, which surprised him when he recalled that he and Tucker had both had to force themselves to drive again after the accident. Jack had flatout refused until the day he couldn't find a ride to the hospital to see Arlie. It had taken him twenty minutes to get the five miles to the hospital.

But it had got better, and he tended to drive everywhere he went as long as he had time. He was always alone, though. There was never anyone pouring coffee for him or holding out her cup for a refill, never a husky voice to mingle with his in singing half-remembered songs, never a scarred hand with pretty French-polished nails to meet and tangle with his on the console between the seats of the car.

He smiled at where Arlie slept with her cheek against one of the pillows she'd brought, the quilt on her lap. He reached over, moving his gaze back to the road, and arranged the blanket to cover her hands.

Road trips were better when they were shared.

"IT'S WARMER HERE." Arlie spoke before she thought. Of course it was warmer where they were—she and Jack had driven eight hours in pursuit of good oysters. Although when she'd used the term "good oysters," Jack had said that was a prime example of an oxymoron.

Chris shivered. "Okay, if you say so." He gestured toward the restaurant beside the motel where they'd met. "They're open. You want to load up on coffee and breakfast before you start back?" He looked past her at Jack. "You couldn't talk her into just staying the night and starting out about nine in the morning? You'd both feel better."

Arlie shook her head. "Mama needs the oysters by early afternoon. But we will eat something that doesn't come out of a sandwich bag, won't we, Jack?"

He nodded, falling into step beside her as they approached the restaurant.

"Mama?" Chris raised his eyebrows. "When did you start calling her that?"

"Lately." Arlie felt Jack's hand capture hers and she curled her fingers into his. "I gave up some stem cells to the woman who gave birth to me and decided Gianna was my real mother. It was a natural process. Only took me twenty-some years."

Seated at a table that offered a view of the nearby interstate and a doughnut shop that screamed at Arlie's sweet tooth, she asked, "So how's it going for you? How's Heather?"

He hesitated. "I'm all right. Heather's in-laws found out about us. We were having dinner together—her kids included—after they left the nursing home for the day and someone from their church saw us. They must have broken all kind of speed limits letting Will's family know what they'd seen—which was nothing, by the way, because Heather won't even let me buy their dinner. They were at Heather's house within a couple of hours."

"Oh, no." Arlie shook her head. "Poor Heather. Were you there when they came?"

"No, I never go there after dark—we're so correct we'd fit right into one of those TV shows about the Victorian age. The kids were in bed and Heather had just settled in to read when they arrived. Will's parents, his sister, and even his grandmother, complete with a walker."

Just then, the waitress brought their food and more coffee, and Arlie thought she might never find out the rest of the story. Finally, when Chris and Jack had both doused their food in salsa, catsup, salt and pepper and compared notes on Chris's western omelet versus Jack's biscuits, gravy and eggs over easy, Arlie sighed mightily and said, "What happened?"

They looked at her, their forks suspended. "To what?" said Jack.

She sighed again. The curtains should have moved with the power of it. "We were having a conversation."

Chris nodded. "We were. Now we're eating."

These two men who'd played such large parts in her life, who'd known each other since training-wheels days and never been friends, were suddenly having a good-old-boy chuckle at her expense. Arlie scowled at them both.

"Okay." Chris relented. He wiped his lips with a napkin and took a sip of coffee. "What they did was ask her what she was waiting for. They appreciated her love for Will but understood she needed to have a life for herself. For the kids. They wanted to know what they could do to help and apologized all over themselves for not having done more already."

Arlie clasped her hands in front of her, even though she was holding her fork. "That's wonderful."

"It is," he agreed. "They've always been good to Heather, but it took a lot for them to set her free, so to speak. They had to let go of the hope that Will would someday wake up and be himself again."

"So what now?"

Some of the light disappeared from his eyes. "It doesn't really change things that much. She won't divorce Will, ever. I'd love to marry her and become a real dad to the kids, but I'm pretty sure if I issued an ultimatum forcing her to choose between her husband and me, I'd lose." He shrugged. "I lose anyway. I understand that, but the worst day with her in my life is better than the best day without her, so that's the way it goes."

Arlie met Jack's eyes, so bright blue behind his glasses. For just a little piece of time, with her knee bumping against his thigh under the table and their forearms coming together on its top, the years fell away. They were teenagers again, wrapped up in each other and cherishing the moments.

They left for the return trip twenty minutes later. In the restaurant's parking lot, before Chris went to the motel and she and Jack got back on the interstate, the two men shook hands with appreciably more warmth than she'd ever seen them share. "Be careful going back," said Chris. "I didn't like it, you know, when Arlie started seeing you again."

Arlie huffed. "It wasn't any of your—"

"Business. Yes, I know, although I still think a pretend girlfriend of two years' standing *was* my business, but I was talking to Jack, not you." Chris grinned, his eyes twinkling in the light from the restaurant windows. "Anyone who'd drive eight hours down and eight hours back for the purpose of getting oysters has my vote for old boyfriend of the year."

Turning, he swept Arlie into his arms. "Stay safe, laker."

She hugged him. "You, too, preppie."

Jack captured her hand in his as they

walked to the car. "It's been a good day." He laughed, tugging her to him in a hug before opening the driver's door for her. "Oysters and all."

CHAPTER SIXTEEN

ARLIE LOVED THE clubhouse Christmas party. It was the only social event that nearly everyone on the lake got involved with. Even William Detwiler loaned horses and a wagon—or sleigh, depending on weather—for horse-savvy volunteers to drive around the lake and deliver meals and gifts to shut-ins.

One corner of the club's central ballroom was designated as Santa's Workshop, where children presented their tickets and received a gift and an ornament from the ceiling-height spruce. Yet another corner was filled with donated silent-auction items, which earned enough money to buy gifts the following year.

Cloth-covered tables and chairs filled the middle of the room. When the meal was finished, the tables were folded and put away and chairs were placed in rows for the pageant. Holly and everyone she could strong-arm into participating had a part in the production.

Unless her sister needed her to play the piano, Arlie had learned to hide from being drafted for the pageant. She usually stayed in the kitchen until the last dish was washed, then grabbed a seat near the back to watch the show.

This year, her date came into the kitchen and got her, untying the apron she wore over her sparkly green sweater and black silk skirt. "I haven't seen one of these since my senior year in high school," he said. "Come sit with me." He smiled, dipping his head to kiss her so lightly she almost pulled him back to deepen it. "You did then."

When the pageant—it was *Scrooge* this year—was over, the chairs were moved once again for the dance. Musicians took their places on the stage and dessert was set out along with paper plates and plastic forks. Paid babysitters herded their charges into a side room where they would play until they fell asleep on the premade pallets borrowed from Once Upon A Time Daycare.

Jack looked at his watch. "I have to run out to the plant to check things. Luke, the night watchman, is at the party and I don't want him to have to leave. Will you dance with me when I get back?"

Arlie looked up at him, feeling the tenderness in his blue gaze, the gentle possession of his hands at her waist. A sense of belonging slipped over her as warm and shiny as the sequins and rhinestones on her sweater. It had been so long since she'd felt that, since she'd wanted a man's kiss to go deeper, since she'd wanted to dance.

"Only the last dance?" she asked.

The twinkling Christmas lights hanging from the rafters reflected off the edges of his glasses, and the color of his eyes sparkled with the shards of dancing light. "Any one you like," he promised. "Or all of them."

"I'll wait." She went to sit beside Libby Worth, watching the dance floor fill as soon as the band began to play "Begin the Beguine."

Libby smiled, nodding toward the trained ballroom dancers who swept gracefully through the crowd. "It's like time got to the middle of the twentieth century and stood still, isn't it?"

"It is." Arlie waved as Max and Gianna passed them. "Are you all booked up until Christmas?" The tearoom's business was slow in wintertime, with December the exception to that rule. It was everyone's favorite place for a small party.

"Yes. Even on Christmas Day."

Arlie was horrified. "Oh, no, Libby, you don't want to work on Christmas."

"It's better for me than being alone or horning in on someone else's celebration. This is a family that's been apart and are trying to come together on neutral ground. They're renting the large cabin at Hoosier Hills and I'm preparing Christmas dinner for them." Libby's eyes shone, and Arlie thought—not for the first time—what a gift the other woman's gentle nature was.

They watched the dancers switch up from the waltz to a jitterbug that had the spectators' toes tapping against the wood floor. Arlie was certain if Jack came back now, they'd sit this one out. Although Holly didn't—she and Paul Phillipy were cutting the proverbial rug.

"What about Jesse?" Arlie asked. "Don't you and he see each other on Christmas?"

Libby waved a dismissive hand. "He doesn't celebrate at all, so he's always the vet on call for the area. We usually have dinner together on Christmas Eve before the service at St.

Paul's and exchange gifts, but that ends it for him."

"You don't have other family?" Arlie knew their parents were dead, but the Worths were both very private; she didn't know much else about them.

"No. Our parents were older, remember, and they were both only children, so when Dad died a year after I graduated, we were all that was left." Libby grinned at her. "I love the lake as much as you do, because if it wasn't for the people here, no one would even know I'm alive."

"Libby, that's so sad." Arlie clasped her hand.

"No, it's not, because I *do* have the lake. I have the tearoom. I have Jesse if I really need him. And I have friends. It all works." She grinned suddenly, her freckles standing out in relief on her cheeks. "And here come the Llewellyn boys. I'll bet we can get them to dance." Arlie looked up and spotted Jack and Tucker in the doorway. Jack was talking, his head bent toward his brother's good ear. They laughed together, then looked around the room. When Jack's eyes came to rest on her, he raised his brows in an unmistakable invitation.

She pulled Libby to her feet. "I'll bet you're right."

"Was everything okay at the plant?" Arlie asked when Jack led her to the dance floor. The jitterbug had ended and the band was playing a fox-trot.

"Yeah, it was fine. I just didn't want Luke to have to leave the party—he was having way too good of a time for that. He's the balloon-animal guy." Jack grinned down at her. "Let's count off first."

Halfway around the floor, Arlie gazed up at him in startled appreciation. It was like dancing on delicious musical air. "Okay, when did you learn to do this?"

"Remember the women I told you about at the party-favors plant?"

She nodded.

"Most of them belonged to a ballroom-dance group. They got me to agree to fill in if anyone's partner couldn't make it. From then on, one or another of their husbands managed to have something going on every week, so I learned to dance whether I wanted to or not." He swung her wide. "Want to dip? I'm good at that."

"Let me get my breath back first."

He did, almost, then took her on a twirl and a dip that left her breathless once again.

Holly and Nate danced close. "Jack, you are so wasted on her," said Holly. "I saw that dip and I'm cutting in."

"Well, I'm hurt." Nate handed her over and pulled a laughing Arlie to him. "After I shared my Juicy Fruit gum, too. Don't even ask." He shook his head sadly. "She took it all. All I have is an empty yellow package in my pocket with all the lint."

Arlie laughed. "I'd just get it stuck to something anyway. So are you going to North Carolina to work on that golf course? I thought you'd still be there."

"I flew in there yesterday and flew back here this afternoon, and I admit I am tired. I don't know how people do that all the time. But, yes, I'm going to go down there for a few months."

She smiled. "You love it, don't you?"

"I do. I mean, I'd have loved being a pro golfer. You know how much I wanted that when we were kids. But designing is— Man, it's just wonderful. For a guy who barely passed industrial arts in high school, I couldn't feel any luckier. I still get to play, though not that well. I get to go to courses all over the country—even the world. And I get to design, which is to me like dancing is to your sister, the one over there showing off that she can do more with one foot than most of us can do with two. It doesn't get much better."

Across the dance floor, moving much more slowly than the music called for, the very pregnant beautician from the It's De-Lovely Salon danced with her husband. Arlie thought of catching babies, of being in the arms of the only man she'd ever really loved, of singing old songs with him even though she didn't like her voice anymore. It didn't get much better than that, either.

The music sped up again, flowing into another jitterbug, and Arlie caught sight of Holly, her dark head thrown back as she laughed at something Jack had said. Nearby, Max and Gianna danced slow and close, oblivious to the beat of the music.

Emily, an employee of Rent-A-Wife, still reeling from recent and unexpected widowhood, sat with Mrs. Benteen. Their heads were together, and as Arlie watched, Nate's mother leaned in and said something to the younger woman that made Emily laugh out loud. It was a good thing to see.

"Your mother," said Arlie, looking up at

Nate. "How's she doing? How's your aunt? Isn't that who she went to see?"

"Mom's fine and so is my aunt. I'll tell you, Arlie, Rent-A-Wife is a godsend for her. Between your family's business and living next door to the Phillipys, she's able to be entirely independent. I can travel without worrying and my sister can raise her family in Texas without running back to Indiana every few months to keep an eye out while I'm gone. You don't know how many people you help."

"I'm cutting in." Jack's hand fell on Nate's shoulder. "Holly has worn me completely out. That music better go back to what we danced to in high school. You know, when we didn't really move."

Nate kissed Arlie's cheek. "See you all later. I'm going to grab a dance with Libby."

Evidently sensing that the dancers were wearing down, the band began a slow number, and Jack's hands slipped to Arlie's waist. "Want to go grab a drink at Anything Goes after this? I love the Christmas party, but it's been a long evening."

She laughed, reaching to tug at his beard. "You're just worn out from the oyster run."

"That's likely," he admitted. "But a mug

of the Grill's special hot chocolate sounds good."

"To me, too."

They said good-night to friends and family, found their coats in the cloakroom and started across the parking lot. "Want to walk?" he asked when they reached his SUV.

"No." She winced. "I'm wearing heels. I've probably already danced myself into a blister."

ARLIE WAS ASLEEP before they made it to Anything Goes. Jack turned around in the parking lot and drove back to the Toe. "Hey," he said softly, "wake up, sleeping beauty."

She opened her eyes—what beautiful eyes they were—and looked around to regain familiarity. "Some date I am. I hope you realize my falling asleep is no reflection on the quality of your company."

He grinned, then leaned over to kiss her, keeping his hands on his side of the console. "That never occurred to me until you mentioned it. Come on. I'll walk you to the door and take Wally and Caruso out for you."

They stood in the doorway while the puppy and cat did their perimeter check. "I wish Charlie had been here. He'd have liked the party." Arlie hugged herself for warmth—she'd already taken off her coat—and he put his arm around her.

"Me, too." Her mention of Charlie intensified the ache he always felt when it had been too long since he'd seen his son. "He'll be here soon. He's spending Christmas break with his grandparents in South Bend and he'll be here part of the time, too."

She looked up at him, and he could see questions in her eyes, but he didn't want to answer them, didn't want to address his failings as a father. It had been a beautiful night that had capped off a wonderful week. He didn't want to think about failings of any kind.

"I had fun tonight." He drew her against him to allow Caruso and Wally room to run into the house. "You look beautiful."

"Thank you."

"What do you think? Will you be my girl again? If I dig up my class ring, do you want it?" She was the only one who'd ever worn it—Jack didn't like rings—but it had been on a chain around Arlie's neck until the night of the accident. A sheriff's deputy had found it mostly unscathed in the wreckage and given it to Jack. He still had it, though he wasn't sure where it was.

She shook her head. "I don't think we're ready for that. Do you?" Her voice was so soft there was almost no rasp in it. "When you see Charlie, how often do you end the visit with thoughts of not seeing him again? How often do you almost decide his life would be better without you in it?"

For just a split, suspended second, he didn't understand why she'd asked that. For longer than that, he didn't want to answer.

"I don't doubt for one minute that you love Charlie with all your heart." It was a mere whisper now. He had to bend his head to hear her. "And I don't doubt you care for me. But I don't believe you'll stay, Jack. I just don't."

CHAPTER SEVENTEEN

JACK SET THE bottle of Vermont maple syrup in front of Arlie where she sat at his kitchen table. He'd called her early Saturday morning, and she'd walked to the Dower House with Wally prancing on his lead and making frequent forays into the piles of dirty snow left by the snowplow along the lake's narrow streets.

"I got the building," he said. "The Realtor texted this morning."

She had to think about what he meant. "Oh, the drugstore. Are you going to put a bike shop in it? Have you decided?"

"I don't know," he admitted. "I'm not sure it fits. I'm not much on buildings talking, but it seemed to me it was saying no. What do you think?"

She knew what would fit. She'd mentally set up the offices of A Woman's Place on the Lake at least ten different times in the days since Sarah had lost her baby. She'd even shown Kari Ross the realty website's photographs of the building the day the doctor had come to sew.

Looking at the man in whose kitchen she sat, at his tired eyes and wrinkled white shirt with the tie hanging loose down its front, she knew if she told him what she thought, he would move heaven and earth to make it happen.

As close as they had become, it wasn't his to do. Their renewed friendship was deep and—she hoped—abiding, but a friendship was all it was destined to be. With their genetic backgrounds and what had gone before, not to mention the lack of faith in him she couldn't seem to get past, they weren't meant to be spouses or parents.

That was more than she could think about right now.

She took another bite of pancake and forced herself to swallow. "The closest one is Breakaway in Peru, and almost everyone on the lake rides—there's even a riding club."

Jack gave her more pancakes, and she stifled a groan. "Good thought," he said. "I owned one in Vermont for a while, the Chain and Sprocket. It was a lot of work and not all that much money."

"Is that why you sold it?" She took another bite.

"Nope." Jack set a yapping Wally on the stool beside him and gave him a bite of bacon. "I sold it because the people who worked there loved it more than I did and they wanted to buy it. We were making a profit by the time they took over and they're making a bigger one now. The fun was in the work. It always is. I still fill in there once in a while if they're shorthanded."

Arlie finished her pancakes and put her dishes in the dishwasher. "That was a delicious breakfast. Now, I'm going to take my obnoxious puppy and walk home and you're going to get some sleep. Have you made it to eight hours for the entire week yet?"

"I'm about to," he promised, following her to the back door and holding her coat for her. "Got your gloves?"

She made a face at him. "You sound like Mama."

He laughed when she pulled on a red one and a green one. "At least they're in the spirit of the season. Be careful walking home. It's snowing again this morning. I feel like I never left Vermont—all we need are some good mountains and a whole lot less wind."

She meant to kiss his cheek, really she did, but he moved. And then they both stood still, their hands at each other's waists and their hearts beating solid—and maybe a little fast—against each other as their lips met and held. Exploring a little. Or...oh, yes... more than a little.

"A good way," said Jack, his breath coming short and quick, "to start a day."

She smiled, her mouth against his, and felt his lips curve in response. "Yes," she said. "Yes, it was."

Nearly an inch of sugary new snow lay on the roads when she left Dower House. Wally was still having a wonderful time running beside her, so she walked on past the Toe and went to the saltbox house at the end of Christensen's Cove. Max's car was in the driveway. Arlie noticed—and was embarrassed to have done so—that he'd just got there. There were still fresh tracks in the newly fallen snow.

Gianna opened the back door as soon as Arlie stomped her feet on the stoop. "You're just in time for breakfast."

"I just ate pancakes with Jack." Arlie hugged Gianna and took off her coat, leaving it on top of the washing machine. By the time she was ready to pick Wally up to clean his feet, Gianna was already drying him with a fluffy towel from the clothes dryer and telling him what a good boy he was. "You should have had boys. Holly and I always cleaned our own feet and you never gave us warm towels or told us we were good girls."

"No, I should have had puppies. They don't talk back." Gianna laughed and led the way into the kitchen. "Come have coffee anyway. Is everything okay?"

"I was just thinking of something. Hi, Max." Arlie waved. It was getting easier seeing him in Dad's spot at the table. She poured coffee for herself and joined him. "Sorry to interrupt your breakfast."

"You're not interrupting." Gianna brought plates to the table for Max and herself. "You're sure you don't want some breakfast? Wally looks hungry."

"Wally always looks hungry." Arlie gave her dog a disparaging frown. "I have a question for you two. You're a mother and a school administrator, so I'm counting on expertise."

"Oh, go ahead." Max rubbed his hands together. "I love being an expert."

"Do you love being an administrator, too? Is the fun in the work?"

He thought for a minute. "I don't necessarily love my job," he said finally. "I love being in a building filled with kids and schoolteachers, because they are the absolute top of the crop when it comes to people. I like playing basketball at lunchtime and being the butt of *all* the jokes at the school talent show. I like sometimes saying the right thing at the right time so I do something good for a kid who needs it. The paperwork and the politics and going to meetings whether I want to or not—no, I don't love that."

"I remember—" And suddenly, she did. "I remember you telling all of us who survived the accident that it wasn't our faults Dad and Linda died. You said the same thing I don't know how many days in a row. You told Holly and me Daddy would have died a hundred times over if it would have kept us safe. Mama said the same thing and so did our grandparents, but you were the principal—we knew you wouldn't say anything you didn't mean."

"I like being that guy, the one who doesn't say anything I don't mean, and that's an important part of the job." Max took a bite of a gravy-covered biscuit and chewed, a thoughtful expression on his face. "So, yes, I'd have to say I love being a principal, and the fun is definitely in the work."

"Thank you." Arlie turned her attention to Gianna, who was sharing her breakfast with Wally. That was just disgusting. "What about you, Mama? You stayed at home to raise us when it wasn't a popular thing to do because… Why did you?"

"Your dad and I talked about it. You two had already had a lot of drama. Your mother's leaving was difficult for you, and Holly was a daddy's girl whose father died without any kind of warning. We thought you both needed the stability of a full-time parent. We were both pretty good ones, but the truth is your dad made a lot more money at Chrysler than I did as a secretary." She laughed, her dark eyes soft with memory. "He was also horrified by the challenge of doing two little girls' hair every morning."

"Did you miss working?"

"Sometimes I did. Rent-A-Wife has been great for that. I get out of the house and keep what skills I have sharp, but I don't work long days. The truth is, though, that overall I loved being a homemaker. If you and Holly would just get busy, I'd love being a grandma, too, but that's not what we're talking about, is it?"

"No." Arlie gave up fighting it and went into the kitchen, coming back with a small bowl full of biscuits and gravy. She carried the coffee carafe, too, and refilled everyone's cups. When she was sitting again and had demolished half a biscuit, she confessed, "Remember the plans we looked at? I want to go back to midwifery, to open a practice here on the lake just like we talked about. Jack said this morning that the fun was in the work just like you did, Max, and you're both right. I like being a nurse, but I *love* being a midwife, and I don't think I can make the business go if I keep working at the hospital."

She sipped coffee and ate another bite of biscuit. If she finished the whole bowl, she would have to unsnap her jeans for the walk home, but worse things than that had happened. She captured Gianna's attention. "But I need a financial partner. Mama, would you think of investing some of the money we talked about?" She named an amount that sounded horrifying to her. She set down her fork. "Never mind. Forget I even asked that. I'm thirty-three years old and I'm not going to build my life on my mother's retirement."

Gianna and Max met each other's eyes, and Arlie was reminded of when her father was alive. Dave and Gianna's conversations about the girls had taken place in complete silence, but there'd never been any doubt they understood each other.

"Actually, Arletta Marquetta Brigetta," said Max, taking license with her name that hadn't been given, "your mother and I had another idea."

Arlie didn't glare at him—he was still the principal and she didn't have the nerve—but she spoke stiffly. "I certainly hope it's a good one, since you called me that awful name and being in Mama's house means I can't throw a tantrum or kick your shins."

"What we thought," said Gianna, still holding Max's gaze, "was that we'd both like to invest."

CHAPTER EIGHTEEN

"IT'S BEAUTIFUL, ISN'T IT?" Arlie stood in the middle of the wide-planked floor of the old drugstore and turned in a slow circle.

"It is." Jack leaned against the wall. "In better shape than I originally thought, too. Did you know it had an elevator?"

"No, really?"

"Back here." He led the way to the back of the room. "The owners lived upstairs, remember? The Proctors were old even when we were kids—or they seemed old, like everyone over forty did—but one of their fathers lived with them and he couldn't handle the stairs, so they put in an elevator. It's not huge, but it'll hold several people without a problem. It's entirely functional, too."

The upstairs of the building was dusty but dry, with two bathrooms, three bedrooms and a bigger kitchen-living area than Arlie had at the Toe.

"Have you decided what to do with the building?" *Say no. Please say no.*

"Halfway." He smiled at her. "Someone I know suggested a bike shop."

Hoisted by her own petard. Arlie didn't remember where the term came from, but she knew when it applied. "Well," she said, giving enthusiasm her best shot, "what a great idea. Wasn't I the smart one?" *Oh, yeah, the smart one all right.* And now she was back to square one.

Jack smiled at her. "I thought so, and I appreciate you having it. Len, who owns the shop in Vermont, might come and help with the setup if that's what I decide on. You'll like him."

"I'm sure I will." *Maybe I can get a job here selling bicycles. I ride pretty well.*

"What do you think is a good name for a shop? Breakaway is already taken locally—Zac and Shannon See have that over in Peru. Chain and Sprocket's been used, though Len wouldn't mind another one a thousand miles away from his store." Jack walked the perimeter of the room, eyeing the old beadboard ceiling.

"It needs to be a Porter."

"What?"

She rolled her eyes at him. "Cole Porter, the songwriter, remember? Most of the shops on the lake have names taken from the titles or the lyrics of his songs. Please don't tell me you didn't know that."

"I knew it." He looked embarrassed, as he should have. "But I have to admit I forgot about it. Family lore says my grandmother wanted to change the name of Llewellyn's Lures to 'Something for the Boys,' but my grandfather stuck to his guns on that one. Said it could have all kinds of connotations, none of them good and none of them having to do with fishing."

Arlie hesitated. "You made that up."

Jack laughed. "Not exactly. Grandmother was laughing at the business names one time—I was just a little kid—and Granddad was the one who actually suggested 'Something for the Boys' to get her dander up. As I remember, it really worked."

"She didn't like the Porter titles on the businesses?" Arlie had never been all that fond of the theme, either, though she had to admit the names usually fit the businesses they were assigned to.

"She didn't like anything about the lake. I'm amazed she stayed here after Granddad died, but she didn't want to leave. She spent a few winters in California and made long visits to the Indianapolis house, but most of her time was at the Hall."

"Memories, probably. Mama says she won't leave her house until we carry her out. She had two happy marriages and raised two excellent daughters there."

"Hmm." Jack frowned. "Were those Gianna's exact words?"

"Close. I may have added one or two." Arlie grinned at him, but it was hard. She squinted at her watch in the dim room. "I need to go home. We're sewing this afternoon."

"I'll walk you."

"No, don't. You're going to the Colts game with Tucker." She zipped her coat and pulled on her gloves. "I thought Charlie would be here by now. He said Friday was his last school day till after New Year's."

"He's with his grandparents. I'll pick him up Christmas Eve."

"That's too bad. He'd have enjoyed the game." She took a last look around the room. "I love the building, Jack. It'll be a great bicycle shop if that's what you decide on, and it will be great for the lake even after you go back to Vermont."

It would have been a great women's clinic, too, but she couldn't say that. It would make him feel bad about something that wasn't even remotely his fault, and there had been more than enough of that between them. If Jack's guilt was made of ice, Miniagua would be completely frozen over by now.

Knowing that didn't make her feel any less sorry for herself as she started the walk to the Toe. She moved more slowly than usual, taking stock of the buildings in what the lake association euphemistically referred to as the "business district." Most of them were occupied, though winter commerce on the lake was abysmal. The Silver Moon Café opened for breakfast and lunch, closing at two. Its greatest summer competitor, Anything Goes Grill, obligingly opened at four o'clock. Libby kept the tearoom open from eleven till four, so there was always a place on the lake to find a good cup of coffee and some conversation.

The buildings that were empty weren't viable options for a medical facility. Two of them needed to be torn down. A third was too small and in the middle of the block, so parking was limited. The fourth and final one used to be a gas station—it still looked like one.

She thought it would make an excellent bicycle shop.

The snow had melted in the weak December sunlight, but more was due that evening. Until it arrived, Miniagua—both lake and community—were as gray as Arlie's mood.

Walking the last block to the Toe, she considered looking for office space in Sawyer. It was only five miles away and as convenient for the Amish community as Miniagua was. It even had the added conveniences of a pharmacy and a small hospital. Holly lived there, too, so Arlie would always have a place to sleep if the town got snowed in.

She'd had her heart set on practicing in Miniagua, though. She should have known better than to let her heart get involved at all. That never worked out well for her. Never.

Driving home from Indianapolis after the game under seriously lowering skies, Jack and Tucker talked about their grandmother, something they never did.

They agreed that she had probably done the best she could, but her capacity for compassion and understanding had been seriously lacking. His grandfather used to urge the boys to cut her some slack. "Her emotions are all out of whack," he'd said, "but she means well."

That had been their father's modus operandi, too, but Victor always took the line of least resistance. When his mother had said it would be better if Jack and Tucker lived at the Hall with the advantages their grandparents could offer, he'd signed over his progeny without blinking twice. Ellen Curtis, with whom both boys had lived before moving into the mansion, had fought to regain custody, but to no avail. The onetime bartender who wasn't a United States citizen stood no chance against the Llewellyns and their squadron of attorneys.

In her later years, Margaret Llewellyn had mellowed. Some. She'd loved Charlie, which had surprised no one more than herself. She'd been, according to Sam, a good customer. Paul Phillipy had even said she'd become more cognizant of workers' needs, although they were never considered if they got in the way of the plant's bottom line.

"She tried to make amends." Jack stared moodily out the passenger window of Tucker's Camaro. It had been too little, too late, but she'd tried.

Judging from the ticking sound of precipitation hitting the car roof, what had begun as a feeble drizzle of rain was becoming a not-so-faint fall of ice.

Tucker slowed down, moving into the right lane and staying there. "Reminds me of you."

Jack jerked his head around. "What?"

"Good grief, Jack, you're going to make yourself old before your time trying to make up for the things Grandmother and Dad and Janice have done to everyone. You still mentor Nate's business even though he's very successful on his own. You've done your best to make sure anyone who was in the accident got whatever money they needed at an interest rate below and beyond what they hoped for even when it meant you were nosing in other people's business. You hardly ever see my mother because of some unfounded guilt, yet you're better at seeing to her needs than I am. You won't let yourself love Arlie because you're afraid she'll be hurt again." Tucker fishtailed a little on the ice and slowed even more, flicking a quick glance to meet Jack's gaze.

"I don't do all that. And while you're at it, leave Arlie's name out of the conversation."

"Yes, you do. When Gianna had her heart surgery, she had no out-of-pocket expenses.

The Linda Saylors and Dave Gallagher scholarships are full rides to any state university. It's been over sixteen years since the accident and I'll bet most of the donations to those scholarships stopped coming in a long time ago, but the full rides are still paid. Every year."

Jack chuckled, smacking Tucker's shoulder. "Someone else pays a large part of those."

His brother's cheeks reddened. "Make no mistake, I think we should give—and give a lot. We have more money than we need, money we haven't earned, and I have absolutely no quarrel with you giving it all away if you want to—my share included. It's easy for us to say the fun is in the working and the earning, both because it is and because we've never for one day in our lives done without. But I take exception to your reason for doing it."

Jack hesitated. "Did Dad ever tell you when the mental illness surfaced in Janice?"

"I don't think so. I just thought she'd always had it."

"Until I was born, she didn't. She was flighty, I guess, and tended to get depressed easily, but the real psychosis came after I was born, and it never went away." Jack smiled grimly. "Her mental health was one thing that Llewellyn money couldn't fix."

"You can't spend the rest of your life single-handedly anticipating the community's needs and fixing its problems, either." Tucker felt for his cup, nodding thanks when Jack put it in his hand. "How much money did you give this year's senior class?"

"I don't know."

"Yes, you do. You gave them enough to cover the prom, didn't you? You bought enough magazine subscriptions that the nursing-home residents won't run out of reading material until at least the tercentennial. You paid enough for your Christmas tree to plant a forest."

"There's nothing wrong with—"

"It's not the giving that's wrong, Jack." Tucker caught his gaze again quickly before looking back at the road. "But you can't keep them safe. You can't keep anyone safe all by yourself, even Charlie. Until you get that, you're never going to be able to let go the way Arlie and Holly talk about. The accident and the dysfunction in our family are going to own you, body and soul."

Jack's phone buzzed in his pocket, signaling a text message. Before he even read it, Tucker's phone rang over the speakers in the car. Tucker pushed a button on the steering wheel and Paul Phillipy's voice came through, nearly buried in crackling interference. "The plant's on fire and it looks pretty bad. I'm here. If you can come safely, it would be good. I can't tell if you're on the other end or not—too much static."

CHAPTER NINETEEN

"It's KIND OF a weird thing." Arlie sewed quilt blocks, "assembly line" style, stitching identical combinations together in a long row. "I know as sure as I'm sitting here that if I told Jack I wanted to lease the building, he'd not only rent it to me, he'd do the improvements needed according to my specifications. But I can't do that. It would end up being the clinic that guilt built."

"That's poetic." Holly wasn't sewing—she was sitting in a rocking chair with her computer on a lap desk and Caruso snoozing happily beside her. She was on deadline and the characters in her story weren't cooperating with her plans for them. "These people are just like my sister. They won't do what is obviously best for them," she complained, her fingers tapping on the keys. "I should have already worn a maid-of-honor dress by now and be practicing for perfect aunthood. Instead, we're obsessing over where you can start your next business."

"Holly," Gianna reproved, "be nice." She patted Wally, not surprisingly curled up in her lap.

"I am being nice. I'm telling her to do what she's always done when life hasn't gone as planned—make a new plan." Holly paused, her fingers in the air. "Which is exactly what these people need to do, too. Thank you! That's it. That will get them out of this miserable corner I wrote them into. I love you, sis."

"I love you, too." Arlie snipped apart the blocks she'd just sewn and went to the ironing board to press the seams. "But you're still a pain in the—"

"Arlie." Gianna sighed, though laughter trembled in her voice. "You be nice, too." She started the embroidery machine and, carrying Wally over one arm, stepped away from its noisy stitching to take a seat beside Holly.

"What is that sound?" Holly tilted her head.

Arlie nodded at the embroidery machine. "That?"

"No. It's outside."

The three of them crowded around the big

window at the end of the room and stared in dumbfounded silence at the spectacle before them. "Good heavens." Gianna was the first to speak. "Look at the ice."

The trees were loaded with it, snapping and crackling in the wind. Branches whipped against the side of the building, making the sound that had been loud enough to hear over the machines. The grass below looked like a field of diamonds in the gathering dusk. Beyond the yard, the lake crashed against the shore, small wavelets standing frozen in its wake.

"Wow. Looks like sleepover time." Holly shuddered. "Driving on ice is way beyond my capabilities."

"Mine, too," said Gianna. "I don't walk on it anymore, either."

Arlie texted Jack.

Ice storm at the lake. Don't come home.

He didn't answer, and she frowned. Cellphone reception wasn't great around the lake, but texts usually went through pretty well. *Usually* being the operative word.

The women prepared dinner together and were just taking seats at the table when the sound of sirens bounced off the ice-covered windows. The women went still in the broken silence, trying to gauge both the distance and whether the sirens were police, fire or ambulance.

"Fire." Gianna closed her eyes and crossed herself. "It seems as though every time there's an ice storm, there's a fire. When I was a kid, stores burned in downtown Peru and there were pictures in the paper of firefighters working with layers of ice all over them."

The sirens quieted, and the women went from window to window, searching for telltale signs of the blaze. A pink cast across the sky in the direction of Sawyer was the only clue, but it was an ominous one.

They ate supper, subdued by thoughts of the destruction that could be wrought and worries about the firefighters. More sirens interrupted the meal, and Arlie shuddered, exchanging looks of dread with the others. It must be a bad one. The freezing rain slowed and stopped, but ice still covered everything. The glow in the western sky grew redder.

Arlie texted Jack again. He still didn't answer.

"Have there been bad fires on the lake?"

asked Holly idly, stacking dishes. "I don't remember any. Do you?"

"The clubhouse burned when I was in elementary school," Gianna remembered. "The building was old and dry, with terrible wiring. I don't remember exactly what happened, but it went up like wadded-up newspaper. That one happened in an ice storm, too. I couldn't understand how the building could be dry with all that ice on it, but it was.

"Another summer, several boats were burned. That was the year a few Sawyer kids thought they'd try out being a gang, but some jail time convinced them otherwise. It was one of those things that in the long run probably did some good, but the people who lost their boats sure didn't see it that way."

Arlie's phone dinged a text, and she looked at the screen.

Fire at the factory. We are almost there. Will call when I can.

He'll never stay now. Even as the thought crossed her mind, she was ashamed of it. *Sometimes it's not about you.*

They'd gone back to the sewing room and were working on different projects when her phone rang. She stared at it before picking it up and sliding her fingers over the screen. "Are you all right?"

JACK LOOKED AT his brother's hands as they gripped the steering wheel. "Do you want me to drive again?" It would have been a good day to have driven his SUV instead of Tucker's sporty car, but neither of them mentioned that—the ice storm had been unexpected, as was the fire.

"I'm good." Tucker turned on his flasher and moved into the turning lane. What little traffic there was—mostly a few intrepid 18-wheelers—was crawling. The reflection of headlights gleamed and splintered on the icy road. The trip from Indianapolis had taken three hours, and even though they'd taken turns driving, they were both exhausted.

Jack spoke because he couldn't do anything else. "I can't imagine the factory being gone."

"We don't know how bad it is. It may just be some smoke damage."

"You don't believe that."

"No."

Before they'd lost the connection, Paul Phillipy had been terse, with little real information, but he hadn't left much room for hope, either. "I can't tell how bad it is. There's too much fire water and ice and mud to tell. You boys just be safe coming—"

Paul loved the plant as much as Jack's grandfather had. He'd worked there all of his adult life. The term "you boys" sounded good in Jack's ears. Comforting.

"What if it's gone?" Tucker asked the question they'd been avoiding.

"We'll still have the other plants." Even to his own ears, Jack's rejoinder sounded hollow.

"The Miniagua facility is the heart of Llewellyn's Lures. If the heart's gone, we may as well sell off the others."

Jack wasn't ready to talk about that. He'd walked away from what was important one time, and it had made his life into a sketchy shadow of things dreamed of and planned for. He wouldn't do that again.

Twenty minutes later, as he walked through the mud and the mire around the decimated factory with his brother, the fire chief and Paul, he wasn't so sure. Looking down, he couldn't tell where the ice left off and the shattered glass began.

The chief was matter-of-fact. "With so

much wood and glue in there, plus it taking us at least twice as long to get here on the ice, it could have been a lot worse. The office part is gone, but the rest of the building is still standing. A ton of smoke, but the structural damage is limited."

"No one was hurt, though, right?" Jack had already asked once, but he had to be sure. Nothing was that calamitous if no one was hurt. "No firefighters? The night watchman?"

"The sheriff took him home," said Paul. "He was pretty shaky and feeling guilty because he thought he should have seen or smelled something sooner."

"A firefighter caught some smoke, but I've already heard back. He'll be fine come morning." Relief lightened the chief's exhausted features.

"Any ideas on how it started?" asked Tucker.

The firefighter hesitated. "It didn't look deliberate to me. We'll get out here when it's daylight to take a better look. But the fire's out. There was no damage to any but the main building."

What if there had been injuries or even death? The inventory that was housed in the other buildings on the property could have been lost. The paper accounts that had just gone up in ice and water and smoke used to be the only records Llewellyn's Lures kept. Jack had fought his grandmother tooth and nail while he and Tuck were in college to bring the plant into the computer age. In one summer, Tucker had overseen the modernization of the offices while Jack entered archived records onto electronic media.

Even during the years they'd scarcely talked, they'd worked together. It was an unsettling thought, and Jack felt a wash of regret for decisions he'd made.

"There's nothing you can do here now," the chief assured him. "The fire marshal will be here in the morning and I'm sure you'll have insurance people you'll want to call." He squinted up at the sky. "It's starting to warm up—the ice will be gone by then."

Paul Phillipy left at the same time, walking with them as far as his car.

"Thanks for coming so quickly," said Jack.

"It's all right." Paul looked back at the building and shook his head. "Sad, though. I don't think Llewellyn's Lures has missed a day of production since it opened. Even before I was born, in the forties, it manufactured things for the war effort. I don't know exactly what, but my dad worked here then."

"We won't miss one now, either." Jack exchanged a look with his brother. "There'll be a week's paid vacation while we set up temporary office operations in the old drugstore building. We'll transfer production to Tennessee while we repair and replace whatever needs it in the main building."

Tucker nodded. "I'll fly down there tomorrow if you want to handle things here." His smile was weary but relieved at the same time. "Start-up is your middle name, isn't it?"

"It is." Jack laid an arm across his brother's shoulders as they walked on to the Camaro. "I'm good at starting up, but I'm not sure how I'll do with starting over."

Tucker gave him a light elbow in the ribs. "It's time you worked on that in more than one area."

Jack's phone signaled a message. When he'd fastened his seat belt, he withdrew it from his pocket. At some level he heard Tucker answer the hands-free signal in the car, heard him say, "Hi, Tracy. Yeah, he's right here," but he felt as though he was in a cave with no way out. The garbled, echoing sounds of his ex-wife's voice bounced off the walls of his mind.

The screen on his phone screamed Tracy's delayed text message at him even after it wasn't lit anymore.

Charlie missing. Tried to reach you. He left a note at Mom & Dad's saying he was coming to your house. Has his cell phone but isn't answering. Police have been called. Please call me ASAP.

Jack couldn't breathe, couldn't speak even as Tucker grasped his arm and Tracy's voice, hysteria defining it, came over the car speakers. "Jack? Jack? You haven't heard from him? Not at all?" before the call dropped.

Not Charlie. Please dear holy God, not Charlie.

CHAPTER TWENTY

THE POWER WENT out within minutes after the phone call so that they argued in darkness until Gianna could get the emergency candles lit.

"Stay here and take care of Caruso and Wally. And each other. Keep trying to reach Jack and Tucker—I'm not getting through to them at all." Standing between her mother and sister, Arlie felt their love as surely as though they were hugging her.

They'd both wanted to join her for the trek to the Laundromat that housed Miniagua's bus stop—where Charlie waited—but she'd talked them out of it. Finally. Neither her mother's iffy heart nor her sister's prosthetic foot was a good match for icy surfaces and unrelieved darkness.

"I love you both." She blinked back tears that appeared from nowhere and reached past Holly for her boots. She wound her scarf around her neck twice, covering her mouth and chin. The soft teal wrap had been Holly's first crocheting project—she hadn't known how to end it, so it was extra long and wonderfully flawed.

Gianna handed her a flashlight. "Try to call or text when you get there. I know they're not going through, but one of them might."

Arlie's grandfather's walking sticks were still propped in the corner of the Toe's breezeway. She found one that felt like the right length and wondered distractedly if it had belonged to her grandmother.

The sky was both moonless and starless, and the flashlight made little impression on the inky blackness brought on by the power outage. Icy trees snapped and popped eerily overhead, and Arlie thought belatedly that it might have been a good idea to wear a bicycle helmet.

She had to cross the bridge at the end of the business district, a dark and scary undertaking. The wind was intense, the lake loud below her feet. Had Charlie come this far on foot before he'd gone back to the relative safety of the bus stop? Arlie's heart ached for the fear he must have felt. That he still felt, if his voice on the crackling phone call was any indication.

Arlie didn't think she'd ever been afraid in Miniagua—a crime wave usually had to do with vandalizing the soda machines outside the convenience stores—but she didn't recall it ever being this dark before. She sang. Loud. Halfway across, with a misstep and a shriek that interrupted her rendition of "White Christmas"—they'd watched the movie that day—she slid toward the edge of the bridge, stabbing at the ice with the walking stick until she gained enough purchase to stop herself. When she did stop, it was because her foot found a spot on the pavement that was completely dry. She cast a grateful glance upward. "Thanks, Superdad," she mumbled and moved on.

Charlie waited outside the Laundromat, looking small and lonely in the darkness. When he saw Arlie coming, he ran toward her, his backpack bumping from side to side. He slid the last several feet so that he landed hard against her.

She held him close, rocking back and forth and absorbing the tremble of his body with her own. He was taller than she was and smelled like cold, sweet, adolescent boy. Holding him felt like nothing she'd ever experienced before.

This was what being a mom was like. This all-encompassing love was what Gianna felt and what Jack wouldn't claim for fear that he'd do it wrong. It was what Arlie had lost. Tears burned hot and sudden, stinging as much as the ice that struck her face.

She made herself sound firm. "You're okay now. My mom will let your mom and dad know you're with us. It will be fine."

"No, it won't." His voice wavered and sighed against her ear. "My dad's going to kill me."

"Only once and not seriously," she promised. "Why are you outside? Isn't the laundry open?"

"Yes, but the people in there were weird." He sniffed, a sound that further broke her heart. "So were some of the ones on the bus." He drew back, though not far. "Not geek-weird like me, but scary-weird like on TV shows."

Thanks again, Daddy, for watching over this boy.

When they were walking back toward the Toe, Charlie asked, "Did you ever run away?"

"Once." Arlie squinted against the driving needles of ice that had begun falling again. "I was mad at Mama over something, and I

packed a bag and took off on my bicycle—
Holly and I shared a car and I knew she'd
never forgive me if I took it. I got as far as the
cemetery, where I stopped to say goodbye to
my dad. Pretty soon, here came Mama with
Holly. She said if I was running away, they
were, too, because we were in this together
whether I liked it or not. We parked my bike
behind a tree and went to Indianapolis for the
weekend. We went to a concert." She gave
him another squeeze. "I wouldn't count on
the concert if I were you. You should probably just go with your dad only killing you
once."

"It was probably dumb, running away," he
admitted.

She nodded. "It usually is. You want to talk
about why you did it?" She slipped on the ice
and grabbed his arm. "You need to help hold
me up—I'm getting old."

"My mom's going to Germany to work.
She's done that before. I either stay with my
grandparents or board at school while she's
gone. My dad makes sure he's around for
weekends—he's always good about that.
The food's good there and Mom really is
the worst cook in the Northeast Kingdom.
Some of my friends board, too, so it's not

that big of a deal. But this time she's going to be gone for a couple of years. I can go with her or I can stay with my grandparents." He shrugged, and Arlie felt the tension in him. "Those are some pretty sucky choices. If I go with her, I'll be boarding at school there because she works all the time, and if I stay with my grandparents... Well, they're nice and everything, but jeez, Arlie, they really *are* old."

"What do you want to do?" She thought she knew, but she wanted to hear him say it.

"I want to stay with my dad. I'd really like to stay here on the lake, but I don't know what he's going to do. Even if he's based out of here, he'll travel a lot and I'm pretty sure he wouldn't leave me here by myself while he goes back and forth between the plants. Uncle Tuck travels as much as he does."

You could stay with me. She had to bite down on her bottom lip to stop the words from jumping past it. "Have you talked to your dad about it?"

"No. He's been way busy, and he's never wanted me to live with him before. But...do you know I have to wear a tie to meals at my grandparents' house? And if I live with them while Mom's gone, they're going to send me to a military school near them and I'll be boarding again but it will be worse because I'll have to wear a uniform."

She gave him a little shake. "They make movies about kids like you, don't they?"

"Oh, heck, no. Except for those ones that come on TV on Sunday afternoons in black and white."

"Oh." Those were some of Arlie's favorites, but she wasn't going to admit that. "You know they all want what's best for you, right?"

"I know." He sighed, and she felt it move through his body. "But you know what? I'd just like to be twelve. I'd like to play sports instead of doing academic stuff all the time, even if I'm not all that good at them. I'd like to go to school where you and Dad went and never wear another tie as long as I live. Do you know I've never even been in a public school?"

"You need to talk to your dad." She and Holly used to talk about being wealthy and going to boarding schools where they wouldn't have to do household chores or share their clothes. Their discussions hadn't got much past those two points.

Charlie shrugged again. "It won't help."

"It won't hurt."

They were only a few blocks from the Toe when headlights broke the darkness. The car fishtailed madly before it came to a stop in the middle of the road. Both the passenger and driver doors opened, and Jack and Tucker ran toward them, slipping and sliding but never falling.

Charlie met his father halfway, and Arlie drew in a sobbing breath. Tucker came to her side, putting an arm around her, and she leaned into him.

"What were you thinking?" Jack held on to Charlie, the hands on the boy's shoulders trembling visibly. "You scared your mom, your grandparents…everyone… You scared them to death, Charlie." He held him away and shook him, not hard or angrily, then pulled him back in, burying his face in the boy's damp hair. "What were you thinking?" he asked again. His voice was strangled, and when he lifted his head, tears streaked his face.

Charlie gazed up at his father, his features still. "What about you, Dad? Did I scare you?"

Jack looked over his head at Arlie. "The worst night of my entire life was over sixteen years ago," he said, holding her gaze, "and I'd live through it again and again if it meant you were safe."

She smiled at him. *Yes, that's the right thing to say.*

He turned his attention back to the boy in his arms. "I think we probably have things to talk about." He stroked a hand through his hair. "Since you're grounded until you're at least old enough to vote, we'll have plenty of time."

"Let's take the dumb, cold nephew back to the Toe before he freezes fast to the road," Tucker suggested. "We'll talk Gianna into making hot chocolate and something to eat."

Jack hugged Charlie again before they maneuvered into the car. "I don't know how you're going to give your mother and me back the ten years you just scared off our lives, but I'm pretty sure we'll find a way," he warned.

Gianna fed them soup and hot chocolate, then went back up to the sewing room. Holly, Libby and Tucker followed, with Tucker professing a newly discovered desire to learn how to knit.

Charlie put his empty dishes in the dishwasher and sat on the living room couch with

Wally in his lap. Both he and the puppy were asleep within minutes.

Arlie laid a quilt over them and looked up at where Jack stood watching his boy sleep. "Are you going to make him go back to his grandparents?"

Jack sighed, gazing out at the lake through the window over the kitchen sink. "I don't want to, but if I let him stay here, isn't that rewarding bad behavior?"

She thought of the weekend in Indianapolis all those years ago with her mother and sister. "No. It's letting him know that no matter what happens, he's your family and—" she smiled at the memory "—you're in it together."

He hesitated. "I'll see what Tracy says. She's the custodial parent and I try not to interfere with her decisions."

"You know she's going to Germany?"

"Yeah. She just told me tonight on one of the thirty-second conversations we managed. She knew Charlie was upset, but he's always gone along, always stayed with her folks and didn't make waves."

Arlie rearranged glasses in the dishwasher, needing something to do with her hands. "He's twelve. He's *supposed* to make waves."

"I guess that's true, but I hope he doesn't make any more like he did today. My heart can't stand it. Tonight, when Charlie was missing, I thought of your mom the night of the accident. Your dad was already gone, and Holly had lost her foot, and Gianna sat there for hours on end not knowing if you were going to make it. I don't know how she survived."

"He wants to live with you." It wasn't Arlie's place to tell him that—the life he and Charlie shared was nothing to do with her. Except that it was. She wasn't just someone who thought Charlie was an okay kid. No, she was someone who loved him. He was her business.

She joined Jack at the window, not objecting when his arms came around her from behind, holding her close and warm.

Power was coming back on around the lake. It looked magical, with house windows brightening and mercury lights beginning their slow warm-up.

"I know he does." Jack sounded both resigned and jubilant.

"What are you going to do?"

"That I *don't* know." She could hear the indecision in his voice. "What do you think?"

"I think you need to talk to him. And I

think you need to listen to him. Not to your own past and fears and wants, but to his." She turned in his arms so she could smile into his face, enjoying the tightening of his embrace. "Channel Gianna Gallagher—you can't lose."

It was Tuesday evening after the fire and Jack's face was drawn tight with fatigue, but he'd wanted to have dinner with her and he'd wanted to cook it. Arlie had argued, but he'd been insistent. In the end, she'd decided there were worse things than having her dinner prepared by a handsome man. Especially this one.

"Where's Charlie?" she asked when she got to the Dower House. "He didn't go back to South Bend, did he?"

"No. They're having a pizza, popcorn and movie overnight at the church. He wanted to go. I'm pretty sure he's going to use his church attendance and making new friends as leverage to move in with me even though the sleepover is costing him an entire extra week of being grounded."

Smart boy. "Will that work?"

Jack shrugged. "It will with me, but I'm already convinced. Did I tell you he wants a dog for Christmas?" He handed her a glass of wine.

"He's twelve. Of course he does." A dog would anchor Charlie to his father's house. She wondered if Jack realized that.

"His mother's allergic and his grandparents don't want pets around. The dog would have to live here whether Charlie does or not." Jack swirled his wine in the glass and looked pleased.

"Have you talked to Tracy yet about Charlie staying here?"

"Not yet. She'll be at her parents' for Christmas. I'll talk to her then."

What are you waiting for? But she knew without saying the words aloud. Although Jack Llewellyn had been successful at many things in his life, the relationships he'd been part of had been epic failures. He was afraid.

Arlie was good at minding her own business. It was something you learned when you lived in a small community with an inexhaustible grapevine. It was one thing to *know* about other people's concerns—making yourself a part of them was something else again.

But this was Jack. More important, this was Charlie.

"You need to talk to her right away." Arlie

set down her glass and met his gaze. "You're both emotional wrecks right now. I get that. I know you don't want to take advantage of a situation, but if you leave Charlie's life in limbo, you're going to force him to run away again. Or do something else stupid. Like we keep saying, he *is* twelve. Stupid comes with the territory."

Jack frowned, shaking his head. "I need to get the aftermath of the fire taken care of before I try to settle anything about Charlie. What if he stays here and I end up being busier than his mother is? He knows he's loved now. It'll be okay to leave it till Tracy's here."

Arlie frowned back at him. "No. It won't be okay. He knows he's loved today. By tomorrow, he may not."

Jack didn't look away, but she didn't know what he was thinking. That was one of the bad parts of a sixteen-year separation—reconnecting was spotty in places.

And then he reached for the phone.

When Tracy answered, he went into the office he'd created in the dining room, waving for Arlie to follow him. She shook her head, mouthing "I'll make the salad" and going to the refrigerator.

The conversation lasted long enough for

her to finish the salad and wash all the dishes
in the sink. She watered the poinsettia on
the windowsill and wandered into the living
room and up to the library to make sure the
Christmas tree lights had been turned on.
She stopped at the door of Charlie's room
and noticed with glee that it wasn't very neat.
The bed had been straightened—sort of—
but there were clothes on the floor and in the
wing chair. A bath towel hung over the desk
chair. The bulletin board she'd hung for him
was cluttered.

He'd made himself at home. She hoped
Jack and Tracy understood that.

Arlie heard Jack's pounding feet on the
stairs and turned when he spoke. "I can't believe it. If he comes here to live, that mess
is going to be everywhere. There'll be video
games in the living room and he'll tell gross
jokes and it'll take a gallon of milk and a
family-size box of cereal every day just to
keep him alive." He joined her in the open
doorway, looking at the room with barely a
shake of his head.

It was there in his voice, the unrestrained
glee she didn't think she'd heard since high
school days. Her heart jumped, then melted
when she saw the expression on his face.

"Without a doubt," she agreed. "That's why girls are so much better than boys, but I guess no one could tell you and Tracy that."

He took her hands. "We're going to have shared custody—she'll bring papers when she comes to her folks' for Christmas. She was thrilled." He shook his head again. "Have I been wrong all this time? Have I been shortchanging Charlie in a misguided attempt to protect him?"

Arlie thought he probably had, but she wasn't going to toss rain on this particular parade. Not tonight. "Remember to check under his bed for pizza crusts and candy wrappers and to not complain when he dresses funny. He's supposed to."

He took her into his arms, holding her close and rocking back and forth. "Yeah, he is. Isn't it great?"

CHAPTER TWENTY-ONE

"WE DON'T HAVE to have the steaks. It's so late, we can just have salad and dessert and call it dinner," Arlie offered when they returned to the kitchen.

"I'm too hungry for that, if you don't mind waiting."

"I don't mind." And she didn't. She loved sharing space with him, whether it was his or hers. "You mentioned the aftermath of the fire. How are things going?"

"I couldn't believe it." Jack set the steaks under the broiler. "They had a week's paid vacation while we put reopening plans into action. So what did they do? Took one day off." He held up his hands in supplication, one of them holding the spoon he had stirred the mushrooms with.

"No one could get on the grounds Monday because the fire marshal and insurance adjusters and all kinds of officials were all over the place. They ruled the fire an accident, a wiring glitch of some sort, and this morning, out of fifty-nine employees, more than forty of them were at the site to help clean up. Those people were amazing."

Arlie knew those people. She'd worked with them, socialized with them and played softball with them. She wasn't really surprised. She'd have been more surprised if they hadn't shown up.

She poured the homemade dressing she'd brought with her into little side dishes. "Where will you get new machinery for inside the plant?"

He put the steaks on platters and added the baked potatoes from the warming drawer under the oven. "Sorry. I know we should have the salad first, but I never time things right. Plus, my call to Tracy delayed things some."

"Doesn't matter. My stomach doesn't care what order it gets filled in."

When they were seated, he answered her question. "We ordered all new office furniture and machines from a distributor in Peru and they'll be here tomorrow."

"What about manufacturing equipment? That will take longer, won't it?"

"It will, but Paul flew to Maine, where

we've gotten replacement tooling for as long as he could remember. He'll order what he can. Tuck's in Tennessee and will be able to get some from there, too."

She chewed thoughtfully on her steak, mildly resentful that he cooked as well as she did and Gianna Gallagher wasn't even his mother. "Sam said his mom went along, too. Is that usual?"

Jack cleared his throat and didn't meet her eyes. "You know Sam's sister and her family live in New Hampshire. It would have been silly for them not to have taken a few days to drive down and see them, especially this close to Christmas."

"You're hard as nails, aren't you, Jack of several trades?" She smiled at him, waiting till he looked at her. When he did, she felt as though she might very well fall into the tenderness in his blue eyes.

"Family means more to me than it ever did before," he admitted. He set down his fork. "Not that I love Charlie more or that Tuck is more my brother than he ever was, but I think in the past I concentrated more on the word *dysfunction* than it deserved. And I thought family was who you shared blood with. I wanted to do something for the Phillipys because they've been family to me. To Tuck. To this whole community."

"What about me?" She couldn't believe she'd asked the question, but now that she had, she wanted to hear the answer. "Am I family?"

"Yes."

Silence fell between them and their gazes skittered away from each other as if neither of them knew what to say next.

Arlie took a deep breath and another bite. "I truly believe I'll be hungry on my death-bed. I'm sure it's Mama's fault that I love food so much. All that Italian cooking."

He smiled at her, his eyes crinkling. "She used to bring it in every day while you were in the hospital, just in case you were able to eat that day. Then she'd take some to Kokomo to Holly." He laughed, the sound sending ripples along Arlie's nerve endings. "I think it's what made your throat heal so fast, the fact that you wanted to swallow normally again."

Arlie didn't want to cry. She hated it when she did, but the tears were there, pushing themselves out to trail down her cheeks. "You were there whenever I woke up and there whenever I went to sleep. Even when Mama was dividing herself between Holly and me and never having time to grieve for Daddy, you were there for me every single day. You were family even more than you were my boy-friend."

She got up, carrying her dishes to the dish-washer. Her hands trembled. "All the time you've been back," she said, her voice tight, "I've felt so righteous about letting go, about putting it to the back of my mind that you left me that fall."

"I wish I could go back in time." He brought his dishes over, adding them to hers. She tried not to notice that his hands shook as much as hers did. "I would do things so differently."

"Me, too, probably." She rested her hands on his chest, reveling in the solid warmth of him. His heart beat steadily against her fin-gers, and they curled in response. When he put loose arms around her waist, she leaned into them. He would never let her fall. Never. "We need to talk about when you left and make peace with it. You're starting over with Charlie, with the company. Start over with our past, too."

He nodded agreement, his arms tighten-ing, the blue of his eyes going dark.

She rose on tiptoe to brush his lips with hers. "The truth of it is, I've always focused on you leaving, not on how you were there for me every single day while I got better. Even when you couldn't make yourself drive a car, you got to the hospital. When I came home, you still came every day. When I finally—" She stopped.

"You don't have to do this," he said, a little belatedly. "You don't have to remember."

"Yes, I do. The day I came home, when I had no choice but to accept that Daddy was dead, there was nothing anyone could say to give me comfort. Nothing anyone could do. I was walking, screaming hysterically, and you waited it out with me. When I turned on Mama, you stopped me. When I started to tell Holly he wasn't *really* her dad, you stopped me again. Because you knew the things I was going to say were ones people couldn't forget. You remembered even when I didn't that Mama and Holly had already lost one husband and father. Losing Daddy was history repeating its miserable self for them."

"They would have understood, Arlie. You know they would."

She took a deep, sobbing breath. Even considering the passage of time, the memories were agony—how could she have wanted to hurt the mother and sister she loved more than anyone except Jack? He was right when he said they would have understood, but they'd never have forgotten. Ever. "That day in mid-July when it was hotter than Hades out there and raining so hard the entire state of Indiana was a steam pit, you took me to the cemetery and sat there with me at his grave until…until I could stand it."

Not that she could stand it now, either. But now, as then, Jack made it bearable.

He turned her in the direction of the living room. "Let's sit on the couch. Your mom's not here, so we can even neck and drink beer if we want to."

Arlie laughed, a hitching little effort that sounded pathetic to her own ears. "I never drink beer." And she hadn't necked with anyone in a very long time.

"Wine, then." He poured them some and they settled on the couch in front of the fireplace.

She sipped the wine, taking momentary comfort in the Sycamore Hill zinfandel Chris said was mediocre this year and she loved anyway. "I've concentrated so hard on being noble and letting go that I forgot to hold on to the things I need to keep. I let go of midwifery because that was easier than trying to set up my own practice when the doctor in Sawyer didn't want me here. I thought it would be too hard to have a real relationship, so I spent two years in a false one, because then no one asked me when I was going to get married and have children. When my Olivia Newton-John sound leaned toward Bonnie Raitt, I let it go rather than try to work with it and come up with something new." Her voice, smoky at the best of times, failed her entirely.

"No." He shook his head, turning a troubled blue gaze from the flickering fire to meet her eyes. "You're wrong. You've been successful and you've made yourself that way."

"So have you."

He hesitated, biting down on his bottom lip, then nodded. "To a certain extent."

"But before you were successful, you let me go. You let Tucker go. You left Miniagua behind." She shrugged, not knowing how to make her point clear, then went for what she thought might be the jugular. "You're a Jack of several trades instead of a furniture builder, which is what you wanted to be growing up. Was it worth it?"

He flinched, and she wished she hadn't

said it—where was all her big talk about letting go?

It was his turn to shrug. "Most of the time. Being…uh…diversified doesn't mean I can't be a carpenter. It just means I'll probably always be a tinkerer instead of a master like Caleb Hershberger. I can live with that. It's not perfect, but most things aren't."

Arlie thought of helping babies come into the world, of laughing with new mothers and teasing new fathers and those precious moments with new life in her hands. He was right. Most things weren't perfect. But some came really close.

She remembered his jubilation earlier in the evening, his sprint up the stairs after talking to Tracy, his satisfaction that his son was going to live with him. Oh, yeah, really close.

Sometimes, letting go was the wrong thing to do. Jack knew it, had known it for all these long years—Arlie was just now figuring it out. She didn't know how long it would last or how far she would take this new knowledge, but she'd always been taught that a step at a time was a good way to get most anywhere you wanted to go.

"You know," she said, "a bicycle shop is a good idea, but the old drugstore isn't a good location for it. As soon as you get the office rebuilt out at the factory, I'd like to lease the building from you. Or buy it." She smiled at him. "It will be perfect for the Miniagua branch of A Woman's Place."

CHAPTER TWENTY-TWO

JACK STOOD WITH Gianna on the ground floor of the old drugstore building, watching it become a women's clinic right before his eyes. He didn't know why he hadn't thought of it himself—maybe because it wasn't his field of expertise. The closest he'd come was cutting the cord after Charlie's birth and waiting with Caleb while Miriam gave birth to little Daniel and Rebekah.

"She didn't want to say anything to you." Gianna watched her daughters taking measurements. "She was afraid you'd say yes out of old and needless guilt." She laid a hand on his arm. "Was she right?"

He smiled at her, thinking how lucky Arlie was when Gianna Christensen Gallagher had stepped neatly into the place Glennis vacated. "It wasn't guilt. I said yes because it was Arlie who asked."

"Ah." Gianna nodded, then called, "Don't forget you'll have walls in here, girls." Smiling back at Jack, she said, "Do you have intentions toward my daughter, Jack? Should I be worried?"

He hesitated. "I probably do, though I'm not sure at this point what they are." His gaze followed Arlie as she zipped around the cavernous room making absolutely no effort at containing her excitement. "But don't worry."

With a wave, he left, driving back to the plant.

Llewellyn's employees and a host of volunteers had expedited the cleanup from the fire. Paul and Tucker had both returned from successful trips. And with the help of Amish friends and extra crews hired by the insurance company, the repair of the main building had been done in record time.

Less than two weeks after the fire, Jack was working with construction crews on finishing the building's interior. The new equipment would go in after the first of the year. Construction of a new office wing would start at the same time, although the top floor of the drugstore building was working out better than he and Tucker had expected.

"The clinic can wait till you get the office rebuilt at the plant. We'll probably be in the way," Arlie had said when they signed the lease agreement for the building.

The office staff had other ideas. "They won't bother us at all," a clerk had said. "The lake needs a medical facility. By yesterday if Arlie can manage it."

Jack had looked around at the wall-to-wall mess. "If you say so. It won't be for long. The new building will be up by March."

"No hurry," said the office manager. "We can walk to lunch from here. It's a nice change from the break room at the plant. Plus, we'll be able to go downstairs once in a while and give Arlie and the doctor she's working with all kinds of advice on how to arrange the clinic."

That conversation had ended with plans drawn on a paper towel from the bathroom for a new cafeteria at the plant. Which was how Jack found himself laying new flooring with Caleb Hershberger, their nail guns popping rhythmically on the boards.

"You should open your own shop." Caleb grinned at Jack as they nailed their way backward across the wide plank floor. "I wouldn't be—what was that you said that time? *Ja*, training my replacement—because there's more than enough work for both of us."

"Would you still be willing to help me to learn new stuff even if we were competitors?"

The grin widened into a laugh. "*Ja.* Only I'd charge you for it." Caleb gave the board a satisfied slap.

Jack drove around the lake on his way home, making the ten-minute drive into twenty-five by stopping at the overlook that edged the golf course. He got out of the SUV and stood for a long few minutes, staring out at the choppy gray water. In an hour or so, thousands of Christmas lights would be twinkling all around the lake, but for now it was just cold, windy and dreary.

He didn't know why he felt so unsettled. He had Charlie, the answer to every prayer he hadn't even realized he had. Things at the plant were going far better than anyone could have expected. He'd regained the closeness with his brother he threw away all those years before. He saw Arlie almost every day.

Ah. Yes. There it was.

Arlie.

Almost every day wasn't always enough— leaving her was hard every time, and the messages in her eyes told him it wasn't easy for her, either. When they were together, they talked nonstop. They hugged each other in greeting and farewell and laughed long and loud at the same things. He and her pets even had a mutual-admiration thing going on—it seemed Wally had not forgotten who rescued him from the dark, scary mailbox. The dog and cat loved Charlie, too, and Jack had a re-signed feeling he knew what his son would be getting for Christmas. The boy loved Wally, but he wanted a "real dog," and he wanted it to be his own.

The same chemistry that had sparked be-tween Arlie and himself in high school was a bonfire now—at least for him. Sometimes he thought it was for her, too, but most of the time they were too busy to even think about their relationship. If *relationship* was the right word. Did they spend time together only because they knew each other so well and because right now they were swimming in the same social fishbowl that was life on the lake?

Or was it because it was only when they were together that life was special? Sometimes when the sun slipped up over the lake on a red-sky morning, the color faded away to leave the most beautiful burnished gold in its wake. The light would shine on the water and the waves would wash up in all shades of silver and copper.

Those colors and the shine and sparkle that went with them—that was what loving Arlie felt like.

He wasn't even surprised when he thought the words, because in sixteen years of loneliness, loss and wrong decisions, that was one thing that had remained the same. If anything, it had grown stronger.

He loved Arlie.

Arlie thought of the Toe with its barn-red paint and green metal roof, and of the color Gianna Christensen had brought with her when she'd married Dave. In the past twenty-six years, Arlie realized, nothing in her life had been beige. Not everything had been easy and she was almost sure she'd cried as often as she'd laughed—there had been months after the accident when physical, mental and emotional pain had been a constant companion—but she'd never been bored, never thought living was like that song she'd sung in a high school revue, "Is That All There Is?"

She closed her eyes and imagined Jack's blue eyes dancing behind his glasses and the shine of his streaky hair. She pictured walking and riding bicycles with him around the lake and laughing over—oh, Lord, everything. The sharing of that laughter was music in her heart.

Her mind skittered over his tendency toward feeling guilty over things beyond his control, his fear that anger would become a force he'd have to deal with and mental illness an even greater one. She thought of the ominous knell of the breast-cancer bell in her own genes, of the fact that she'd been a child even her own mother couldn't love.

She thought of Charlie, whom she loved in a way as pure and uncomplicated as any she'd ever known. But what if she inherited Glennis's mothering capabilities instead of Gianna's?

That had been something she and Jack had shared from the beginning. Neither of them had been loved by their mothers, but they had been rescued and cherished by Gianna and Ellen. Both had been afraid to have children, afraid they'd inflict untold damage on yet another generation. Yet here they were with Charlie, and neither of them could look at him and think he'd been a mistake.

Their lives, even allowing for the pain that had infiltrated them, had never been without color. They still weren't.

CHAPTER TWENTY-THREE

ARLIE HAD JUST put on her boots when her phone rang. "Can you pick up the turkey at Detwilers'?" Gianna, who was never frazzled, sounded as though she was bouncing on her last nerve. "It's Christmas Eve. I don't know how I managed to forget that. It was right on my way home from Kokomo."

Arlie laughed. "You can blame Max for that, unless he's there to defend himself. I'm going into Sawyer, then taking Wally to Jesse's for his shots, so I'll go right by Detwilers'. I have to go to the country club, too. They hired us to shop for staff gifts and their party is this evening after they close—I promised Holly I'd do the job, then forgot it."

"Be careful. It's snowing and blowing out there today."

"I will," Arlie promised, pushing her arm into her coat sleeve. "Gotta go. Love you, Mama."

"You, too, Arletta Marquetta Brigetta."

Not knowing about what awaited him at the vet's, Wally got into his new quilted carrier eagerly, curling his fuzzy little body around the teddy bear Arlie tossed in to him. He was asleep by the time the red Mini Cooper backed out of the garage.

In Sawyer, she bought the last gifts on her personal list, spending a little extra time at the bookstore making sure Holly's books were all displayed cover-out. She offered to sign them as the author's older, prettier and smarter sister, garnering laughs from the store's owner and from a customer who promptly bought a copy of every one of Holly's books for her niece.

Arlie found a book on woodworking on a table near the cash register and added it to the bookstore gift cards she was buying to have on hand.

She flinched when Wally got his shots, gave Jesse a hug and a Christmas ornament she'd made and drove on to Bishop Detwiler's house. He put the fresh turkey into the back of the Mini for her, adding a quart of his wife's home-canned salsa because the Detwilers knew Arlie loved it.

She was nearly to the lake road when she remembered the gifts in the back of the car that needed to be delivered to the country club. She turned around in the golf course's driveway, mumbling a few words that Gianna would have scolded her for and laughing when Wally barked his own remonstrance.

She delivered the gifts, exchanging Christmas wishes with the club manager, then headed home. She drove slowly. The curvy road hadn't straightened any since the night of the accident, though it was wider than it had been then. Her gaze flicked involuntarily to the two small crosses that stood silent sentinel where her father and Linda Saylors had died. As usual, there were flowers around the markers, most of them poinsettias. At prom time, the sheer number of corsages and boutonnieres left there covered the crosses altogether so that the site looked like an eclectic flower bed.

Every few years, someone replaced the crosses. It looked as though it had been done recently. She pulled into the driveway adjacent to the little memorial—the people who lived there were gone for the winter and would never know.

"I'll be right back, Wally." The wind was fierce when she got out of the Mini Cooper and walked over to look down at the crosses. Rather than pieces of two-by-two-inch lumber cut and nailed together, the new crosses had been carved from walnut wood and assembled with mortise and tenon. They were stained instead of painted.

Arlie knelt, wiping away clinging snowflakes and squinting to read the small letters etched on the cross bars. The inscription on the smaller, more delicate cross was Linda Saylors's name, and beside it, a tiara had been carved with rhinestones carefully embedded in the wood—she had been a prom princess.

The words on the larger cross were *Dave Gallagher—Dancing King*.

"Oh, Daddy." Tears blinded her and her hands shook when she aimed the viewfinder on her phone. She took several shots and texted them to Gianna and Holly. The wind rocked her with its strength, and snow stung her face, but she stayed where she was.

What would he tell her to do if he were here? He'd always been the stern parent when he and Gianna played good cop, bad cop with her and Holly, but he'd been fun, too. When they and their friends had performed the can-can for a fund-raiser variety show, he'd been the dancer on the end. The Sunday morning the girls had been baptized, he'd wept with Gianna. He'd been Sonny Bono in a skit when

Arlie had deepened her voice and sang "I got you, babe."

"We miss you so much, Superdad." The tears fell, tumbling to the scarf that hugged her chin. "What was it like for you after Glennis left? How did you fall in love again after you'd been hurt? Were you able to jump into the great life we had without looking back and being afraid it would all happen again?"

It *had* been a great life. Dave and Gianna had loved each other and both girls so much and so well that pain from the past had seldom even been a player on the stage of their lives together.

Her phone dinged that she had a text, and she looked at the screen.

THEY'RE BEAUTIFUL. BLESS JACK'S HEART.

Jack. Of course it had been Jack. She tapped in Gianna's number. "Mama?"

"Are you okay?" Gianna sounded concerned.

Arlie took a second to calm her voice. "If you had it to do again, knowing Daddy was going to be gone so soon, would you have married us anyway or would you have taken Holly and gotten out of Dodge?"

Gianna laughed, and the sound settled over her so warmly Arlie thought the snow should have melted away. "I wouldn't give up a minute with you and your dad for anything. We had ten years that we were all together, Arlie. *Ten years!* There are people who never have ten *minutes* of that kind of happiness. So yes, you bet—if I had it to do again, I'd do it in a heartbeat."

After she'd hung up and responded to Holly's Beautiful! text, Arlie took another picture of the crosses and tapped in Thank you! on the phone's miniature screen. She located Jack's number and hit Send.

JACK CLIMBED INTO the SUV to drive to a meeting with Tucker at the company's temporary office. It was closed until after New Year's, but he wanted to make sure nothing had been left undone—the fire had made him paranoid about loose ends.

Although the last loose end had tied itself neatly in a bow—they had found a viable candidate to manage the Miniagua plant. Jensen Cathcart was a veteran of the Iraq war Paul had met on his trip to Maine. Paul had been so impressed that he'd paid for the man's plane ticket to Indiana. The ink was still wet on Jensen's MBA, but Jack and Tucker knew by the end of the introductory interview that he was perfect for the job. They hired him on the spot.

Far from jubilant, though, Jack felt depressed. It was only two months ago, wasn't it, that he was itching to get back to Vermont? When he was worrying about missing skiing and mountain biking and his house. Of course, the house was rented anyway—he'd have to find a place to live for the length of the lease. It would be good to see friends he'd missed, to spend an evening with music and laughter and a well-poured Guinness at McGuffey's Tavern. He'd be able to get Charlie settled into Fionnegan Academy and maybe get the "real dog" that seemed to be injecting himself into every conversation these days.

If they went back, would he and Tuck lose the closeness they'd managed to regain? Would he mourn the lake itself, as he had done sixteen years ago? He would miss Miniagua's businesses named after Cole Porter songs—hot chocolate tasted better at Anything Goes than it did anywhere and he had his own coffee cup at the Silver Moon Café.

If he didn't manage to stop at Libby's tearoom on the days she baked cinnamon rolls, she saved him some. He enjoyed time spent with Nate and Sam. They had even ambushed Jesse Worth at Libby's and talked him into joining them and Tucker for occasional poker nights.

But it would be good to go home. To ski and snowboard on Wish Mountain. To check in at the Chain and Sprocket. And there was nothing that said he wouldn't come back to the lake more often now on school holidays. Stay longer. He'd be like Chris Granger, living in two places and enjoying both worlds.

But Arlie wouldn't be in Vermont. The words took the bleak forefront of his thoughts, accounting for the depression that dogged his every step.

Maybe he could ask her to go to Vermont with him. She loved Charlie. Jack thought maybe she loved Charlie's dad, too.

At the temporary office, he double-checked everything, answered a few emails that weren't as urgent as their senders had deemed them and locked the door behind him. Downstairs, he opened the new door that gave access to the space that would house A Woman's Place on the Lake.

The clinic wouldn't open for weeks yet,

but it was as though Arlie was already there. There were bright colors everywhere—no institutionally off-white paint had been allowed. The painting was artistic—every time Penny Phillipy had said, "What do you think?" Arlie had nodded enthusiastic agreement, and the interior of the old drugstore showed warmth and welcome everywhere you looked.

He could never ask her to leave this. He could almost feel her heartbeat in the bright rooms.

A Christmas tree lit one front window, a nativity scene the other. Twinkle lights draped from the exposed ceiling beams. There was no furniture yet, so the space echoed as he walked through, but it wasn't a lonely kind of sound—more of a waiting one.

Waiting. What was he waiting for? To stop feeling responsible for every setback in everyone else's life? It probably wasn't going to happen—he'd worried ever since the day of Jensen's interview that Llewellyn's wasn't doing enough for veterans. Tucker said somewhere in Jack's ancestry there was an overactive Jewish mother who was still passing guilt down to all her descendants.

He waited for other things, too, for the

other shoe that was mental illness to drop its heavy weight on him and everyone he loved. For the old angers to reassert themselves so that he never knew what would set them off. He'd talked to Charlie about them, told him what to do if he thought his father ever leaned too far over the edge of being reasonable. Charlie had just said, "You'll never hurt me."

Let him be right.

He loved Vermont. It would be safe there, and as long as he had Charlie, he could be happy—or contented, maybe. Not really happy. Most of the guilt and the fear would be back at Miniagua, where he'd left it sixteen years ago.

So would Tucker. So would the friends he'd grown close to.

So would Arlie Gallagher.

Could he leave her again? Even knowing she would be better off without her life littered by him and his idiot hang-ups, could he kiss her goodbye and climb into the SUV and drive away without looking back? Because that was the only way to do it.

In the car again, with its engine purring and the defroster blasting at the snow blowing against the windshield, he drove to the plant, parking outside the stark frame that would become the new office. The buildings and the grounds wore light coats of snow. Unless one was looking very hard, all physical evidence of the fire had been erased.

They'd done a good job, the factory's employees and the Amish construction workers and Tucker and Jack. They'd worked hard and hidden the wounds inflicted by a fire that had been an unforeseeable accident.

He'd miss Llewellyn's Lures—there was no denying it. However, it wasn't the family business he couldn't bear to leave, but the family itself. *What about me?* Arlie had asked. *Am I family?*

Oh, yes. Oh, dear God, yes.

Jack's phone chimed, signaling an incoming text, and he looked at the screen. A picture popped up, showing the crosses he'd placed at the accident site on Country Club Road. Thank you! he read.

Still sitting in the car, he looked again at the grounds of the plant.

Wounds healed. The scars they left were part of life's road map, as unavoidable as the potholes that appeared on the lake roads every spring. The fissures in the pavement had to be fixed by both the road crew and the lake residents. No one ever minded doing the repairs, Paul Phillipy said, because they were a sure harbinger of spring with all its newness and growth.

He picked up his phone and tapped in Where are you?

On my way back to the Toe.

He hesitated. Will you wait there for me?

A full minute passed before the phone chimed again and another ten seconds before he could make himself read the text.

He closed his eyes, drew a deep breath and looked again.

Always.

FIVE MINUTES AFTER Arlie sent the most courageous text of her life, Jack's car pulled in at the Toe. Wally must have sensed his presence, so as soon as she opened the door, the little dog leaped joyfully into his rescuer's arms.

Arlie had just tossed her coat at the row of hooks beside the front door, and her scarf was half-unwound around her neck. Jack grasped the soft wool and drew her to him, lowering his head to kiss her. His arms were at her waist, and her hands linked behind his neck, ruffling the soft hair there. *Don't let go. Oh, please, don't let go.*

A few minutes later, he lifted his head. She shaped his cheeks with her palms, feeling the cold brush of his beard where snow still clung to it.

"The crosses are wonderful."

"Thank you." He smiled at her, his eyes shining bluer than she thought she'd ever seen them. "You are, too." He kissed her again, with sixteen years of yearning filling the space between them. When he drew back, the smile had disappeared. "I wish I could go back."

She shook her head. She didn't want this to be about then—she wanted it to be about now. Besides, they couldn't go back. No one could.

"We have a new plant manager," he said. "Tucker and I are able to return to Tennessee and Vermont."

Arlie stiffened. Had Jack not been holding her up, she thought she might have doubled over with the pain of it.

"But I don't want to go," he went on. "I'm thinking I'd like to open my own woodworking shop and continue to serve in an advisory capacity at Llewellyn's Lures. I'd like for Charlie to wear a Lakers football or basketball uniform if that's what he'd like to do. And I'm thinking—" He paused. Cleared his throat. Pressed his forehead to hers for an intimate moment. "I know no matter how much I'd like to undo what happened sixteen years ago, I can't. I thought when I first saw you again that I still loved you, that I'd always loved you and wasn't that just dandy, but I was wrong."

She drew back enough to look into his eyes. What did he mean? What was he saying?

And suddenly she knew. But she needed for him to tell her anyway.

"What I did," he said, holding her gaze, "was fall in love with you again. I may have loved you when you were seventeen—I *did* love you—but not enough. Not well. Who I love now is you at thirty-three, with the most generous and funny spirit I've ever had the privilege to know. And I'm going to love you forever. With no going back."

The declaration took her breath away, and for a moment she just stood, with his hands tangled in her scarf and hers slipping from his face to the sides of his neck, where his pulse beat strong and fast against her fingers.

"I wanted to die when you left," she said, her voice rough and uneven the way it had been back then. Only now it was emotion that took the music from it, not injury. "Of course, I wanted to die a lot those days, but you and Mama wouldn't ever let me. So even when I wasn't letting go, I owned that, that you made me hold on just by being right there every day." She shook her head, her hands lying flat on his chest. Feeling the warmth of his skin through the flannel of his shirt. "But I was perfectly content just to take and not give."

"No. You always—"

"I loved you," she interrupted, then mirrored his words. "But not enough. Not well. I didn't see how the emotional pain you suffered could be anywhere near as awful as the loss and injuries our family experienced."

"You were right. I didn't lose anything in that accident compared to what you did—"

She placed her fingers against his lips. "Hush. I was selfish, but I was seventeen. Whereas now—" She was starting to enjoy this. A lot. So she paused.

He kissed the fingertips against his mouth, then took her hand. "Now?"

"Whereas now I love you really well. And forever. With no going back."

He slowly unwound the scarf, one loop after another. "How do you feel about marriage? To me, that is. I'm good at woodworking and I'm not a half-bad landlord. I have this kid who's guaranteed entertainment."

"My mother's a good cook and I can deliver babies. And I probably love Charlie more than I love you—he's funnier. I'll bring that to the table. Sounds like a pretty good match, doesn't it?"

"It does to me."

"We're going to be family, Jack. Right?"

"We already are."

He lowered his head to hers again, and she didn't talk anymore for a while. They seemed to have already said the right things.

"When?" she said. "Should we wait? I can, you know. I've got a business to start up—I may not have time to get married."

He laughed, hugging her again. Kissing her again. "We've waited long enough, don't you think. Plus, you're the only thing besides a dog the kid asked for this year. I can't disappoint him."

"Merry Christmas," she whispered.

He kissed her again. "Yes. It is."

"And make no mistake," she murmured against his lips.

"About what?"

"He'll still want the dog."

* * * * *

If you loved this novel,
don't miss

BACK TO McGUFFEY'S

available from USA TODAY
bestselling author Liz Flaherty

and

Harlequin Heartwarming.

LARGER-PRINT BOOKS!

GET 2 FREE
LARGER-PRINT NOVELS
PLUS 2 FREE
MYSTERY GIFTS

Love Inspired®

Larger-print novels are now available...

YES! Please send me 2 FREE LARGER-PRINT Love Inspired® novels and my 2 FREE mystery gifts (gifts are worth about $10). After receiving them, if I don't wish to receive any more books, I can return the shipping statement marked "cancel." If I don't cancel, I will receive 6 brand-new novels every month and be billed just $5.49 per book in the U.S. or $5.99 per book in Canada. That's a savings of at least 19% off the cover price. It's quite a bargain! Shipping and handling is just 50¢ per book in the U.S. and 75¢ per book in Canada.* I understand that accepting the 2 free books and gifts places me under no obligation to buy anything. I can always return a shipment and cancel at any time. Even if I never buy another book, the two free books and gifts are mine to keep forever.

122/322 IDN GH6D

Name   (PLEASE PRINT)

Address   Apt. #

City   State/Prov.   Zip/Postal Code

Signature (if under 18, a parent or guardian must sign)

Mail to the **Reader Service:**
IN U.S.A.: P.O. Box 1867, Buffalo, NY 14240-1867
IN CANADA: P.O. Box 609, Fort Erie, Ontario L2A 5X3

**Are you a current subscriber to Love Inspired® books
and want to receive the larger-print edition?
Call 1-800-873-8635 or visit www.ReaderService.com.**

* Terms and prices subject to change without notice. Prices do not include applicable taxes. Sales tax applicable in N.Y. Canadian residents will be charged applicable taxes. Offer not valid in Quebec. This offer is limited to one order per household. Not valid to current subscribers to Love Inspired Larger-Print books. All orders subject to credit approval. Credit or debit balances in a customer's account(s) may be offset by any other outstanding balance owed by or to the customer. Please allow 4 to 6 weeks for delivery. Offer available while quantities last.

Your Privacy—The Reader Service is committed to protecting your privacy. Our Privacy Policy is available online at www.ReaderService.com or upon request from the Reader Service.

We make a portion of our mailing list available to reputable third parties that offer products we believe may interest you. If you prefer that we not exchange your name with third parties, or if you wish to clarify or modify your communication preferences, please visit us at www.ReaderService.com/consumerschoice or write to us at Reader Service Preference Service, P.O. Box 9062, Buffalo, NY 14240-9062. Include your complete name and address.

LILP15

LARGER-PRINT BOOKS!

GET 2 FREE LARGER-PRINT NOVELS PLUS 2 FREE MYSTERY GIFTS

Love Inspired®
SUSPENSE
RIVETING INSPIRATIONAL ROMANCE

Larger-print novels are now available...

YES! Please send me 2 FREE LARGER-PRINT Love Inspired® Suspense novels and my 2 FREE mystery gifts (gifts are worth about $10). After receiving them, if I don't wish to receive any more books, I can return the shipping statement marked "cancel." If I don't cancel, I will receive 4 brand-new novels every month and be billed just $5.49 per book in the U.S. or $5.99 per book in Canada. That's a savings of at least 19% off the cover price. It's quite a bargain! Shipping and handling is just 50¢ per book in the U.S. and 75¢ per book in Canada.* I understand that accepting the 2 free books and gifts places me under no obligation to buy anything. I can always return a shipment and cancel at any time. Even if I never buy another book, the two free books and gifts are mine to keep forever.

110/310 IDN GH6P

Name	(PLEASE PRINT)	

Address		Apt. #

City	State/Prov.	Zip/Postal Code

Signature (if under 18, a parent or guardian must sign)

Mail to the **Reader Service:**
IN U.S.A.: P.O. Box 1867, Buffalo, NY 14240-1867
IN CANADA: P.O. Box 609, Fort Erie, Ontario L2A 5X3

Are you a current subscriber to Love Inspired® Suspense books and want to receive the larger-print edition?
Call 1-800-873-8635 or visit www.ReaderService.com.

* Terms and prices subject to change without notice. Prices do not include applicable taxes. Sales tax applicable in N.Y. Canadian residents will be charged applicable taxes. Offer not valid in Quebec. This offer is limited to one order per household. Not valid for current subscribers to Love Inspired Suspense larger-print books. All orders subject to credit approval. Credit or debit balances in a customer's account(s) may be offset by any other outstanding balance owed by or to the customer. Please allow 4 to 6 weeks for delivery. Offer available while quantities last.

Your Privacy—The Reader Service is committed to protecting your privacy. Our Privacy Policy is available online at www.ReaderService.com or upon request from the Reader Service.

We make a portion of our mailing list available to reputable third parties that offer products we believe may interest you. If you prefer that we not exchange your name with third parties, or if you wish to clarify or modify your communication preferences, please visit us at www.ReaderService.com/consumerchoice or write to us at Reader Service Preference Service, P.O. Box 9062, Buffalo, NY 14240-9062. Include your complete name and address.

LARGER-PRINT BOOKS!
GET 2 FREE LARGER-PRINT NOVELS PLUS
2 FREE GIFTS!

HARLEQUIN®

super romance®

More Story...More Romance

YES! Please send me 2 FREE LARGER-PRINT Harlequin® Superromance® novels and my 2 FREE gifts (gifts are worth about $10). After receiving them, if I don't wish to receive any more books, I can return the shipping statement marked "cancel." If I don't cancel, I will receive 4 brand-new novels every month and be billed just $5.94 per book in the U.S. or $6.24 per book in Canada. That's a savings of at least 12% off the cover price! It's quite a bargain! Shipping and handling is just 50¢ per book in the U.S. or 75¢ per book in Canada.* I understand that accepting the 2 free books and gifts places me under no obligation to buy anything. I can always return a shipment and cancel at any time. Even if I never buy another book, the two free books and gifts are mine to keep forever.

132/332 HDN GHVC

Name	(PLEASE PRINT)

Address		Apt. #

City	State/Prov.	Zip/Postal Code

Signature (if under 18, a parent or guardian must sign)

Mail to the **Reader Service:**
IN U.S.A.: P.O. Box 1867, Buffalo, NY 14240-1867
IN CANADA: P.O. Box 609, Fort Erie, Ontario L2A 5X3

Want to try two free books from another line?
Call 1-800-873-8635 today or visit www.ReaderService.com.

* Terms and prices subject to change without notice. Prices do not include applicable taxes. Sales tax applicable in N.Y. Canadian residents will be charged applicable taxes. Offer not valid in Quebec. This offer is limited to one order per household. Not valid for current subscribers to Harlequin Superromance Larger-Print books. All orders subject to credit approval. Credit or debit balances in a customer's account(s) may be offset by any other outstanding balance owed by or to the customer. Please allow 4 to 6 weeks for delivery. Offer available while quantities last.

Your Privacy—The Reader Service is committed to protecting your privacy. Our Privacy Policy is available online at www.ReaderService.com or upon request from the Reader Service.

We make a portion of our mailing list available to reputable third parties that offer products we believe may interest you. If you prefer that we not exchange your name with third parties, or if you wish to clarify or modify your communication preferences, please visit us at www.ReaderService.com/consumerschoice or write to us at Reader Service Preference Service, P.O. Box 9062, Buffalo, NY 14240-9062. Include your complete name and address.

HSRLP15

READERSERVICE.COM

Manage your account online!

- Review your order history
- Manage your payments
- Update your address

We've designed the Reader Service website just for you.

Enjoy all the features!

- Discover new series available to you, and read excerpts from any series.
- Respond to mailings and special monthly offers.
- Connect with favorite authors at the blog.
- Browse the Bonus Bucks catalog and online-only exculsives.
- Share your feedback.

Visit us at:

ReaderService.com

RS

REQUEST YOUR FREE BOOKS!

2 FREE INSPIRATIONAL NOVELS
PLUS 2 *FREE* MYSTERY GIFTS

Love Inspired HISTORICAL

YES! Please send me 2 FREE Love Inspired® Historical novels and my 2 FREE
mystery gifts (gifts are worth about $10). After receiving them, if I don't wish to receive
any more books, I can return the shipping statement marked "cancel." If I don't cancel,
I will receive 4 brand-new novels every month and be billed just $4.99 per book in the
U.S. or $5.49 per book in Canada. That's a saving of at least 17% off the cover price.
It's quite a bargain! Shipping and handling is just 50¢ per book in the U.S. and 75¢ per
book in Canada.* I understand that accepting the 2 free books and gifts places me under
no obligation to buy anything. I can always return a shipment and cancel at any time.
Even if I never buy another book, the two free books and gifts are mine to keep forever.

102/302 IDN GH6Z

Name _____ (PLEASE PRINT) _____

Address _____ Apt. # _____

City _____ State/Prov. _____ Zip/Postal Code _____

Signature (if under 18, a parent or guardian must sign)

Mail to the **Reader Service:**
IN U.S.A.: P.O. Box 1867, Buffalo, NY 14240-1867
IN CANADA: P.O. Box 609, Fort Erie, Ontario L2A 5X3

**Want to try two free books from another series?
Call 1-800-873-8635 or visit www.ReaderService.com.**

* Terms and prices subject to change without notice. Prices do not include applicable
taxes. Sales tax applicable in N.Y. Canadian residents will be charged applicable taxes.
Offer not valid in Quebec. This offer is limited to one order per household. Not valid
for current subscribers to Love Inspired Historical books. All orders subject to credit
approval. Credit or debit balances in a customer's account(s) may be offset by any other
outstanding balance owed by or to the customer. Please allow 4 to 6 weeks for delivery.
Offer available while quantities last.

Your Privacy—The Reader Service is committed to protecting your privacy. Our
Privacy Policy is available online at www.ReaderService.com or upon request from
the Reader Service.

We make a portion of our mailing list available to reputable third parties that offer
products we believe may interest you. If you prefer that we not exchange your name with
third parties, or if you wish to clarify or modify your communication preferences, please
visit us at www.ReaderService.com/consumerschoice or write to us at Reader Service
Preference Service, P.O. Box 9062, Buffalo, NY 14240-9062. Include your complete
name and address.

LIH15

REQUEST YOUR FREE BOOKS!
2 FREE WHOLESOME ROMANCE NOVELS
IN LARGER PRINT
PLUS 2
FREE
MYSTERY GIFTS

HEARTWARMING™

Wholesome, tender romances

YES! Please send me 2 FREE Harlequin® Heartwarming Larger-Print novels and my 2 FREE mystery gifts (gifts worth about $10). After receiving them, if I don't wish to receive any more books, I can return the shipping statement marked "cancel." If I don't cancel, I will receive 4 brand-new larger-print novels every month and be billed just $5.24 per book in the U.S. or $5.99 per book in Canada. That's a savings of at least 19% off the cover price. It's quite a bargain! Shipping and handling is just 50¢ per book in the U.S. and 75¢ per book in Canada.* I understand that accepting the 2 free books and gifts places me under no obligation to buy anything. I can always return a shipment and cancel at any time. Even if I never buy another book, the two free books and gifts are mine to keep forever.

161/361 IDN GHX2

Name _____ (PLEASE PRINT)

Address _____ Apt. #

City _____ State/Prov. _____ Zip/Postal Code

Signature (if under 18, a parent or guardian must sign)

Mail to the **Reader Service:**
IN U.S.A.: P.O. Box 1867, Buffalo, NY 14240-1867
IN CANADA: P.O. Box 609, Fort Erie, Ontario L2A 5X3

* Terms and prices subject to change without notice. Prices do not include applicable taxes. Sales tax applicable in N.Y. Canadian residents will be charged applicable taxes. Offer not valid in Quebec. This offer is limited to one order per household. Not valid for current subscribers to Harlequin Heartwarming larger-print books. All orders subject to credit approval. Credit or debit balances in a customer's account(s) may be offset by any other outstanding balance owed by or to the customer. Please allow 4 to 6 weeks for delivery. Offer available while quantities last.

Your Privacy—The Reader Service is committed to protecting your privacy. Our Privacy Policy is available online at www.ReaderService.com or upon request from the Reader Service.

We make a portion of our mailing list available to reputable third parties that offer products we believe may interest you. If you prefer that we not exchange your name with third parties, or if you wish to clarify or modify your communication preferences, please visit us at www.ReaderService.com/consumerchoice or write to us at Reader Service Preference Service, P.O. Box 9062, Buffalo, NY 14240-9062. Include your complete name and address.

HW